Catherine Dunne

THE WALLED GARDEN

MACMILLAN

First published 2000 by Macmillan
an imprint of Macmillan Publishers Ltd
25 Eccleston Place, London SW1W 9NF
Basingstoke and Oxford
Associated companies throughout the world
www.macmillan.co.uk

ISBN 0 333 78583 5

3 5 7 9 8 6 4 2

A CIP catalogue record for this book is available from
the British Library.

Typeset by SetSystems Ltd, Saffron Walden, Essex
Printed and bound in Great Britain by
Mackays of Chatham plc, Chatham, Kent

For my father, Charles MacAlister.

In memory of my mother,
Elizabeth (Lil), née Sheridan (1916–1989).

Acknowledgements

The Tyrone Guthrie Centre at Annaghmakerrig in Co. Monaghan has been a real haven for writers and artists for many years now. I was lucky enough to be there for the month of October, 1998, surrounded by the peace and tranquility of Bernard Loughlin's autumn garden. My thanks to Bernard and Mary, former directors, who have since moved to warmer climes.

My thanks, too, to all the others who were resident at Annaghmakerrig during that time. It was a pleasure to be with those who took their work, but not themselves, very seriously indeed.

Special thanks are also due to Shirley Stewart, Literary Agent, for her sheer hard work and dedication, and for her unfailing sense of humour in times of stress.

ONE

Homecoming

IT WAS ALWAYS like this, on the last leg of the journey.

Everything conspired against her: the pale, yellowish light slanting irregularly across the airport motorway, the droplets of rain crowding on her windscreen, the menacing approach of speedy headlights in her rear-view mirror. Cars were hurtling along, ducking and weaving from lane to lane like large, demented insects, keeping her senses on edge. Even the motor-cyclists seemed to be more casually reckless than ever.

Beth hated this surge of unreason, this uncharacteristic road-rage. She was normally a good driver. But coming home was never normal. Coming home, coming back, whatever – it was always the same. She was glad to turn off to the left, onto safer, more familiar territory.

But even here, as she drove down Griffith Avenue, she could feel the backs of her knees growing stiff, the slow crawl of tension like a steel bar across her shoulder blades. She had always disliked hire cars. It took her too long to grow used to them. They had a mind of their own. The indicators would somehow manage to be on the wrong side, or the lights in an impossible position. This time, it was the driver's seat that wasn't right. She had already tried to ease herself into it, but the back stayed bolt upright, unforgiving. Her foot was beginning to cramp, resting at an awkward angle on the accelerator. She tried again, fumbling beneath her this time, keeping her eyes on the road ahead. Even a couple of inches back would ease the strain, surely. If she couldn't do it on the move, then she'd have to pull over. Anyway, there wasn't too much traffic around; the pubs wouldn't close for a couple of hours yet.

'Come on, come *on*,' she urged out loud, crossly, as her right hand closed over the resisting lever. She never knew from one car to the next – was it push back or pull forward?

Suddenly, there was a swift, sudden movement of oiled metal. It was enough to shock Beth's hands off the steering wheel, enough to distract her eyes from the road ahead for a split second. The seat shot back. The car waltzed crazily, giddily, gleefully over the white line.

She watched its mad dance with fascination. From somewhere way above, she could see her hands back on the steering wheel again, her eyes forward, her feet in the correct position. Through the rhythmic windscreen wipers, a huge lorry lumbered towards her. Bulk Cement Supplies, she read. She was surprised at how clearly she could see the letters. The headlights on the cab were bright, blinding. The drops of rain on her windscreen were crudely efficient magnifying glasses.

The blare of a horn startled her then, and she jumped, finally alert, wrenching the steering wheel to the left. She went flying forward, hitting her chin painfully off its rigid surface. Then the seat belt locked and jerked her suddenly back again. The car lurched obediently out of the lorry's way. It mounted the kerb, and came to an abrupt, muddy stop on the grass verge.

It had all taken only a couple of seconds. Beth was surprised at how suspended she'd felt. She hadn't even been afraid. Strangely, she had been rather interested, watching the way the windscreen wipers had measured the lorry's rapid approach. Swish, swish.

A face loomed suddenly at her, out of the darkness. A fist hammered angrily on glass. Calmly, she watched as the electric window slid down. She knew that its rainy surface would have been cleansed by the time she closed it again.

'What in Christ's name d'ye think you're *at*, woman?'

She saw the man's black fingernails as he held onto the open window. He was huge in his grey padded jacket, bulky. Like his cement supplies, Beth suddenly thought. She wanted to laugh. His voice was loud, angry, but his red, creased face looked more frightened than threatening. His pores were huge, staring at her blackly. She looked around her. He had parked his lorry: the hazard lights were flashing. She thought that that was a sensible thing to do; she should do the same. There was no one behind her, she had only two wheels on the road, but still, just in case. She began to push at the switches in front of her on the dashboard. Now she couldn't even remember which one it was. She shook her head.

'I don't know which one it is,' she said, puzzled, looking down at his fingernails again. Square, they were, and broad. The hands of a man used to manual labour. When he spoke again, his voice was different, distant.

'Are y'all right, missus?'

'Yes, yes, thank you. I'm fine. Now I must be on my way.'

She dismissed him with a wave of her hand and made to close the window. He stuck his head in then and filled the car with his rage. Drops of rain were beading across his forehead, running down the cracks and lines of his face.

'Ya could'a killed both of us, ya stupid bitch? D'ya realize that?'

Dimly, she was aware of the lilt of his accent, the slight interrogative lift at the end of each sentence. It was an accent she had never liked.

'I'm sorry,' she said, firmly. 'I was trying to adjust my seat and it slipped. I got distracted. I'm sorry if I gave you a fright.'

He glared at her, disbelieving. He jabbed a squat, solid forefinger in the air, pointing at her.

'I'm takin' your number. I'm goin' to report *you*, so I am. *You* shouldn't be let out, so ya shouldn't!'

He slammed his open hand on the roof of the car. Its whole body shook slightly. The sound he made was sharp, metallic, as though he wore a heavy ring. She imagined she had seen a thick, gold wedding band. Beth watched him as he ran across the road and hoisted himself up into his cab, his jeans straining at the waistband. The internal light was switched on, and he began to scribble something, leaning forward furiously on the dashboard. The stiff set of his shoulders told her:

I'm goin' to get you; you'll pay for this, so you will. Then
the sickly light went out and he eased the lorry back
into the outer lane again. She could feel his glare on the
back of her neck as he drove away, could imagine him
muttering obscenities to himself.

She rested her arms on the steering wheel and leaned
her forehead on her hands. Her chin had suddenly
begun to hurt. A broad band of sweat started at her
hairline, sliding its way hotly down the back of her
neck. She closed her eyes and saw it all again – the dark,
gleaming road surface, the big painted letters on the
lorry's cab, the back and forwards of the windscreen
wipers. Then she remembered the man's fingernails,
could see them still, right under her nose. She could
imagine the smell of diesel from his hands, the stale
stench of damp clothes and male sweat in the lorry's cab
where he sat for hours on end. Her stomach began to
shift restlessly as the smells grew stronger; something
black and sour plucked at the back of her throat.

'It's just shock, it's only shock,' she whispered to
herself. 'Fresh air. I'll be fine.'

She turned the key in the ignition and opened the
window again. She breathed in lungfuls of the sharp
October night. Cars passed up and down the avenue,
squashing the winter leaves to a yellow and brown
sludge. Her hands plucked weakly at her seat-belt, not
able to undo the buckle. She sat where she was, breathing deeply, dragging her damp hair back from her
forehead a couple of times. Gradually, she began to feel
better; the nausea subsided. The grey lights before her
eyes cleared and she glanced at the clock on the

dashboard. The numerals glowed redly. The steady, pulse-like rhythm of the passing seconds made her begin to feel sleepy. She made an effort to sit up straighter. She *had* to get going. She was nearly there.

She checked both mirrors several times, indicated right and drove slowly off the slushy grass. The low skirt of the car made a pained, grinding sound as it bumped in slow motion off the high kerb. Once she was on the move again, she began to feel suddenly better, almost light-hearted. Nothing awful had happened. She was safe, the car was in one piece. She felt cleansed, her anxiety calmed. Maybe she didn't need to feel so full of dread about what was waiting for her. Maybe this near miss was a sign that things wouldn't be so bad, after all. Even the memory of dirty fingernails and diesel smells began to lose their power to sicken.

She steadied herself at the traffic lights, willing them to stay red a little longer. She tried some more deep breathing. The road to home was quiet, its rush-hour evening chaos long over. Once in her own street, she welcomed its silence, the orange glow of the lamps, the winter-night emptiness. Its narrowness was even more exaggerated by the long files of parked cars on either side. It was a street made for trikes and two-wheelers, for scooters and roller-skaters. It was just about wide enough for hopscotch. It had never been made for the growing gridlock that was now Dublin traffic.

Beth eased her foot off the accelerator. Now that she was almost there, she felt a little thrill, a small stirring of hope. No matter how often she came back, each time a part of her believed that, this time, things would be different. No matter how reluctant she had felt, this time it was the right thing, the only thing to do. She had a sudden vision of herself as, finally, a competent adult – calm, responsible, rising to the crisis. No one need know how she really felt. She owed it to James, and he would be waiting for her.

He was standing at one of the downstairs windows. He had a book in his left hand, closed over the index finger, marking his place. The short, capable fingers of his right hand restlessly combed the grey hairs of his beard. Beth had known he would be standing there, just like that, felt the familiar mix of tenderness and impatience as he stooped, peering short-sightedly through the bottom pane. Making sure it was her, she supposed. She wondered what he would do if it were someone else. Would he not answer the door anyway, no matter who it was? Why stand so thoroughly on guard, all the time?

The thought made her feel guilty. He was worried about her; she was late. It was normal: a warm, brotherly reaction.

She turned the car in the broad driveway and pointed it towards the house, the wheels spitting out gravel. The hazy sweep of headlights caught the wooden plaque on the right-hand side of the front door. *Woodvale*. Even the name started a tug somewhere towards the bottom of Beth's heart. It spoke of tranquillity and shelter, something which she felt this house had not offered her, not since she was a very small child. Somebody, no doubt James, had picked out the black lettering again, and the wood was shiny with new varnish. She had never known a man with such passion for detail.

He was at the car window even before she'd switched off the ignition.

'Beth? Are you all right? I was getting worried.'

His eyes were a deep blue, magnified behind the solid lenses of his glasses. Before she had time to reply, before she was even properly out of the car, he put both his arms around her and pulled her to him. She was at least a head taller than he was, and she had the impression of being hugged by a large, overgrown boy. He was doing his best to balance a huge umbrella over their heads.

'I'm fine,' she smiled at him. 'We were almost an hour late taking off. Fog at Heathrow.'

'I thought you might have had car trouble at this end. I was going to ring Laura in a little while, but I didn't want to worry her. I'm glad you're here.'

He was taking her case out of the boot, folding her coat over his arm, motioning towards her for the car keys. Minding her again. She took the umbrella from him.

'I can do it, James,' she began, handing over the keys nevertheless. Although his hands were full, he managed to lock the driver's door with ease. The tail-lights flashed twice as he switched on the alarm.

'Nonsense. You look exhausted, you're like a ghost. Come on inside. The fire's lit.'

Beth followed him into the large front sitting room, feeling too tired to argue. The familiar pattern of the leader and the led was instantly re-established, as though all the intervening years had suddenly fallen away, crumbling to nothing under her feet like a rickety bridge in a bad dream. It was almost as if the past decades had never happened: they were swept away abruptly, completely, by this surge of the familiar. Beth was irritated and comforted at the same time by all the old assumptions she could read in her brother's broad, slightly stooped shoulders. They obviously weren't going to talk about anything until they were inside, until he judged that she was ready. Even in times of crisis, James's instinctive hospitality had never deserted him.

She handed him the duty-free bag.

'Your namesake.'

He peered inside, knowing exactly what he would find.

'Jameson,' and he beamed at her, eyes glinting. He became immediately busy. 'A gin and tonic for you?'

Beth nodded.

'Let me just give Laura a quick call, to let her know I've arrived. I'll be back in a minute.'

When she returned, glasses had appeared from the cabinet in the corner, there was the chinking of ice. There was even a lemon, sliced, waiting damply under cling-film. How long had he been standing there at the window, prepared, waiting for her?

'You sit down, Sis; I'll get the drinks.'

Sis. The word suddenly brought Beth back forty years. Their first trolley, a proud wooden structure, with ball bearings for wheels and a steering mechanism made out of string. She remembered its smooth planed seat and the smell of oil from the sturdy handles her dad had fixed at either side. She could see herself, in tears of frustration, unable to go either forwards or backwards. Her legs were too short: she couldn't get the necessary momentum to send her whizzing down the grassy slope. Suddenly, two warm hands were on her back, James's voice at her ear.

'Hang on tight, Sis, and I'll push you. Keep your feet on the steering bar and don't move them until I tell you.'

Rippling shafts of sunlight pierced the bright green of the trees on either side as Beth hurtled down the hill. She had liked the feel of stronger, older hands on her back.

'Here you go.'

Beth took the glass James offered her, and settled herself in the armchair on the opposite side of the fire to his. His book was now open, face down on the floor beside his chair. She strained to see its title: a biography of Cromwell this time. Sometimes, Beth felt that James kept on reading while he waited for his life to begin. She had never understood his passion for history. All those dates, all those long-drawn-out battles, all that endless rummaging around in the past. Even as a child, he'd never gone through an Enid Blyton phase like everyone else had. He'd never hungered for the next Secret Seven or Famous Five adventures, where children led lives impossibly different from theirs, where parents were conveniently absent and picnics were an everyday wonder on islands, in caves, near mountain-tops, with three types of lemonade and lashings and lashings of food. He'd always preferred reality, badgering his mother to get him books from the adult library from the time he was ten.

'How is she?' Beth asked finally.

He shrugged.

'You know, much the same. The nurse will come in at this time every evening, to settle her for the night. Sometimes she gets restless, but most of the time she just sleeps. I think the sedative they've prescribed for her is pretty heavy stuff.'

James sipped at his glass thoughtfully. Beth had the feeling that he was choosing his words carefully.

'Does she know you, James?'

'Sometimes I think she does. A couple of times in the hospital, she pressed my hand. And she's opened her eyes once or twice. But to be honest, I don't even know if she saw me. It's very hard to tell.'

James's voice had gone quiet. He turned his back to Beth and began to poke the fire vigorously. The silence between them was not an uncomfortable one. Beth looked around the room, taking in its shabby grandeur. It was a big, sprawling old Victorian house, but every time Beth came back she was struck by how small it was compared to her childhood memories. Then the rooms had been vast, bright, honey-coloured deserts in summer; huge, bare, freezing plains in winter where a game of hide-and-seek could take all day. The broad, pock-marked floorboards had been varnished again, but the old rug was now badly worn in places; the fabric on the sagging armchairs was threadbare. She felt suddenly overwhelmed by a sense of being home. A great wave of affection washed over her as she watched James's bent back, heard the orange and red sigh of turf briquettes as they hit the flames. When he turned back to her, his round face was glowing from the heat.

'I'm sorry I couldn't come sooner,' she said.

He smiled down at her, his back to the fire, hands spread behind him towards the flames.

'That's okay, Sis. They only let her home this afternoon. The easiest thing for me was to move some stuff in straight away. I'm glad you're here now, though.'

'Are you still going to stay over?'

Beth did not want to be left on her own. Ever since James's phone call, she had felt as though she were drowning in quicksand. She had flailed uselessly from one activity to the next. She'd have delayed for much longer, too, had it been up to her. Even her own daughter had been puzzled by her slowness. On the night of James's call, it was Laura who kept saying: 'But Mum, you have to go *now*.' And Tony had been angry, which had surprised her. She'd hardly ever seen him angry before, not even while they were still married. It was his strength of feeling that had finally jolted Beth into some form of reality. Without it, she knew she'd have allowed herself to be dragged down by a creeping paralysis, sucked under by inertia. She had moved, dreamlike, from one urgent task to the next, her limbs leaden, her mind soggy and unresponsive. Now that she was finally here, the thought of being left on her own filled her with alarm. Especially as the dying woman upstairs was her mother.

James was nodding, looking at her over the tops of his glasses.

'Yes. I want to be here. They don't think she'll hang on too long.'

Beth felt herself gaze stupidly at her brother. There was nothing to say. She knew she should feel shocked, sad, anything. But there was nothing there. The earlier feeling she had had in the car, of being suspended, beyond reality, had not gone away. It was as though all her emotions had been hung up somewhere and were waiting quietly, like clothes hanging limply in a wardrobe, until Beth came back to fit them around her again.

'I almost had an accident on the way from the airport, you know,' she confided suddenly.

She hadn't meant to blurt this out to James, but she felt a need to make up to him for her lack of connectedness, her inability to feel grateful to him for the awful few days he had just been through.

He was immediately concerned, as she had known he would be.

'I *knew* something was wrong with you. What happened?'

Beth told him, feeling her chin begin to throb.

'It was a really stupid thing to do . . . I was lucky he didn't come ploughing right into me.'

'You're upset, that's why you got so distracted. Do you need anything for your chin? I think there's some painkillers down in the kitchen.'

Beth shook her head.

'No, I'll be okay. What really worries me is that he

threatened to report me. I saw him take down my number and . . . God, that's the last thing I need.'

James took her glass.

'Here, let me get you another one. Don't worry about that, Sis – there's no way he'll do that. He won't want to get tied up in paperwork over something that didn't happen. Trust me.'

Beth was about to respond when there was a soft tap on the sitting-room door. They both looked around. A young woman entered almost at once.

'She's comfortable now, Mr Keating. I think she'll sleep through the night.'

James stood up straighter as the woman was speaking. He gestured towards Beth.

'This is my sister, Beth. Beth, this is June, our ministering angel.'

The nurse smiled at him. Then she turned to Beth and shook hands.

'Pleased to meet you.'

Still holding on to Beth's hand, she looked pointedly at James.

'I hope this means you'll be getting some sleep, Mr Keating.'

Beth felt instantly guilty. She drew her hand back at once. The nurse looked right at her.

'He needs a bit of looking after. I don't think he's slept since last Sunday.'

Her tone was cool, her handshake had been unemphatic. James had always had the ability to inspire fierce loyalty. Beth now had the long-familiar sensation of falling short of everyone's expectations. She felt suddenly, thoroughly, depressed.

He was leading June towards the door now, his hand under her elbow.

'Thanks again, June. We'll see you tomorrow. We'll call Dr Crowley if there's any change.'

'Good night,' called Beth.

''Night.'

Beth heard the scrunch of her feet on gravel, saw her fling a scarf around her neck as she went, head bent low against the wind and rain. She watched at the window until the young woman was out of sight, battling her way towards the bus stop.

When she turned around, James was watching her. She hadn't heard him come back into the room.

'I chose to sit with her in the hospital, Beth. I'd have done it every night, even if you'd been here, right from the very start.'

Beth nodded; it was suddenly necessary to bite down hard on her lower lip. She smiled at her brother.

'I know you would. Now that I'm here, at least we can keep each other company.'

He held out his hand to her.

'Do you want to go up and see her now?'

She hesitated. James immediately gestured towards her chair instead, as though he had just had a much better idea.

'Tell you what, let's finish our drinks first. Then we'll go up together, okay?'

They sat quietly in the firelight. Beth knew she was

on the edge of something momentous. It existed separately from her sense of gratitude and her brother's kindness; it was something else, something that hung heavily in the air between them. She waited, sipping, hoping for courage to fill her.

*

The bedroom was in darkness, filled by an intense, dry heat. There was a peculiar smell in the air that Beth instantly recognized but could not name, and a depth of stillness which she had never known before. James lit a new night-light on his mother's dressing table. Together, they turned to face the bed.

Beth's first reaction was a start of surprise. *This* was not her mother! Had there been some grotesque mistake? Where was the cloud of robust energy, the unmistakable air of authority and *capability*? Although Beth had thought she'd understood the implications of her mother's sudden, massive stroke, she had not expected to find her so thoroughly absent from herself.

James was caressing the soft hair back from her forehead, murmuring to her. Beth was horrified. She saw that one corner of the half-open mouth was curving sharply downward, that the whole left-hand side of her face seemed to have collapsed, defeated by years and gravity. Abruptly, she moved away from the bedside and left the room. At the top of the stairs, she paused, holding on to the banisters.

Steady yourself.

James followed her out onto the landing almost at once. Anxiety was everywhere, clouding all around him.

'Sis? Are you all right? She's not in any pain, you know.'

Beth nodded, trying to swallow. Her throat and chest felt obstructed somehow, she had difficulty breathing deeply. How did he do it, night after night? How come he was able to face it, and she wasn't?

'Sorry. It's just the shock – seeing her so unlike her old self. It's okay. I'll be fine.'

From a point somewhere beyond feeling, Beth forced herself to make the return journey back towards her side of the bed. She understood that James, from a position of long standing, occupied his mother's right side, the side towards which her head turned automatically. That had always been his privilege. Had she opened her eyes, his gaze would have illuminated everything for her. Light of my life.

Beth had always understood her place.

She sat now on the little armchair by the window which James had thoughtfully provided for her. It had been hers since early childhood, a permanent resident in her old room. The bo-bo-dee. Her childish efforts to name this chair had christened it for ever. No one in the family ever knew it as anything else but the bo-bo-dee. The bedside seat; the seat her mother had occupied during so many bedside vigils in the past. Nights of steaming basins of water, warm towels and Friar's Balsam. Times when she, Beth, had been sick with croup, bronchitis, asthma. Now its newly upholstered seat spoke to Beth of those times. She would rather have not remembered. They carried a debt which she didn't know if she was able to repay.

'She's very peaceful, Sis, isn't she?'

There was a note of pleading in James's voice which Beth hadn't ever heard before. It shocked her. Surely he wasn't looking to *her* for reassurance? He was way older – a full five years, just recently past his half-century. He had to have all of this under wraps; *he* was in charge. If he weren't, then where did that leave her?

Beth reached out tentatively and took her mother's left hand in hers. It was surprisingly warm in her grasp. The skin was papery, almost translucent, with blue veins prominent. The thin gold wedding band sat loosely on her ring finger, held in place only by the protruding, shiny knuckle. Beth felt her breath begin to ease some-where at the back of her throat as she stroked the old, freckled skin. The warm hand resting in hers felt real and solid, a weight that would be reckoned with. Beth was glad; there was no slipping away here. This was still a woman of substance.

Her own fears began to dissolve as she held on to her mother's hand, covering it with her own, protec-tively. Some of that old, familiar strength seemed to seep through the fingertips into Beth's, so that she felt suddenly hopeful, more grounded, as she relaxed into her chair. It was as though a long period of waiting had finally come to an end. This was not going to be as bad as she'd feared. She answered James quietly.

'Yes, she looks as though she's just . . . resting.'

Beth would have continued, but the doorbell startled them both. Its shrill unexpectedness made each of them look questioningly at the other.

'That'll be Olive,' James offered, finally.

Ah, Olive.

'You go down, James. I'll stay with her.'

'Are you sure?'

Beth's heart was no longer racing. It was peaceful here, nothing else was expected of her but her presence.

'Absolutely. Take your time.'

James noticed the way his mother's hand lay quietly in Beth's. He left the room quickly, satisfied.

Beth leaned towards her mother.

'Tell you what, Mam,' she whispered, 'I'd much prefer to sit here with you all night than have ten minutes of the lovely Olive.'

It pleased Beth to see her mother's fixed grimace as a sardonic smile. No love lost there.

She could hear voices downstairs. She hoped Olive had come on her own, that she wouldn't have to face any nieces and nephews just yet. Somewhere, a door closed, too loudly. Beth could feel her mouth going dry. Please, God, not a scene. Not now, not tonight.

Quick, urgent, footsteps up the stairs. She braced herself.

Olive's head and shoulders appeared abruptly around the bedroom door. Beth was shocked at the sudden, discordant notes which seemed to swell from her in waves, disturbing the air all around the room. For an instant, the absurd blackness of Olive's hair and her heavily painted face made Beth think of Hallowe'en. Olive held on to the edge of the door with both hands, her red fingernails standing out sharply against the white paint. Finally, she motioned towards Beth with her head, barely meeting her eyes.

'Can I talk to you for a minute?'

Her whisper was urgent, almost aggressive.

Beth sighed inwardly. She laid her mother's hand gently on the bedspread. She was surprised at how *offended* she felt by Olive's intrusion; she had to make a promise to herself not to lose her temper.

Olive was standing on the landing, her arms folded. Beth noticed how dressed-up she was, her skirt and jacket much more in keeping with the cut and thrust of the boardroom than the sick room. She tried to manage a smile, conscious of James beginning his slow, heavy ascent up the stairs. Olive began speaking, almost at once.

'You can manage Alice on your own for one evening, can't you? After all, James has been cooped up in the hospital non-stop for almost a week.'

Her voice was full of sharp edges. Her movements, too, were uneasy. She was smoothing her hair, straightening her skirt, her hands restless; she did not look directly at Beth.

'Hello, Olive,' said Beth quietly. 'You're looking well.'

Her own response startled her. It was as though she were suddenly floating in a bubble of lightness and brightness. It took no effort to glide over the solid wall of Olive's resentment. Up, up and over; down the other side.

James was almost at her shoulder.

'Of course I'll stay on my own tonight,' she said. 'I'm very conscious that James has had to do everything all week; on his own.'

She was still able to keep her voice soft. She allowed no trace of the earlier shock of fear she'd felt at the thought of having to do this alone, so soon. Olive looked right at her, reacting to the sting in the tail. *On his own.*

He's been on his own for twenty-five years, ever since he married you.

Beth turned to James, now beside her on the landing.

'Why don't you and Olive go out for the rest of the evening? I'm quite happy to stay here. Just show me where Dr Crowley's number is and you head off. I'll be fine,' said Beth, emphatically, watching her brother's frown deepen. He knew, of course he did. Now he would try to protect her.

'But you've only just arrived,' objected James. 'You haven't even had anything to eat yet.'

'I'm not hungry,' she said, keeping her voice steady. The palms of her hands felt all warm and prickly. 'I can always get something later on. Go.'

And she gave him a gentle shove.

Olive's arms were folded again. Beth noticed, irrelevantly, that her sister-in-law's earrings actually matched the intricate gold buttons of her cuffs. She thought, suddenly, how nice it would be to slap her face.

'How are Keith and Gemma?' she asked instead.

'Fine, thank you,' replied Olive, keeping her eyes on her husband, hurrying him.

'Good,' said Beth politely. 'I hope I'll see them soon. The twins still taking New York by storm?'

There was no answer. Olive wanted to be gone. She

was already making her way downstairs. James turned back to his sister, his eyes troubled.

Beth shook her head at him.

'Go on; I'll still be here when you get back.'

She kissed the top of his head. He followed his wife, without a word.

Beth waited until the front door closed behind them. Then she went back into the bedroom, back to her side of the bed, back to her little seat.

'You'd have been proud of me just there, Mam,' she said. 'The lovely Olive didn't win that one, and I didn't lose the rag.'

There was no reply; of course there wouldn't be. Nevertheless, Beth had the strange feeling that she was on the brink of something that approached conversation. Her mother had rarely stayed silent before. Their words had, more often than not, collided in mid-air, becoming missiles hurled at one another. Beth had never felt that she had been really listened to. Her mother had always insisted it was because she spoke no sense.

The silence in this room was almost like being heard for the first time. Each of them now had to play a different role from the usual. Her mother was unspeaking, but it was not the angry silence that was the prelude, or the sequel, to a row. Beth was neither defensive nor belligerent; she knew that this time her words would have the shape and sense that she intended. They would not become warped and loaded as they negotiated the gap between her intention and her mother's understanding.

Listening to the uneven breathing of the frail, elderly

woman beside her, Beth hoped it wasn't already too late for her to feel beyond the years of sharp exchanges, the slow foxtrot of anger and disappointment that had kept each of them at arm's length from the other, dancing to the same old tunes.

'I think you and I are going to get on just fine,' she said softly, straightening the already immaculate sheet.

'It's nice to be home.'

*

It was a new feeling for Beth to be sitting still, to be doing nothing. For two hours, she had sat almost unmoving, watching every breath taken, every rise and fall of the thin, flat chest. She had not noticed the time passing; she was intent on her vigil. The woman in the bed did not yet look like her mother, although from time to time, Beth thought she saw in the ravaged face something which inspired recognition. The pink bed-jacket with its delicate ribbons and lacy edging drew her gaze back, again and again. She thought how absurd it was to be so moved by something as ordinary, as prosaic as a knitted pink bed-jacket.

The collapse of feeling that had followed James's phone call, the creeping sense of life being hung up somewhere, far out of her reach, now began to recede. Something akin to pain began to seep into all the cold spaces inside her chest. Being watchful, being attentive to this someone else, Beth could feel the lifting of the heavy curtain between her and the reality around her. In the absolute stillness of the sick room, yellow light guttering, sensation flooded back so suddenly, so ferociously that her heart began to speed up. She was afraid to move, to stand, didn't want to disturb it. It was a tremendous relief to hear the front door close, and James's heavy step on the landing.

'Everything okay?' he asked.

She nodded, suddenly choked by the unbearable tenderness with which he stroked his mother's face. For the first time, the long overdue tears began to well and fall, and Beth made no attempt to wipe them away. Their warmth was comforting. It was almost like melting. James looked at her anxiously. She had never been a weeper.

'I knew I shouldn't have left you alone. It was much too soon.'

She shook her head.

'No. No, it was just right. I haven't been able to cry since I heard the news. This is a relief.'

She half-laughed at him, resorting to wiping her eyes on her sleeve. There was no effort to this grieving, no sobbing. The tears were simply releasing themselves; they demanded nothing from her.

James handed her some tissues from the box on the bedside locker.

'Here,' and he grinned at her. 'Bet you haven't used your sleeve since you were a kid. You used to be a snotty little urchin.'

'I know. Some things never change.'

She blew her nose, loudly. He was looking at her kindly.

'Why don't you go downstairs and make us both a

cup of tea. There's plenty of food in the fridge; get yourself something to eat. Go on,' he urged.

Beth's stomach felt empty, but it was not the cave-like hollowness of hunger. It was something else, something she didn't yet recognize, couldn't put a name to.

She patted her mother's hand before she stood up. It was a reassuring touch; it said, don't worry, I'll be back in a minute. It would be wrong to withdraw her comfort abruptly, just to stand up and go. How much, she wondered, did anybody really know about what dying people felt? Maybe, like a blind person whose other senses become more acute to compensate for the loss of sight, the dying develop a kind of third eye, alert and watchful in the middle of their forehead, seeing and understanding things hidden from the rest of us. It gave Beth comfort to think like that; it went a little way towards explaining the growing sense of closeness between her and the small figure in the pink bed-jacket. Perhaps, if she believed in this other way of seeing, this frail old woman beside her might just become her mother again, in time.

Beth made her way downstairs, then along the narrow passageway beside the dining-room. The bulb was blown so she felt carefully, with familiar feet, for the two steps which led down to the level of the kitchen. Switching on the light after the darkness of the hallway was like an electric shock. The kitchen looked suddenly floodlit. The red floor tiles, the scrubbed pine table, the press-doors which her mother had lovingly beeswaxed once a year, every year, just before Christmas. All of this was familiar to Beth. But it was familiar now in a different way. It was almost as though someone had reconstructed the kitchen to conform to her memory. It was a copy, not the real thing. Its core was missing. Beth realized with a shock, that never, not even once that she could remember, had she been in this house without her mother's central presence in this room, at this table. She had a sudden, vivid image of a greying head bent over the Singer sewing-machine, competent hands easing yards and yards of fabric under the shiny foot, producing perfectly straight and even lines of stitching every time. An aproned figure sat with her back to the dresser, peeling and chopping vegetables, the old cracked baking-bowl full of salted water set in front of her. Her absence gave the kitchen an eerie stillness, quite unlike the reposeful silence of the bedroom upstairs, which now claimed her.

Beth plugged in the kettle, looking out at the straggly, blackened grass. The big muddy field behind their home had long ago been transformed into a cluster of houses, each one with its own tiny front garden. The streetlights now cast long shadows over Beth's old back garden, occasionally lighting up some corner as the glow was filtered through the swaying branches. She remembered her dad planting a line of spindly new trees near the solid oaks which had been there since his childhood, and way before. He'd told her they'd grow tall, reaching even higher, in time, than the stone walls of his sheltered garden. He'd been troubled by all the new house-building on his tranquil territory, upset by the intrusion of unwanted neighbours. But that, he'd told Beth, is life.

A gust of sudden wind threw a shaft of streetlight onto the big apple tree, now gnarled and ugly in its winter bareness. Beth could only ever remember it as full and leafy, part of endless childhood summers. With a bright-green jolt of memory, she saw the swing her father had made for them, the toy with the edge of danger that had kept the neighbourhood kids swarming all over them one July, begging for a go. She had wanted to charge them a penny, she remembered, instinctively understanding the value of novelty. Her mother had been adamant that she should do no such thing. It was the first of many battles they had had over that swing. Beth had been cross that she had had to wait her turn. It wasn't fair. It was *their* swing, in *their* garden. Why did they have to share it and wait in line, like the other kids?

'You're a selfish little girl, Elizabeth Keating. Why can't you be more like James?'

God, if she'd had a penny for every time she'd heard that, growing up. It was a wonder she didn't hate James's guts.

Beth searched in the press beside the sink for the old wooden tray her dad had made.

'You can have my go, Sis. They'll all go home for tea soon and then we can have it to ourselves.'

James, pleading, ever the peacemaker. Even as a very small child, she had known when to stop, when to surrender. His generosity had been irresistible. On the few occasions when she did persist, it was James who, unaccountably, ended up in trouble.

'Stop giving in to her, James. She has to learn how to share, to be patient.'

The kettle clicked off. Beth saw that the window-pane had become clouded by steam. It was cold in here. Shivering, she turned to the painted dresser in the corner where her mother always kept an array of old china. She had hardly ever thrown anything out: she'd believed that most things could be mended. Still there, on the second shelf beside the yellow one that she used every day, was the old willow-patterned teapot. Its glaze was cracked and spidery. Beth lifted it and shook it gently. It had been broken and jigsawed back together many times. There was no sound. She smiled to herself.

It had always been known as 'The Bank'. Into this, her father had put his wages on a Thursday evening, an unopened envelope. Her mother would divide the notes and coins into different piles, handing her father one of them, the smallest, for himself. On a Wednesday night, she would lift The Bank and shake it. Sometimes there was no sound at all; more often, there was the chinking of coin.

'Only a rattle left, Jack,' she would laugh. 'Time to go again!'

Beth poured boiling water onto the tea leaves. Her mother had never believed in tea-bags. She put the milk-jug and the two china cups and saucers onto the tray. Mugs were *not* suitable for tea, her mother had sniffed, on more than one occasion in the past when Beth had come to visit. You had to drink tea out of bone china. Beth's eyes were drawn to the wall behind the kettle, where dozens of little yellow reminders were stuck to the tiles. *'Set alarm'*, *'Lock downstairs doors and windows'*, *'Water plants'*, she read, in her mother's familiar, distinctive handwriting. Beth smiled. She was in the habit of leaving such notes to herself, too.

She pulled the woollen cosy over the teapot, and went in search of sugar. James still took it; or perhaps Olive had won that battle, too. There were a couple of packets of Jacob's Mikado, James's favourite biscuits, in the tin; a chocolate cake was still in its cellophane wrapper. Beth grinned when she saw them. Evidently, the war was still in progress.

She lifted the tray carefully, waiting for her eyes to grow accustomed to the dark hallway again. Must get a bulb tomorrow. Must get something to make a meal, too. James's idea of a full fridge and hers were quite different. And she didn't want to survive on chocolate cake.

Slowly, she went up the stairs, feeling as though she had already been back for a long time.

*

After two cups of tea, Beth felt suddenly alert, all her earlier tiredness replaced by a surge of energy which made her feel she could stay up all night. She now wanted to; she was almost impatient to resume the silent conversation which had drawn her close, closer than ever before to the mother who was now listening to her presence with undivided attention. She turned to face James. They hadn't spoken in quite some time, each content to watch and wait in the flickering silence.

'I'll stay with her for tonight. You must be exhausted.'

James was finishing his second slice of cake. It was a little while before he answered. Beth noticed that he was having difficulty in stifling a yawn.

'It's funny, you know – before you came this evening, I hadn't even felt tired, not once. Now that you're here, I can't keep my eyes open.'

She smiled at him.

'You're off duty, James. We'll take it in shifts tomorrow; for now, she's all mine. Go on to bed.'

'Are you really sure?'

'Cross my heart.'

He smiled at the childish echo. But still, he didn't move. Beth prodded him again, understanding his need to be reassured.

'I'm quite happy to stay, James, honestly. I'll call you if she gets distressed.'

Looking less reluctant now, he stood up.

'You'll also call me if *you* get distressed – deal?'

'Deal. Now go on, it's almost one o'clock. Get a good night's sleep.'

James kissed her on the cheek. After he left, Beth renewed the night-light on the dressing table, and lit an extra one on the bedside locker. It gave her pleasure to perform these little tasks, as though the ritual of light-making could somehow increase her mother's comfort. Shadows danced on the walls until the flames settled.

Her mother murmured and moved a little, her hands shifting. Beth stood up at once and leaned over her. In the pale, yellow light, she could see how dry and cracked the old woman's lips were. There must be lip-balm somewhere.

She did a quick mental check on the contents of her make-up bag. She had left home in such numb confusion that she could no longer remember what she had packed and what she had left behind. Anyway, she didn't want to leave this room, not even for a minute. This was her night, her responsibility. She wasn't going to let anyone down.

'It's all right, Mam, I'll find something here; your poor lips look very dry.'

Beth laid her hand on her mother's forehead, glad to repeat James's gesture, to learn from him. She bent down to the bedside locker and pulled at the wooden door. To her surprise, it wouldn't give. She tugged harder. Pulling the night-light towards her, she peered at the doorframe, moving the light above and below the little ornate handle. A shadow confirmed it; the door was locked. Beth sat back on her heels, puzzled.

'What are you doing? You are *not* to go poking around where you have no business!'

Guiltily, a little girl sat on the floor, legs tucked under her, treasures arrayed all around her. It had been like finding her way into Aladdin's cave. A gold locket wrapped in a red velvet bag, a plum-coloured lipstick in a shiny black case; a silver mirror that made your face huge, or smaller, depending on which side you used. A small, round bottle with a stopper that made a glassy sound when you pulled it out, and a delicious smell filled the room.

Caught red-handed.

'Those are my private things, and I'll thank you not to go where you're not wanted.'

Her mother's mouth was a tight, angry line as her hands swept the child's treasures off the wooden floor. Beth wondered why her mother didn't wear the lovely plum-coloured lipstick, or dab the delicious perfume on her wrists, or behind her ears, as she had seen other mothers do.

'Now go downstairs and play. James is waiting for you.'

Beth felt the pins and needles starting from her uncomfortable position on the floor. Was it ever since *that* day that her mother had begun to lock away everything that was precious to her? She tried hard to remember what age she had been. Younger than six, or older than six? It was important to know. If she'd been older than six, then her dad was already dead and such private memories should not have been disturbed. Her mother would have been right to be angry.

But if she had been younger than that, and just a little girl playing among her mother's things? Beth stood up, rubbing her right foot vigorously.

There was a sudden movement from the bed. Instantly, Beth leaned over, taking her mother's hand.

'It's all right, Mam, I'm here.'

The eyes flickered open, focusing suddenly on Beth. There was a slight, but distinct, pressure from her hand.

'Let her,' she whispered, the undamaged side of her mouth moving urgently.

Beth felt the first stirrings of panic. She was raving. Let who do what?

'Of course I will. Don't worry. I'm not going anywhere.'

'*Let* her,' she whispered again, and this time Beth saw some of the old energy in her eyes, in the expression that suddenly lit up half her face.

'Don't worry. I will. It's all under control, I promise you.'

Beth held her hand close, smiling down at her. She knew that her voice had acquired conviction, authority. Her mother would respond to that.

As quickly as the wakefulness had begun, it slipped away. But at least contact had been made. Alice had allowed herself to be reassured by her daughter. Beth felt suddenly happy at the thought, felt that she could do whatever was asked of her now.

The puzzle was, who was the 'her' and what was Beth to allow her to do? Maybe it was nothing at all, just the incoherent ramblings of a dying woman. But her eyes had been clear and direct. Maybe there was a clue somewhere in the room, she just had to find it. Beth knelt down again beside the locker and pulled harder on the handle. There was still no give. She looked around her. Where would someone hide a key? Where would *she* hide it? Her eyes lit on the jewellery box on the dressing table. James had given her mother that, years ago, for Christmas. Mahogany, inlaid with mother-of-pearl; he had bought it and restored it because it was the same age as the house.

Beth lifted the hinged wooden lid and carefully took out the red velvet-covered tray. Underneath, there was a tangle of glass beads, old necklaces, a silver brooch or two. Beth moved them about, as though trailing her hand through water. Suddenly, she felt a small shock of recognition. There it was, the brass key. Now that she saw it, she remembered it again, remembered the abrupt way her mother had used it that day long ago, placing it when she had finished into the pocket of her apron.

'Now go downstairs and play. James is waiting for you.'

Beth fitted the key into the lock, moving the brass escutcheon out of the way. The door yielded at once. She put her hand inside, involuntarily glancing up at the bed. If she were caught in the act again . . . Her hand grasped at something large and silky. She pulled it out, into the dim light. A make-up bag. The one that she, Beth, had given her for her seventieth birthday. Purple silk, shot through with gold. Her mother had had a dress like that, once. Beth had thought that the memory would please her. And it had: she had written at once, warmly, saying how much she liked it. Beth had been very surprised. It was the first time in several years that her mother had written to her with such affection.

She pulled the plaited drawstrings apart. Perhaps she would find the lip-balm here, or Vaseline, or her mother's cure-all – a tin of Ayrton's pink ointment. It had been a permanent feature of her childhood, the ready answer to wasp-stings, skinned knees and, occasionally, sunburn. Her mother's response to every physical crisis had been to reach for the pink ointment. But there was nothing like that here. Instead, tied primly with Christmas-cake ribbon, were two packets of fat, white envelopes.

Beth cautiously took out the first parcel. In her mother's copperplate script, the word 'James' was written in thick, black ink. Beth's mouth went dry and she experienced the familiar falling-down-inside sensation of disappointment. She turned over the second parcel, telling herself to expect nothing, wanting to find something.

In the same confident handwriting, 'Elizabeth' leapt out at her. She *knew* it; she knew she'd felt their conversation begin the minute she had sat by the bed and taken the thin hand in hers. *Let her.* Of course, that was what she had meant. Nothing to do with permission. It was the *letters* she had wanted to signal.

Carefully, she replaced James's parcel in the silk bag, pulled the drawstrings tight, and replaced the bag in the locker. She turned the key in the lock once more and put it back in the jewellery box. Then she sat by the bed and stroked her mother's hand.

'I've found them, Mam. I've found the letters. You can rest now. I have them.'

There was no movement. Beth leaned forward, willing the next breath to be taken, holding her own in fear. The pink bed-jacket rose and fell, almost imperceptibly. Beth sat back again, filled with a sense of urgency.

She pulled the first envelope out from behind the

ribbon. She was careful not to disturb their order. Her hands had begun to tremble slightly. She wondered if it was a delayed reaction from the incident with the cement lorry.

She retied the ribbon carefully. If she knew her mother at all, their order would be important. She moved the bedside light closer to her and opened the first envelope.

TWO

The Green Tricycle

ALICE CLOSED THE front door behind her and stood for a moment in the hall. Shafts of July sunlight pierced the stained-glass panels, making crazily-coloured patterns on the wooden floor. She watched as the streams of light were filled with dust motes, dancing giddily around each other.

She hung up her light summer jacket on the hallstand. She opened her handbag and took out a comb, patting her hair into place. She noticed that even the touch of barely-pink lipstick had feathered around the edges of her lips, making her mouth look, if anything, older than its years. She wouldn't bother touching it up again. Recently, she had begun to see old women wearing make-up as somewhat pathetic. The first time she'd felt that way had been quite a shock: she had never before thought of herself as old. Elderly, yes, getting on, no spring chicken – but never as finally, irrevocably – *old*. The garish blur of colour on eyes and lips, the heavy powdering over the facial cracks, had begun to embarrass her; she'd begun to find such blue and red notes of defiance sadly off-key. Today, in particular, she had been assaulted by the messy outlines of lips and eyes

37

which had seemed to her to be everywhere – leafing through magazines in the hospital waiting room, queuing up for coffee, standing at the bus stop. Such a lot of *waiting*.

Alice leaned closer to the mirror, as though her eyes were drawn by something else, something she hadn't seen before. She peered at her reflection for a moment, looking straight and deep into clear-blue eyes that returned her steady gaze. Was there a difference to her face now that could be seen by others? Would she have to avert her eyes even from strangers on the street? Abruptly, she pulled away from the mirror, turning her back on it. The silence of the house surrounded her. She could have gone to James's, of course, but a stronger instinct had brought her home.

She snapped her handbag shut and placed it on the hall-stand. Then she walked down the passageway to the kitchen. She wouldn't think about anything, just for the moment. Put the kettle on first; everything else could wait. Alice stood at the kitchen window, waiting for the water to boil. Looking out at the back garden, with its ivy and creeper-clad stone walls, always soothed her. The shrubs, most of which Jack had planted years and years ago, stood out in curious relief, their shape and colour heightened by the intense summer-green of the grass. Over the years, she had been careful to replace those that hadn't thrived with members of the same flowering family – Jack's eye for shape and colour, she thought, could never be equalled. Keeping to his plan for the rambling old walled garden had been almost like keeping in touch. Today, Alice had the strangest sensation that she was only now seeing this garden, in all its familiarity, for the first time.

At this time of year, the screen of trees at the end wall obliterated almost completely all signs of the new houses. Of course, they weren't new any more. New almost forty years ago, but for Alice, they still intruded on to the landscape of her memory. She and Jack had resented those new houses: their upper windows were prying eyes into the sheltered intimacy of their family. The two oaks, planted long before Jack's parents had bought the house, and the ageing apple tree, no longer any good for bearing fruit, all looked in some way different. The garden looked almost expectant, poised for change.

Shrub, she suddenly thought. What a funny word. It was one of those she had lost recently; it had strayed away from her, like a disobedient child. Ever since its return, she had regarded it suspiciously, in case it eluded her again. She could no longer take it for granted; it had acquired a strangeness in its absence, and had still not quite recovered its old familiarity. She could still see its size and shape, the curl of the letters as she would write them. It was a surprising word, spoken aloud – bare and functional, straggly, blunt like winter. It bore no relationship to the extravagance of the growth spreading out in front of her. *Clematis, Cistus, Hebe. Hypericum, Lavandula, Olearia.* Liquid words, green and lush, darkness-scented. *Passiflora, Potentilla*: vibrant-sounding and vigorous as their colours. And then the dreamy, floaty ones: *Hemerocallis, Nymphaea, Mimulus.* That part of the back garden nearest the house was a gently undulating carpet of shades of purples and whites, blues and yellows, defying the eye's need for gravity as it seemed to sweep upwards, blurring the harshness of the line between the boundary wall and the ground below. Her eye was drawn back down again, as usual, to the pool of still, reedy water, off-centre and irregularly shaped, with its shock of cup-like, crimson flowers. When she'd first come home with baby James, Jack had proudly taken both of them into his July garden and shown them the pond, newly dug, carefully lined and filled with *Nymphaea* 'James Brydon'. He had been bright-eyed, almost child-like in his pleasure that he had found a water plant to celebrate the naming of his new son. Throughout the years, he had added to his garden with the slips and bulbs provided in the main by the people whose houses he painted; it had added to his pleasure that so much beauty had been created for nothing. Alice had often thought that he derived a special delight from the cuttings he pinched from gardens when he had failed to cajole the owner, or when he simply hadn't bothered to ask, sure that nobody was looking. The majority of the great plan had happened before Elizabeth was born. The final rhododendron, the one which bore her name, had been planted one September, and obedi-ently produced large trusses of scarlet flowers just in time for her arrival, early the following April.

The loud click of the kettle's automatic switch drew Alice away from the window. She reached for the yellow teapot on the dresser shelf. She pulled her eyes away from the bits and pieces of china arrayed there, and made her way deliberately back to the sink. She filled the teapot right up, and poured milk from the carton into her little white and gold china jug. She couldn't bear cartons or bottles on the table; she hadn't been brought up to that. Jack had been much more easy-going about such things, but he'd bowed willingly to her preference. So had James. Elizabeth had fought it. But then, Elizabeth had fought her on just about everything.

Alice had no idea how long she'd been sitting at the kitchen table when the phone rang. She jumped, the silence of the house shattered, the remembered years scattering away like disturbed mice into the safety of the gradually darkening kitchen corners. She blinked in shock a few times, and stood, holding on to the back of her chair for a moment, as though planting her feet firmly in the present again. She reached for the phone, already knowing it was James.

'Hello?'

'Alice?'

His voice was anxious, as though he didn't really believe it was she who had answered.

'Hello, James.'

'I tried calling at three, but there was no one home. How did you get on?'

'I didn't get back until after four. I've been . . . in the garden ever since; it was such a lovely afternoon. I got on fine. Absolutely nothing to worry about.'

Alice made the decision even as she spoke. She hadn't yet given any conscious thought to what she was going to tell her son, but now she felt sure that she did not want him to know. It was her knowledge, and she wasn't yet ready to give it away. Sharing it had the power to make her crumble, to make her descend into sickness, into the indignity of the invalid. What she'd been told today by doctors wearing white coats and grave expressions, she hadn't needed to be told. She had already known it herself for some time.

'What did he say?'

'*She*. Dr Turner is a *she*.'

'What did she say, then?'

Alice smiled to herself. Dear James. Not even a trace of irritation in his voice. Just concern, and love. And the ever-present undercurrent of anxiety.

'All the tests came back clear. There's nothing to worry about. I'm just suffering from the forgetfulness of old age.'

Alice kept her voice deliberately light, pre-empting the questions she knew James would still want to ask. He had always craved her reassurance.

'But what about ... what you said felt like confusion?'

Alice's tone became firmer. James had never been one to confront her. He would back off if he sensed no weakness on her part, none of the shocked vulnerability of illness and old age which he had been expecting.

'I'm nearly seventy-six, James. I'm not as sprightly as I used to be. That's all. It's not Alzheimer's, my blood pressure's fine and everything else is as it should be. For my age.'

Alice stopped. Just the right amount of sharpness in her tone. Now he would appease her. She could hear the smile in his voice as he answered.

'Did they know what a tough old bird they were dealing with?'

'Absolutely. And this tough old bird has just got to keep on doing what she's doing. Dr Crowley will get the detailed results in a week or so, and I've to go and see her then.'

The subject was closed. Alice waited. Whatever James said next would tell whether she had pulled it off.

'Well, that's a relief. I still wish you had let me go with you, though.'

There was a pause. Alice's tone was gentler now. She could afford to be.

'I appreciate the offer, you know I do. But you know how much I hate a fuss.'

It was a well-aired topic between them. She knew James's feelings; she also knew that he was far too soft-hearted to bully her.

'Okay, okay. I'm just glad it all worked out. Do you want to come over for dinner? I can collect you.'

'No, I won't, thanks. Not tonight. I'm a little tired after walking around town.'

'Of course, of course.'

Alice could almost hear him kicking himself for what he would perceive as his lack of sensitivity. She spoke again, quickly.

'Why don't you come to me for lunch tomorrow? Have you time?'

Yes, he had. He'd be there by one. Alice kept him talking a little longer, asked about the children, about Olive. She was sure that he was satisfied, finally, that he wouldn't want to probe any further. She was tired by the time the conversation ended. Lying seemed to require an awful lot of effort. But she needed to gather her strength around her; she needed the time alone to absorb what was happening to her. And, at the same time, it was more than that – time of itself would never be enough. She needed what her grandchildren referred to as 'space'. She had never quite understood until today what they all meant by that. She did not want to be reduced by James's concern into a *patient*; she did not want the humiliation of seeing herself transformed before his eyes into an old, helpless woman. It wasn't just to spare his feelings, although it was partly that, too. It was more a need to be still, to reflect, to draw together all the different strands of herself, all the loops and twists of possibility and probability which had unravelled before her all that afternoon.

Alice felt that she was dying in small steps. At first, it had seemed like an ordinary forgetfulness, like something being on the tip of your tongue, but the something had become more elusive than formerly. The first time it had happened, she hadn't been at all frightened, merely bemused. She had held the sticky crimson globes in her palm, examining them closely, moving them around with her finger as though she could somehow discover their name by closer inspection. But the word simply would not come. She knew that she was familiar with them, that she had used them in her Christmas cakes since God was a boy. But their name kept slipping away from her. The mixture was ready; *they* needed to be added to the pale creamy mass of butter, sugar and eggs that already filled her baking bowl. The word was in her head, she could feel it there, wandering around aimlessly, lost somewhere among the complex circuitry. Suddenly, like a tiny explosion, it came to her: *cherries.* She had laughed out loud in relief. She'd realized that her forehead was damp; the effort, and the frustration of trying to remember had actually made her sweat. And yet, it wasn't quite *remembering*; that didn't really describe it. It was more like searching for a sense of recognition. It was as though she had never seen cherries before; that even if she had remembered the word, it would no longer fit. She felt as if a whole new language might need to be learned, with rules and grammar to suit the new strangeness of the previously familiar.

She had gone and pulled the little transparent plastic container out of the pedal bin in the kitchen, just to make absolutely sure. There it was, written cheerfully in red: Glacé Cherries. For the rest of that afternoon, Alice had murmured the words over and over again to herself, capturing them on her tongue and in her ear, making sure that they could never escape her again. And she hadn't forgotten them since: she saw them now, large and bold, shackled to the screen of her memory. But she had forgotten others instead, and the frantic search for them had finally distressed her so much that she had grown urgent in her need to know, to find out why. And now she knew. Old age is a terrible thing, she had once confided to James. But she had said it brightly, not really complaining, just ruefully resigned to the inevitability of it all. That was before she had seen the prospect of the oblivion which now yawned before her: physical infirmity she could take, she had no choice, but the obliteration of herself, her memories, filled her with terror. Much more than dying, she feared the incremental loss of the past and present lives which made up the person called Alice. That was now the nameless, formless future she felt condemned to. *Strike, stricken, stroke.* She did not want to become someone who would look at her children from behind vacant eyes and ask: 'Do I know you?'

Stop it, she told herself severely. She stood up from the kitchen table, lifting the tea-cosy a little, and patting the side of the china teapot. Cold. Perhaps she should have something to eat. Or read her book. Or go to bed early. Alice felt suddenly restless, and the sensation disturbed her: she had never been one for indecision. She must *do* something. She pushed herself into the familiarity of her night-time routine. Doing what was normal at this time of the evening seemed to hold out the best chance of making her feel more secure. Midway through checking the bolts on the back door, she stopped and opened the door instead, stepping outside into the heavily scented garden. The hidden jasmine and evening stock brought with them a wave of memory. James and Elizabeth as children, sitting on this back step, shelling peas from Jack's vegetable plot. James and Elizabeth giggling as they spooned ice cream into tall glasses, topping them up with fizzy lemonade, shrieking as the frothy mixture bubbled suddenly up and over. James and Elizabeth on the swing—. An idea was slowly beginning to form in Alice's mind. It was tentative at first, composed of a jumble of sepia-coloured scenes and memories like still photographs. It was as though the sudden blast of perfume had released the genie from the bottle, and her children's lives tumbled out in disarray all around her.

The very simplicity of the idea delighted and startled her at first. She would write to them. While she still had a firm enough grasp of language, while she was still sharp and self-sufficient, she would write to her children. She didn't know how much longer she had before everything familiar was wiped out. The doctors with their sheaves of notes couldn't tell her that, nobody could tell her that. The recent series of small, relentless strokes that she had suffered had already stolen bits of her life from her, spiriting it away, little by little. Perhaps that's the way it would be – small steps towards obliteration. Or, if she were lucky, a thunderbolt; either way, she was on borrowed time. She was filled with a sense of urgency and purpose. Now she had work to do.

Alice locked and bolted the back door. Before she forgot, she went into the hall and punched the four-number code into the alarm. James had insisted on its installation, had even carried it out himself. She'd fought it at first, but not too hard. And now, today, when she was feeling more vulnerable, she welcomed the reassuring wink of its tiny red eye.

She went back into the kitchen and pulled out an old notebook from the dresser drawer. It was a bit dog-eared, but it would do for tonight. She wanted to write things down now, quickly, before they swam away from her again: she knew only too well the strength of the undertow. Tomorrow, she decided, she would buy proper writing paper, a nice fountain pen, a hard-back notebook. It would be a treat, something to look forward to. There were suddenly so many things she needed to say, and the need now felt like never before: new, urgent. Alice knew that she had never been much good at talking about feelings; with James, that hadn't seemed to matter. There was an instinctual under-standing between the two of them: they shared a secret language, like twins. He had stopped calling her 'Mother' in his late teens, and it had felt right. They were friends, equals, soulmates. But Elizabeth was a different matter. With Elizabeth, Alice had always felt out of her depth. Even as a child, she had pulled away from her mother, always swimming in the opposite direction, against the tide. She had silently demanded a response which Alice was unable to give. Her helpless-ness in the face of her own child had made Alice anxious and frustrated. How much more of her did that little girl *want*?

It seemed that all through Elizabeth's childhood, from the time she was four or five, misunderstandings, exasperation and shouting had been the main tools of communication between them. And like all unsuitable tools, they were ineffective. At their best, they were blunt, clumsy instruments that accidentally wounded one or both of them. At worst, the blows they dealt were pointed, cruel, deadly in their accuracy. All that either of them had ever understood was the sharpness of the other's anger. Perhaps, when there was at least an absence of conflict, she might now be able to find the words to reach her daughter. The busy little figure that Alice had imagined with such glass-like clarity this afternoon in the garden, had returned to her with an intense, restless insistence. She showed no intention of going away; she wanted her mother to speak. Alice hoped that writing to her would be easier than talking. She hoped, too, that she was going to have enough time to make her peace. God alone knew how long she had left.

Now, she was going to give Him a run for his money.

'Woodvale'
28th July 1999

My dear Elizabeth—

Alice paused for a moment. Should she call her Beth or Elizabeth? She had never really approved of her daughter's shortening her name. It had been just another part of the endlessly defiant teenage years and, at the time, Alice had let it slide rather than do battle again. There had been far too many other things to fight about, then. But what about now? Should she soften? Would it be right to give in? Alice shook her head impatiently. What a waste of time. This was about *her*, these were her letters, her memories. She could not imagine her daughter properly without her rightful name. 'Elizabeth' conjured up all sorts of early images, tender pictures of babyhood. For a moment, Alice felt that the warm, bath-smelling little body was beside her again. She used to love stroking the little dimpled hands, the fat legs silky with Johnson's Baby Powder. 'Beth', on the other hand, was all the excesses of sullenness and rebellion, all the spikiness and eye-rolling defiance of adolescence. Alice decided to leave the opening as it was. She hoped that this was going to get easier.

I'd like to think that you'll remember me as I am, right this minute, sitting at the kitchen table. Can you see me? I keep seeing you, but not as you are now – I see you as a tiny baby, or a toddler. And it's very strange, not being able to imagine when and where you, the grown-up, will hold these pages in your hands. It's a bit like posting letters from the past into the future – address unknown. But I feel that there are many things between us which I cannot leave unsaid, and it feels urgent to me that I say them now. This afternoon, in the back garden, I had such clear pictures of you and James as children that they took my breath away. It was almost as though you were both there beside me, sitting on the back step. I could even see the little tartan rug, folded over three times, which I used to make you sit on, so that you wouldn't get a cold in your kidneys. Do you know the rug I'm talking about? It's still here, in your old room, under the eiderdown at the foot of your bed. It's been there for years, an extra blanket for your cold feet: you used to suffer a lot from chilblains. Some of the memories of you, Elizabeth, were particularly insistent, and I want to tell you about them. I need to write quickly, in case all that I saw this afternoon slips away from me again. Something tells me that these memories are very important – I have the feeling that there is a key somewhere in there, something to help me understand why you and I were never as close as we should have been, not real 'mother-and-daughter' close. Maybe I expected too

much of you, of both of us, but I have an uneasy
feeling that we have been cheated of each other. I
want to write about all of this to you now, before
anything happens to me.

Alice paused. *Before I die.* That was what she meant,
wasn't it? How come she couldn't write it down? She
smiled to herself. Seventy-six was a bit late to learn
about being tactful. She was beginning to get tired now,
and her fingers were sore from gripping the pen too
hard, but the need to go on was stronger than the need
to rest.

The young doctor I saw today couldn't tell me
how much time I've got left, of course, nobody can,
but I have a strong sense myself that I haven't long.
She said I've been suffering from a series of tiny
little strokes – I can't remember exactly the name
she used, some long, Latin-sounding words. I had
already suspected as much myself; what she told me
was no surprise. Things have been strange, lately –
confused and shadowy at times. James knows there's
something up, but I've been able to fob him off –
you know how he fusses at the best of times. I don't
want to be made to feel old and helpless before my
time. Growing older has never really frightened me
all that much, at least not in recent years. I was
more afraid of it when I was your age – the thought
of being stooped and faded used to terrify me. But
I've grown more accepting lately, and have even
managed to forget about age altogether. Recently,
when I've looked in the mirror, I've been startled
to see the old, lined face that looks back at me.

Sometimes, I wonder if it's really me. Inside, I feel much younger; I don't feel as though I've changed at all and it's been strange, looking out through my own eyes, not to recognize myself. It's the thought of losing my grip on reality that really terrifies me, not the number of years on my next birthday.

I'm going to tell you something now that no one else knows: I'm beginning to lose my words. The names of ordinary things escape me. Not only that, I'm starting to do peculiar things, to find myself in odd places. A week ago, I woke up, sitting on the bathroom floor. I was still in my nightdress, sitting with my back to the bath, with my sewing basket on my lap. I have no idea how I got there. The time before that, I woke up in your old bedroom, picking at old photos in an album of your dad's. There have been other times, too, but I've gradually got used to these midnight wanderings. I never seem to place myself in any danger, or do myself any harm, at least not yet. It's as though some sort of self-protection is at work, shielding me from myself.

Since I came back from the hospital this afternoon, I have felt surrounded by your childhood. The past seems much more appealing to me, now that my hold on the future has been made that bit looser. I've been trying to think back, to go beyond the pictures that I saw. I've been trying to remember times that were significant between you and me. And there is one day that stands out, that keeps drawing me back to it, again and again. Do you remember anything about your fifth birthday? The day we gave you the little green trike? This evening, when I came in from the garden, I began to wonder if that was when you and I began the long process of falling out. Let me tell you the story of that trike, as I remember it. I know that two people often have very different memories of the same event. I wonder what yours might be.

James had got his first two-wheeler for the Christmas before his tenth birthday. It wasn't a new bike, by any means. Your dad had bought it from Tom McManus down the road, sometime in November. Do you remember the McManus boys? I do! *They* got everything new, *they* were allowed to stay up until midnight, *they* got ten-shilling notes for pocket-money every week and didn't have to eat cabbage for dinner! They didn't even have to do homework . . . Do you remember? They were the bane of my life. Anyway, Tom Senior was getting rid of his own bike – he was one of the first men on our street to own a car.

For weeks, late at night when both you and James were in bed, and whenever your dad had a spare minute, he sanded and filled all the rust spots on the bicycle-frame, painted it black, bought new tubes, a new saddle, a bell. He even stripped and painted the carrier at the back. He was a great maker and mender, your dad. When he was finished, the bike looked brand new, and James was thrilled with it. But what I really remember is your face when we gave it to him. You were so little, still only four, but you wanted a bike just the same as his. You hardly left him alone all over Christmas. Even though it was freezing cold, you demanded 'backers' all around the garden until poor James was exhausted! And I watched you as you begged your dad for a bike just like James's. The doll and pram that Santa had brought you were forgotten – we got no peace until your dad promised to buy you a bike when your birthday came.

You were much too small for a proper two-wheeler, of course, but you couldn't have known that. Money was tight after Christmas: there was very little work and your dad was down to a flat wage. So we had to cut our cloth to suit our measure. About six weeks before your birthday, your dad trawled all the junk shops in town, looking for a three-wheeler with a decent frame that would be right for you. You didn't let him forget his promise, by the way – I don't know how many times since Christmas you'd reminded him of the bike you wanted for your birthday. And he really wanted you to have it: he wanted you to have something of your own, something not handed down from James. In the event, just before your birthday, two things happened – he was laid off, and he couldn't find a good second-hand trike anywhere. All this happened shortly before he went to work for Boyd and Sons: after that, he never looked back. Your dad had never been unemployed before, and he was deeply ashamed. He was also furious at himself, that he hadn't seen it coming. He kept saying how useless he was, how old he was. He was pushing forty, and he felt no one would ever employ him again. He became very upset over not being able to buy you a proper birthday present. So, he took the old trike that had belonged to James, which had been hanging on the roof of the shed for years, and started to do it up for you. Talk about a labour of love.

He locked himself away as soon as you both

went off to school, and worked in the shed all morning, every morning. I'll never forget the amount of effort that went into that little trike. He even went and spent money on a little wicker carrier-basket for the front, and new rubber grips for the handlebars. The mudguards got at least three coats of paint – and I can't remember what else. All I know is that every ounce of shame and disappointment at being unemployed went into that little three-wheeler; you'd call it therapy today. I had to button my lip; we were trying to get by as best we could, and there he was, spending money we didn't have, locked away day after day in the shed, refusing to go out and look for work. I'm telling you this to try to explain how that whole birthday was for me. None of this was your fault, Elizabeth – I'm not telling you these things to upset you, or make you feel guilty – it's all much too long ago. But can you understand how all the different strands got tangled up later on, on the day, and how explosive they all were?

Your dad called me out to the shed the night before your birthday, and showed me the trike for the first time. It was gleaming – he'd even resilvered the spokes. To be honest, I hardly recognized it. But you did. The minute you saw it on the following morning, your mouth turned down and you ran to the shed, yanking the door open. You pointed to exactly where it had been hanging, and I remember just what you said: 'That's the *old* bike! I don't want a *old* bike! I want a new bike like James!'

I can still see your dad's face. He looked like he had been slapped. You were only a little girl, I know, but I can't describe to you, even now, how that made me feel. Your dad just turned away; he said nothing, as usual. I grabbed you by the hand, not caring whether I hurt you. In fact, I think I wanted to hurt you. I squeezed your hand much too hard, and you howled. I dragged you upstairs and flung you into your bedroom. I remember smacking you, hard. I was so angry I don't even remember if I spoke. When I went back downstairs, I gave out yards about you to your dad. He just stood there, filling his pipe, not speaking. Eventually, he told me to calm myself, you were only a child. I was so furious, I took off my apron, flung it on the kitchen floor and marched out the front door, slamming it behind me. I think that that was the first real row your father and I had had since James and you were born.

Much later that day, after my walk had cooled me off, I came home again. Everything was very quiet – the calm after the storm. I looked out of the kitchen window and saw you sitting on your dad's knee, on the old cast-iron seat just beyond the shed door. I saw you snuggling into his chest, and he patted the top of your head with one hand, while he held his pipe in his mouth with the other. I couldn't make out if either of you was speaking. What I did make out, though, was a little hard place in my heart, something that hurt like a stone in my shoe. It hadn't been there before your birthday, but it was there now. Sometimes, I think it never really went away.

Alice stopped writing. This was more like reliving than remembering. She could still feel the powerful shadow of the anger that had filled her that day, more than forty years before. Even her hands had begun to shake. It was time to stop. Maybe this wasn't such a good idea, after all. Why stir up all this old stuff? Would it not be better to leave well enough alone? Except that things with Elizabeth were not well enough – better than before, perhaps, but still mainly surface. Surely there was nothing wrong with honest anger, honest emotion? She would go on, tomorrow. Now she was exhausted. She'd had enough for one day. She could feel herself on the edge of understanding something that was almost too painful to remember. How could a grown woman have felt that jealous of a little girl? And who had she really been angry at, that day? Had she, to her shame, chosen her little daughter as the easy target for the rage that should have been directed elsewhere?

I'm going to stop now, but I'll write more very soon. Do you remember anything at all about that day? I think your picture will be a very different one from mine. I'd like you to try to remember whatever you can. I think it's important – sometimes I've felt very guilty for always being the one to punish you. And you were only a little girl, after all. Now, all these years later, I need you to know how I felt, why I behaved as I did.

In some way I'll probably never understand now, seeing the way your dad forgave you made me feel even worse. Was I always an angry mother? I can't remember; nor can I remember being loving as often as I should have been. Maybe you can; maybe your memories are kinder to me. I hope you'll get the chance to tell me. I'd like you to take your time

with this letter, and with the others which I hope
will soon follow. Please don't rush; I need to feel
that you'll take the time to think about what I've
written, in the same way that I've thought about
you, before, during and after the writing.
    All my love for now,
    Mam.

Alice looked at her signature for a moment. It didn't
look right. If her daughter was Elizabeth, then she was
Alice; this had to be between two grown women, a
groping towards an equal, adult relationship, or it meant
nothing. She crossed out the word 'Mam' and wrote
'Alice' carefully underneath. Then she stretched her fingers one by one. She had to pull and knead all the fingers
of her right hand. They were almost completely cramped;
she thought they looked ugly, white and loose-fleshed,
like turkey claws. Pins and needles were beginning in one
foot and she suddenly realized that she felt cold. Nevertheless, she was filled with a strange sense of elation.
The genie was definitely out of the bottle now. She felt
its presence all around her, swirling like dust as other
memories crowded and prodded. They were so vivid
that she was almost frightened by their sharp edges.
Tomorrow, she'd take a sensible look at all of this.
Perhaps it was time she telephoned Elizabeth, to talk to
her, tell her about the hospital. But Elizabeth would
probably feel she should come home at once, and then
James would be upset that he had been shut out, passed
over; she could already see the hurt in the magnified
blue eyes that his mother had called out to her prodigal

child, rather than to the good and faithful son who had remained behind. Alice sighed; adult children were more difficult, if anything, than toddlers. All these *feelings* to be taken into account. She suddenly remembered one more thing, one more thought from the garden. She didn't know why it was important, but it was nudging at her, niggling; she had to write it down quickly:

> P.S. I will also be writing to James, that is my
> intention. Somehow, I feel that you will find these
> letters before he does. If so, I don't want you to tell
> your brother. He will come looking for me when
> he's ready. You and I have much more catching up
> to do. I will also be asking him to keep my secret,
> just in case he finds his letters before you find yours.
> Please do as I ask; it feels important that it should
> be this way.

Alice felt her mind grow suddenly cloudy. She always grew muddled when she was overtired. Muddled, but wakeful: what seemed like a contradiction had kept her edgy recently, unsleeping well into the small hours. She hoped she was going to sleep tonight. But no matter what, she wasn't taking any sleeping tablet, not now, not for as long as she could help it. She was filled with the sensation of needing every moment. If she slept, fine; if not, she would read, or think, or try to remember. For good or ill, she wanted the memories to come.

And tomorrow, she had something new to get up for.

*

Beth had sat very quietly on the little chair as she read through the letter, her eyes hungry for every one of her mother's words. Now she placed the closely written pages on the bed beside her and reached out for the old freckled hand. She pressed it closely between her own, reassured again by its solid warmth.

The date on the letter had shocked her deeply. Almost three months ago! Her mother had known for nearly three months what was happening to her, and she had said nothing, nothing at all. Beth didn't know whether to feel angry or hurt by this show of resolute independence. Such a conflict of feelings was not a new sensation for her: gaps such as this one had been all too common between them, down through the years. She wondered for one jealous moment whether James had known. Surely not: he would have found some way to tell her. And now, ironically, if she were to do as her mother asked her, she had no way of finding out. Clasping the old hand in hers, she realized that now, more than ever, it was useless to wish that things had been different.

'I'm here, Mam – Alice; I'm here. I've read your first letter; I'll do what you want, I promise.'

There was no response. Her mother's breathing seemed to have stilled somewhat. The earlier shallowness was gone and she seemed to Beth to be deeply, blackly, asleep.

She began to speak to her, softly.

'You knew all of this since July and you never said? Don't you know that I'd have come home running?

Maybe we'd have been able to catch up then, face to face. Maybe I could have helped.'

Beth was deeply moved by her mother's letter, too deeply even for tears. The written words had filled her head and heart with a tangle of emotion and memory. She felt as though all her senses had been heightened, that she was seeing and feeling with a sharpness of perception she had never known before. Her eyes began to fill as she imagined her mother's frail figure sitting on the bathroom floor, the sewing basket from childhood nestling in the flannel hammock between her knees. She had always been an excellent dressmaker. Too good, Beth had often fumed. She had never wanted to be the focus of her mother's needle, once she'd left childhood smocking and summer dresses behind. As a teenager, she would fill up with a furious guilt as she stood, unmoving, on the kitchen chair during interminable fittings. She'd known even then that she should feel grateful. Her mother's selfless work, her skill, even, had demanded Beth's appreciation and admiration. But the home-made skirts and dresses were never good enough: they were always too long, just reaching the knee, a frumpy two or three inches longer than those of her friends. Each fitting became a silent battleground, as Beth raged inside at her mother's refusal to concede. Alice, her face grim, her mouth set closely around half a dozen pins, would pull sharply at the hem-line. Beth would fidget constantly, trying to trick her mother into pinning a shorter length. The response was always the same: Alice would smack her daughter's knees with the back of her left hand, a sharp, silent admonition to stand up straight. Beth stroked that same hand now, turning the wedding ring that had often made her kneecap sting.

At fourteen, to be the same as everyone else was all Beth had wanted. And above everything, that meant wearing shop clothes, not home-made ones. She'd longed to take the bus into town on a Saturday afternoon with her friends, to try on the latest in mini-skirts in She Gear. She'd wanted desperately to be part of that knowledgeable, almost arrogant trawling through the new arrivals in Levi's and Wranglers, sorting with practised ease through the rails and rails of denim in O'Connor's. Dressing like everyone else was how you got to feel like one of the crowd. But the very thought of good money being spent on minis and blue jeans had made her mother's lips tighten. 'Shoddy' was a favourite word of hers to describe any piece of clothing not built to endure. Her eye for crooked hem-lines, stray threads and unravelling seams, was hawk-like. Edge-stitched hems, durable wool gabardine, bound buttonholes – these were the hallmarks of quality garments. Jeans were working-men's clothes and mini-skirts were 'common'. There was no meeting halfway on this issue: clothes were the great divide, the yawning Grand Canyon of her teenage years with her mother. And Beth remembered now how she had knowingly, deliberately hurt her by turning up her nose at all that was made on the gleaming old black and gold Singer sewing-machine, hauled up onto the kitchen table night after night.

But all that was much later. Her mother's letter told

of different times, times when such conscious head-on collisions between them were still years into the future. Of course Beth remembered the green trike: she couldn't remember everything her mother spoke of in her letter, but the words had stirred something on the outskirts of her memory. If she could find the details of that day deep inside her now, would the memory of it still be her own, or would it be changed now, transformed into something else by her mother's words? Memory was a funny thing. Beth hadn't even known until now that the day of the green trike had been her birthday. She did remember that she had behaved badly, but much stronger was the memory of the aftermath: sitting on her dad's knee while his caramel-smelling tobacco smoke shrouded both of them as they sat together, close, at the bottom of the garden.

He'd disappeared into the garden shed again once she'd burst into tears. She could still see how he'd moved the shiny trike to one side, quietly, out of his way. She remembered her mother taking her by the hand, back into the house, but it wasn't Alice's anger that she remembered: it was her own. With a five-year-old's complete self-centredness, she had been unaware of her mother's emotions: she did not remember being pulled, what she did recall was dragging, kicking and screaming, at her mother's resisting hands. Even now, she could feel the shards of disappointment that had sliced through her when she'd realized that this trike was not new, that it was yet another hand-me-down from James. Once more, as her child-self had seen it, he had come first; once again, she hadn't been given what she wanted. James always got everything new – his clothes and toys didn't come from cousins. Auntie Peggy had only had girls: Clare, Anna and Margaret. All of Beth's clothes that weren't home-made had been handed down to her from these three. But James's couldn't be hand-me-downs, naturally: his outfits came home from town in big brown bags decorated with gold writing. As the only boy, he was top of the list. Beth was surprised that she could still recall, with the clarity of old resentments, how sidelined she'd felt in this family, even as a very small child.

From her banishment in the back of the house, her five-year-old self had heard the sounds of hammering and sawing coming from the garden shed. She'd opened her window, cautiously, waiting for her opportunity. He'd have to come out soon for something, even if it was only to light his pipe.

Her father's paint-spattered overalls were a vivid palette, a shock of colours against the brown wood of the garden shed as he emerged, finally, into the garden. He patted his top pocket and pulled out his pipe and a tin of tobacco. From her open window, Beth waited until the ritual of filling, tamping and lighting was finished. The sweet, blue smoke had curled almost at once, drifting up towards her.

'Daddy?' she called.

He looked up.

'Can I come down?'

He nodded.

'Will you ask Mam if it's okay?'

'I'm saying it's okay. Come on.'

She clattered down the stairs and pushed open the kitchen door cautiously, just in case. But there was no sign of her mother, apart from her red-and-white check apron, lying carelessly on the tiled floor.

Beth's image of her father now, sitting waiting for her on the white, cast-iron garden seat, was especially clear. It was as though she were seeing a compilation of memories, like paint layered on canvas, the original image being intensified over and over again; only the colour and the tone changed, the substance remained the same. She had seen him sit like that so many times that no one memory could be anchored to the day when she was five. That iron seat was one of the few things to which his attachment had always been obvious. It nestled in the old part of the garden, beyond the shed, close to the high stone wall at the end. It was in the part that was always meadow-like in its tumble of wildflowers. He had never replanted it; it always remained detached, set apart from the sculpted beauty around the house. Beth wondered now whether her father had known even then that this would form part of the L-shape that he would eventually have to sell, in yet another attempt to keep the family finances afloat. He sat there a lot at the end of the garden, almost hidden from the house; he'd usually smoke his pipe, occasionally he'd read the paper. That day, his head and shoulders were wreathed in tobacco smoke as his daughter approached him. There was no wind; the bright Easter-time mid-morning was warm and still. He seemed almost to be screened from her by the puffs of blue-white pipe smoke. She had always loved that smell, burying her face in his jacket and jumpers after he died, sitting in his wardrobe with the door shut tight when her mother wasn't home. She had used all her childish energy to will him back to life again by breathing for him, taking in all the sweet cloudiness of pipe tobacco. She came closer to him, tentatively now.

'Can I sit on your knee?'

'You can,' and he held out his arms to her.

She snuggled into him, feeling safe and sorry at the same time.

'I'm sorry, Daddy. I didn't mean it.'

He stroked her cheek.

'I know. You were hoping for something better, weren't you?'

She nodded.

'I wanted a *new* bike,' and she began to cry again.

'I know that. But you'll have to learn to be happy with what you've got. Life can be very hard for a little girl who is only made happy by the very best. We've all got to learn to live with what we have. Do you understand me, Lizzie?'

Beth remembered smiling up at him through her tears, cuddling close to the sound of his words, rather than the sense. She hadn't really understood everything he'd said, but she was relieved by his forgiveness, and the kindness in his voice.

Of the many memories her mother could have chosen, Beth smiled at the irony of this one. It was one of the few occasions she could remember when she'd known intuitively, almost at once, that she'd been in the wrong. Five was not too young to see the depth of hurt and humiliation on a father's face. Of course, her child-self couldn't have known that he had recently lost his job; nevertheless, she had learned something that day of her own power to wound, of her heedless, childlike ability to twist the knife, a skill that had remained with her right throughout adulthood. Of all the times her mother had been angry at her, this time her fury had been justified. She needed to make no apology.

Beth thought suddenly of her own daughter, of how docile and gentle she was, of how little she had ever needed to be punished. Laura would have suited Alice so much better than she, Beth, had done: she should have been Alice's child, and Beth should have had feisty Granny Mac as a mother. They should all have swopped generations, intermingling with each other in the interests of family harmony. Each one would have known how best to handle the other. Beth sometimes worried that Laura was too placid; she was still waiting for the battles of adolescence to begin. She had tried hard not to make the same mistakes that her own mother had: clothes, make-up, boys – all were cool in Beth's household. The problem was that Laura didn't seem interested in any of them. At fifteen, she had already drawn her own lines of demarcation, and Beth felt every bit as excluded from Laura's life as Alice had been from hers.

Beth kept both of her hands pressed warmly around her mother's. She had a vision of her teenage self again, truculent, moody, aggressive, and felt a wave of empathy engulf her as she recalled her mother's almost constant facial expression: a mixture of anger, bewilderment and, above all, disappointment. Even as she remembered this, Beth realized that she and Laura were already having their differences, that Laura was pulling away from her in her own time, her own way. And the irony of their battle was not lost on Beth: her own daughter was resisting her mother's unspoken demand that she be more assertive, more driven. Beth could see her now, her small pale face framed by long, flyaway hair; her gaze steady, rather than defiant. But she had inherited Granny Mac's chin – a little sharp, a little prominent, endlessly determined.

Beth looked down at the face on the pillow, now resting peacefully.

'Alice, we've a long way to go. But I know we'll end up at the same place together, when all of this is over.'

She replaced the letter in its creamy envelope, and pushed it into the front pocket of her jeans. In case she fell asleep, she did not want to leave these pages lying around for James to find. She decided to put the rest of the bundle back into the bedside locker, just in case, although the temptation to devour them all, now, was enormous. But she would do as she was told. The clarity and intimacy of her mother's written words were to be savoured, not rushed. Not for the first time, Beth was acutely aware of how hardship had dictated the circumstances of Alice's life. She had always been a great reader, an avid letter-writer, particularly when her children were young. It was sad that lack of opportunity had foiled the growth of a lively, enquiring intelligence, a quick and eager mind.

Beth went looking for the locker key again, and then

placed the letters back in the silk bag. She settled into the little chair once more, feeling a stiffness begin to develop around her hip joints. She closed her eyes, just for a while. She hoped that James would not go searching just yet; this time, it would be nice to be first.

*

A strange sound made Beth look at her watch. It was almost seven o'clock and James would be in soon. There was still no sign of daylight through the closed curtains, but it was as though the spell of night had suddenly been broken. It only took her a moment to identify the whine of the milk-float as it lurched its way down the narrow street from the main avenue. Conditioned by years of childish habit, she waited for the chinking of milk bottles on the red tiles of the porch downstairs. But there was no sound. Instead, as though at a secret signal, the whole street began to wake up. The milkman had worked his magic and loosened the morning noises that now hung, like smoke in the air, all over her mother's bedroom. Somewhere, a car door slammed, an engine revved. She felt like the princess in *Sleeping Beauty*, whose whole unmoving kingdom suddenly springs to life again as her eyelids flicker open after hundreds and hundreds of years of enchanted sleep. Her mother's letter had had an extraordinary effect on her, had awakened more than old memories. The intensity of emotion had finally settled into something approaching a new state of consciousnesss: alert and peaceful at the same time. Beth wanted to read her words again, now, privately, in the silence of her old bedroom. She wanted to find that five-year-old again, to put together the fragments of the little girl who had been so suddenly magicked back to life by her mother's words.

She decided to ask James if he minded that she took the late-shift: she had liked the night-time quietness, the mantle of closeness that darkness and candlelight had cast over the bedroom. Then, if he wanted, he could go home to Olive and the children and return early each morning. That was how she would propose to spend her time from now on: awake at night, asleep for some of each day. Turning her life upside-down at this point had a special appeal for Beth. Being awake all of yesterday had, in some way, made her conscious of new possibilities, of a new way of living. It was as though Alice's fragility had shaken her roughly by the shoulders, shocking her into wakefulness, into the realization that she, Beth, would not live for ever either. It was time now to live *inside* her own life, to make every moment into an act of choice, to stop looking on from the sidelines. There was the new awareness, too, that each breath her mother took could be her last. The tension of waiting was not easy, this sharp-eyed watching for the rise and fall of every breath taken, but for the first time that Beth could remember, she felt that she had truly risen to the challenge. Facing its very difficulty had made her test her own strength and she was surprised at the depth of her resources. She wondered at how she could have left them all untapped over the past twenty years.

It had been strangely comforting to sit in the darkness and absorb her mother's presence without any of the distractions of daylight. The memories evoked by their silent, breathy communication had been bright and clear, the emotions clean and uncluttered, in spite, or perhaps because, of the pain they brought with them. Beth had had the sense for the first time ever of starting to untangle all the undergrowth that had stunted her relationship with Alice. She wanted to sit with her again tonight, to wander with her through the timeless space of Singer sewing-machines, walled gardens and green trikes. It was the least she could do: her mother had supplied the maps.

She felt her eyelids begin to grow heavy, finally. She patted her jeans pocket, making sure the letter was safely hidden, pulling her sweater down carefully. She felt a bit guilty about hiding things from James, but this was not the time for sharing. This time, she would, unquestioningly, do as her mother had bid her. Her last conscious thought, before her eyes drifted closed at last, was how strange a thing the passing of time was. It no longer seemed to be a measurable presence – the hours had slipped away in what could have been an instant or a lifetime, and ordinary living seemed to be something that had happened to her a long time ago. Even the flight from London yesterday evening felt as though it had been undertaken by someone else, someone playing at her life. Here and now was the only reality; the rest of time and space existed in another dimension where other people lived and which she could no longer enter.

When James came in at twenty past seven, Beth was sitting exactly as he had left her more than six hours before. He noticed that her eyes were closed. Gently, he reached out and touched her on the shoulder. She jumped, but there was none of the spiky restlessness of the evening before. He was glad; it must have been an easy night.

'Sis?'

She looked up at once, her eyes becoming wakeful.

'Morning, James.'

'Was everything okay?'

'Fine. Very quiet.' Beth rubbed her hands over her thighs, which had suddenly grown cold. 'She had a good night. Are you sure you've had enough sleep? I'm okay here for another while, if you'd like.'

She stifled a yawn. Now that the time had come, she felt reluctant to leave her mother, to pass over responsibility to someone else.

'I've had plenty of sleep. I usually wake much earlier than this. You should turn in for a while, now; I'll take over.'

She nodded. Maybe it would be good to take a break, to climb between clean sheets, to turn off the thoughts for a few hours. In the split second between sleep and waking at James's gentle touch, Beth had felt suddenly overwhelmed. Her dreaming-self had voiced the fearful, troubled questions that her waking-self could not: What if it all led to nothing? What if she never learned to know this woman, her mother? What if it were all too little, too late? Right now, in the slowly dawning greyness of morning, it all felt like too much to take on. She felt suddenly depressed, her limbs heavy. Now she wanted oblivion.

'Yes. I could do with lying down. I'm feeling a bit stiff.'

She kissed the top of James's head as she left the bedroom. Without even thinking about it, she made her way straight to the back of the house, towards her old room. She took the letter out of her jeans pocket and slipped it under her pillow. She wanted to hold it again, to read the words over and over, but tiredness suddenly blinded her. She kicked off her shoes and jeans. Pulling back the old eiderdown and blankets, she slipped in between cold linen sheets.

Curling up in a ball, burying her head into the comforting softness of her old, childhood-smelling pillow, she slept.

*

It was about midday when Beth finally woke. She felt surprisingly alert and refreshed, all her recent sluggishness gone. The room was warm and dim. She knew from the quality of the light that seeped through a chink in the curtains, that it was drizzling again outside. She lay still for a few moments, allowing her eyes to trace the cracks on walls and ceiling, their shapes still familiar despite the intervening years. The old, childish pictures seemed to spring into life again, as though they had all been waiting a long time for her to open her eyes. Here again was the giant's face, with the huge nose and both eyes set to one side, so that he resembled an unfinished Picasso. There was the delicate outline of a seagull, its beak wide open, wings curving into flight. And above the bedroom door, the silhouette of a tree doomed to permanent winter. Cracks in the old plaster and yellowing paintwork had been a constant feature of Beth's childhood years, and the memory of them now made her smile. James had told her, long after they had both left home, that such shabbiness had been the subject of an on-going tug-of-will between their parents. It had frustrated Alice enormously that the one place her husband took no pride in painting was his own home. Meticulous in his preparation and painstaking in his neatness in other people's houses, he seemed never to see the need for decoration in his own. The tailor's children, Alice would say to James, fuming, are always the ones to have no arse in their trousers . . .

With a sudden shock, Beth remembered her mother, remembered why she was here, at home, lying in her old room. It seemed incredible that she could have forgotten, even for an instant. She pushed back the heavy blankets, still smelling faintly of mothballs. She tugged at the curtains, pulling them back to loop them over the ornate brass hooks on either side of the window. The sky was pewter-coloured, the whole street silent, sheltering from the rain. The house felt quiet too; it had lost that depth of stillness brought on by night, but there were no sounds, no signs of anyone being up and about. As she rummaged in her case for her dressing gown and slippers, Beth felt panic begin to grow somewhere underneath her ribcage. Somehow, although she would never doubt James's kind competence for a moment, Beth was overwhelmed by the feeling that her mother had been left suddenly alone, abandoned, and that even now, she was wakeful, restless, searching for her children ... Beth wanted to get back to her, now, at once. All the responsibility for Alice's ease and comfort felt as though it were suddenly, fiercely, hers, and hers alone. She felt that she could keep her mother alive now by the sheer, simple force of wanting it enough.

She opened her bedroom door and crossed the landing, quickly, to her mother's room. James was there, of course he was, and the sleeping figure in the bed was still unmoving, her head turned to the right, just as when Beth had left her. The change that she had been expecting had not happened, and now Beth didn't know which she feared more: that her mother would die during her vigil, or that she would wake up during James's.

He looked up as Beth entered the room. The candles that she had so carefully lit had all gone out, and James was sitting in the old, deep armchair, his eyes heavy with fatigue. Beth noticed how grey his face was, and she felt the return of all the guilt of the previous evening. She was determined that he would see her doing her part, more than her part. She owed him that, and so much more, the old debt stretching way back, as far as she could remember.

'Are you okay?' she asked, resting her hands lightly on his shoulders.

'I'm fine, only I can hardly keep my eyes open. It must be the last week catching up on me.'

Beth smiled at him.

'We're not eighteen any longer, you know. I gave up trying to do without sleep a long time ago. How is she?'

'The same. I think there's even less movement than a few days ago. Last Tuesday, the day after the stroke, she kept raising and lowering her right arm, as though she was looking for something. The nurse said it was a physiological tic, that it wasn't a voluntary movement. But I don't know. She seems to sleep more heavily now, she hasn't even stirred since you left.'

Beth found it hard to swallow. Even as James was speaking, she could feel the impact of his words. She was filled with a troubled, instinctive certainty that she was already too late to make that last, vital contact with her mother. The letters had arrived too late. The one she'd read was not *enough*; and now it looked as though she'd just run out of time. She couldn't answer him. It was all much too close to being over.

James stood up, stretched, and looked at his watch.

'I've asked Gemma to come over at half twelve so that you and I can have a break. She has a half-day. She'll stay until about three, then she's got to go home and study.'

Beth nodded and reached again for her mother's hand. Was she imagining things or did it feel somehow lighter, more feathery than last night? She held it closely between both of hers, squeezing gently, allowing herself to feel reassured by its steady warmth. Then she turned round to James, and managed to sound brighter, more cheerful than she felt.

'Will you stay while I have a quick shower? Then I'll make us something for lunch. I'm sure Gemma will be starving.'

James yawned hugely. 'Of course. Take your time.'

He ran his fingers through his hair and pulled at his beard. Beth was aware of him walking around the room behind her, stretching his legs. There was an air of agitation around his movements: he wasn't his usual self, stolid and contained. Beth felt that he was on the verge of saying something to her, something unexpected. She turned round to look at him, to give him an opening, but he had his back to her. Something in the set of his shoulders decided her that she should let him take his own time; he had never been the impulsive one. She kissed her mother's forehead, stroking the fine, wispy hair that was almost completely white.

'I'll see you downstairs then – half an hour.'

*

Beth had just put the kettle on when the back door was suddenly flung open and a garish multicoloured umbrella made its appearance into the kitchen.

Startled, she took a step back from the sink and a cheerful disembodied voice called out: 'Hiya, Auntie Beth!'

A very wet, gabardined back was abruptly turned as the umbrella was shaken vigorously out into the yard, drops flying everywhere. Then Gemma faced her aunt, her round face flushed and beaming. Beth held out her arms, filled by a great rush of warmth for the small, plump figure dripping water all over the kitchen floor. Of all his children, Gemma was the one who most resembled James, and Beth loved her all the more for it.

Although she had her mother's colouring, dark hair and pale complexion, Gemma's mannerisms and features were all her father's.

'Gemma! Pet! Come here for a hug!'

Beth stroked the damp, rain-smelling hair. She thought she caught a faint echo of cigarette smoke and prolonged the embrace, tightening her arms around the small shoulders.

'Are you still smoking, you monkey?' Beth whispered into the top of her niece's head.

Lively brown eyes looked up at her. 'Me? Whatever makes you think that?'

'Never mind.' Beth kissed her on the forehead. 'I'd scold you if it wasn't such a complete waste of time. Just don't let your dad find out.'

She helped her to shrug her way out of her soaking school coat. Gemma grinned at her.

'Dad? He's a pussycat. You should say make sure your ma doesn't find out – now *that's* what I'd call trouble!'

Beth tried to hide a smile. She arranged Gemma's coat carefully over the back of a kitchen chair, positioning it close to the range. It had always remained lit, right throughout every winter. She wondered briefly when James had had the time recently to tend to it. She must ask him, and make sure she shared the chore. Turning back to face Gemma, she decided it would be much safer to steer away from the subject of cigarettes and parental personalities.

'How's school?' she asked instead.

'Fine,' Gemma shrugged. 'Too much homework;

too many teachers screaming at us for not studying hard enough for the Leaving. You know the usual. How's Laura?'

'She's fine. She sends her love to everyone.'

'Still getting top marks in everything, I suppose?'

Beth laughed at Gemma's comical expression.

'I'm afraid so. What can I tell you – she certainly doesn't take after her mother!'

Gemma grinned.

'Yeah, well – at least she isn't boring about it. Is she going to come over again this Christmas?'

Beth nodded.

'Yes, I think so, but we'll have to wait and see . . . how things work out here.'

Her voice trailed off. She didn't want to imagine this house empty, locked up, silently waiting for strangers to take it over, just when she was beginning to feel at home.

Gemma cut across the thought, quickly.

'Is there anything to eat? I'm starving! Is Dad upstairs with Gran?'

Beth laughed.

'Hold on! The answer is "yes" to both. Do you want to go up and see him while I get lunch?'

'Yeah, I'll just run up and say hello. I'll take something up with me, so's you and him can have a break. I'll talk to you later, 'kay?'

She grabbed a blackening banana from the fruit bowl on the kitchen table, kissed Beth warmly and gave her another hug before crashing out the door and up the stairs. Beth had the impression of a sweep of positive energy, like the sudden illumination of sheet lightning, brightening through the kitchen, crackling in the air long after her niece had left. It was a good feeling, a welcome contrast to the intense, shadowy stillness of the night before. Who said that the dying had to be surrounded only by dim lights and whispered words? Beth felt that if anything could restore her mother to wakefulness, however briefly, it would be the sheer youthful energy of her clumsy granddaughter.

And Beth needed her mother restored to wakefulness. An idea had been forming in her mind ever since James had spoken of his mother's slowing movements. She had to talk to him now, to convince him that what she, Beth, wanted to do was right, urgent, even essential.

James wandered into the kitchen and picked two sandwiches out of the basket that Beth had just filled. He sat down at the top of the table, and Beth's heart lurched as she turned to watch him. In that one, simple movement, he bore an uncanny resemblance to his mother. Even the way he sat, ramrod straight, right out at the edge of the chair, was Alice's way.

'Sorry,' he said, his mouth full. 'Can't wait, I'm starving.'

'That's okay. Fire ahead. Tea or coffee?'

'Tea, please,' and he reached for another sandwich.

'Gemma's looking well. She's as bubbly as ever.'

James grinned, looking at Beth over the tops of his glasses.

'She's an uncoordinated disaster. Herself and Olive

do nothing but fight about it. Sometimes, I think she's clumsy on purpose.'

Beth poured tea for both of them. She said nothing, but it was easy to see how Gemma's apparent awkwardness was the ideal tool of defiance, a perfectly honed instrument for the torture of her poised, elegant mother. She couldn't help smiling as she imagined Olive's pained disapproval of the daughter who continued to reflect so badly on her. She had a sudden, vivid image of Gemma lurching and crashing around her mother's house-of-the-month sitting room, exulting in her own gaucheness, saying, 'See? Can't control this now, can you?' It made Beth want to hug her niece, hard. She was amused for a moment at how, in less than twenty-four hours, she was beginning to feel like something of an expert on mothers and daughters.

'Will I bring a tray up to her?' she asked James.

He shook his head.

'No. She said she'd prefer to come down later. She thinks it would be ghoulish to eat in front of Alice. She wouldn't even come into the bedroom until she'd finished the banana.' James spooned sugar into his tea. 'Not that there's much chance of Alice waking up,' he added.

It was the perfect opening, but Beth felt suddenly nervous. She was afraid that what she wanted was monstrous, that soft-hearted James would be horrified at what he would see as her callousness.

'I need to talk to you about that,' she eventually said, quietly.

'About what?' James stopped, another sandwich midway to his mouth.

'Remember you said that Mam sometimes seemed to come to, and you thought that she recognized you?'

He nodded. 'Yeah?'

'Well, it happened to me last night. She definitely woke up, and she squeezed my hand – very lightly, but I know she knew I was there.'

James's face lit up.

'That's great – I was afraid you mightn't have had that; I thought it might be already too late. I'm glad it happened, Sis.'

Beth swallowed. She tried to make her voice firm. She knew she was on very shaky ground here.

'So am I. The thing is, I didn't really get a chance to say anything to her – she slipped away again so quickly.'

James nodded.

'That's the way it happens. She's sedated just enough to make sure she doesn't feel any discomfort, so she's more or less permanently asleep.'

'Yes, but how do we know she feels any pain?'

He shrugged.

'We don't. The sedation is to avoid her getting distressed, as much as anything. The last stroke left her almost completely paralysed. It's highly unlikely she can even speak.'

Beth almost lost courage. How was she going to do this without James finding out about the letters? How could she possibly ask him to agree to something that seemed so cruel, so totally without reason? Then she remembered the urgency in her mother's expression when she managed the word *letter* and knew she had to do this. She took a deep breath. By now James was looking at her closely, his expression puzzled.

'She tried to speak to me, James, only I couldn't make out what she was saying. She wasn't awake for long enough.'

Beth stopped abruptly. She could see by James's eyes that he was beginning to understand.

'You want to wake her up?' he asked incredulously.

'No, of course not, not wake her up as such. I just thought that if we – if Dr Crowley reduced the amount of sedative for one night, that she might wake up naturally, just for a little while. Then, if she did come to, well, we'd both be there, you know?'

Beth stopped. James had stood up slowly; both hands were now resting palms downward on the table, as he steadied himself. His eyes appeared intensely blue, and she knew that he was furious.

'Jesus Christ, I don't believe you. How can you even *think* of doing such a thing?'

Beth flared back at him, guilt and anguish finally igniting.

'Because I think there might be things she'd like to say. She certainly tried hard enough last night.'

Her voice was tight, her words brittle. God, she hated this. Her brother's rare displays of anger had always had the power to make her feel small and ashamed, like a badly behaved child. She was very tempted to say, 'Stop – wait – let's not do this. There are letters for you upstairs.' But her promise to her mother had a stronger grip. She knew that this time, she had to resist James's anger. She had promised obedience to Alice and this time she would deliver, even though it was rather late in the day.

They both stood, glaring at each other across the table. Beth felt suddenly breathless, as though someone had abruptly cut off her air supply. She had never fought with James like this, and now he was looking at her with a mixture of rage and loathing.

'Are you sure it's not things that *you* want to say? This is about you, isn't it, not about caring for Alice at all?'

His voice was still soft, but his tone left Beth in no doubt that, right now, he found his sister beneath contempt.

'That's part of it, yes. But you weren't there when she tried to speak to me. It's for her, too. I owe it to her.'

'It's a bit late for you to start thinking of what you owe, isn't it?'

James's voice was harder now; he had drawn himself up and was standing very straight, his hands clenched by his side. Beth could feel herself being sucked inwards and downwards by an ever-increasing spiral of anger and recrimination.

'It's never too late. Just because *you* don't feel the need to say anything, just because *your* life allowed you to be here . . .'

'What the hell do you know about *my* life? Just who do you think you are?'

Beth felt as though she had been slapped. James had never spoken to her like that before; she had never heard him use the harsh tone that now seemed to hover, loud and shocked, in the air between them. Before she could even think of a reply, he turned his back on her and walked stiffly out the kitchen door. He closed it very softly behind him. She heard his measured tread creak all the way up the stairs. And then there was silence.

Beth's knees began to tremble. All her anger drained away, leaving her feeling weak, almost light-headed. She sat down at the table and rested her head in her hands, feeling her chin begin to throb again as she did so. She could feel the beat of her own heart echoing painfully in her ears. She'd been right; this was going to be awful; and what made it worse was that it was going to be awful in a way she had never imagined. Nothing could have prepared her for James's contempt.

The kitchen door suddenly opened.

'Auntie Beth? You okay?'

Gemma was standing over her, anxious. Beth managed to smile up at her.

'Yes, love, I'm fine. Tired and emotional, that's all.'

'Did you have a row with Dad? He seems really pissed off.'

'We had a disagreement, that's all. This is a really tough time, Gemma, and we're both exhausted. We'll be fine, I promise.'

Gemma knelt beside Beth's chair and put both arms around her aunt. Beth held her close for a long time. When she was sure that her tears were under control, she pulled away and smiled at the troubled young face in front of her. She cupped both of her hands around the pointy McKinney chin.

'It's okay, I promise. We're both stressed out, but we'll get over it. Promise.'

'Yeah, well, I don't want you two falling out.'

Gemma's eyes were wide, all traces of colour gone from her cheeks. Looking down at her, Beth saw echoes of Laura's blue eyes, her grave expression. The memory of her daughter and of last night was suddenly enough. Beth decided at once what she wasn't going to do. She wasn't going to drive a wedge between herself and James, not now. This was shaping up to be the sort of row that never got fixed in some families, that could leave brothers and sisters not speaking to each other for decades. It was the first drop out of a well of poison that could affect not only her, but Laura and Gemma too; all the cousins. Beth was determined that she would not be party to that. She and Laura had little enough family as it was. She would find a way around this; it would not be right to leave everything for James to fix. It was time that she, too, learned how to be a peacemaker.

'We won't fall out, I promise you. It was mostly my fault, and I'll go up right now and say I'm sorry. And that will be the end of it.'

Gemma pulled her coat off the back of the chair.

'Yeah, well, if I'm not needed, I'll head off home. But you'd be much better giving him time to cool off. I wouldn't go near him for another hour or so, if I were you.'

Beth nodded, smiling at her.

'I'll take your advice.'

'Go for a walk, or something. It's almost stopped raining.'

Gemma retrieved her umbrella from the sink and picked up her schoolbag.

'I'll see you later, then, okay?'

'Okay,' Beth agreed. 'Don't you want anything else to eat before you go?'

Gemma shook her head.

'No thanks; lost my appetite.'

She blew her aunt a kiss, and then she was gone. The kitchen seemed to sag suddenly without her and Beth felt that the air had been emptied. She poured the last dregs of tea into her cup. How was she going to handle this? Was she being heartless and selfish, as James had just accused her? Or was she right to fight for this, for her mother, as well as for herself? She sighed. It always seemed to happen the same way, every time she came home. She was always at the centre of conflict, except that now, she wasn't fighting any childhood ghosts, but rather the most loyal, substantial ally she had ever had.

Beth left her uneaten lunch on the table, and went to get her coat from the hall-stand. She hoped the walk would clear her head, soothe her heart. When she came back, she was going to have to find some way of giving all three of them what they each needed.

*

He was downstairs in the kitchen, waiting for her. The dishes had been piled neatly in the sink. A pot of coffee and two mugs sat in the middle of the kitchen table.

'It's all right,' he said, as soon as she stepped inside. 'Keith has no lectures this afternoon, so he stopped by to see Alice. He's with her now.'

Beth nodded, her mouth suddenly dry. She no longer knew what to say. There was a strange edginess between them, something which was not familiar to her, not with James. Her eyes were drawn away from him to the side of the range where the bucket of anthracite stood. The fire was newly stoked, the doors cleaned, chrome handles gleaming. She had been found wanting again, she supposed. She had a sudden thought that being here, with James, made her feel less than significant, somehow. No matter what she did now, or had done in their shared past, it seemed that she could never measure up. Like now, he'd always been there first, before her, doing the right thing.

'Coffee?'

She nodded, still not trusting herself to speak. It was James who broke their silence, pushing a mug towards her.

'I'm sorry about what happened, Sis. I shouldn't have spoken to you like that.'

Beth's eyes filled, moved beyond words by his simple generosity. He had done it again: he had always been the first to say sorry – to Alice, to friends, to her, even when the responsibility for wrong-doing was still in question. She envied him the ability he had, to soothe and defuse conflict. It took her a moment to regain control, to measure her words. She could feel the gap between the two of them closing again, but she was cautious, still. She felt suddenly resolute: this time, she was not going to let him soothe her out of her need for her mother.

'I'm sorry, too, James, but I really need to do this.'

James's head was bent. He seemed to be peering into his mug. When he answered her, his voice had grown very quiet.

'I know. I was thinking about it upstairs. I've had lots of chances to say my goodbyes, and I still don't find it easy to let her go.'

Beth swallowed hard, trying to ease the words around the hard lump in her throat.

'I just want to feel close to her for a little while, and to tell her that. I didn't know how else to ask for it.'

James combed his fingers through his beard, looking at her steadily. He seemed to be making up his mind about something.

'To be honest, it was your assumptions about my life that really got me going.'

Beth returned his gaze, not understanding. He took a sip of coffee, and she could see him deciding whether to continue.

'Olive and I have been going through a very rough patch, lately and, well, maybe that's why I barked at you like I did. It really pisses me off when people assume my life is all sewn up.'

Beth felt embarrassed by James's admission. It was

like being a child again, made speechless by hot confusion. What could she say? He was probably the only man in the whole world who wouldn't see life with Olive as a *permanent* rough patch; if he was suffering now, then things must be really bad.

'I'm sorry,' she said. 'Is there anything I can do?'

He shook his head.

'No, thanks, Sis. I'll have to sort it out for myself.'

'I know, but if you want to talk – God knows I'm no expert, I seem to spend half my life fucking up. But I can be a good listener.'

Stop babbling, she said to herself. The words came tumbling out, tripping over one another. It was an astonishing sensation to be offering James comfort and sympathy – it had always been the other way around. She was sure that he would regard her offer with amusement: what could she possibly do for him, after all? To her surprise, he took her seriously.

'Thanks, Sis. I may well take you up on that.'

He poured more coffee and held up the pot, looking quizzically at her. She shook her head. She knew that for now, the subject was closed. Peace had been restored. Beth felt almost happy, as though something had shifted between them and finally settled into a place long prepared for it. All of her anxiety drained away, and a sense of calm filled her. Now that she felt able, she was going to see this through.

'What about the sedation, James? What should we do?'

Her question was just right, it had the tone she'd

intended. They were in this together, now more than ever.

'I'm happy for you to ring Dr Crowley and talk to her about it. If there's any question of Alice suffering . . .'

'There'll be no question of that, James. Give me some credit.'

Her smile softened the words she had spoken, and he patted her hand.

'Of course; I didn't mean to—'

'It's okay, I know you didn't. But I'm not totally heartless, you know.'

Beth pulled her hand away abruptly. She felt a sudden burn of bright red anger where he'd patted her.

'I'll ring Dr Crowley this evening.'

She stood up from the table. She'd been unable to soften her tone, this time. A new, unfamiliar irritation with her brother was beginning to take root. His air of patient wisdom was suddenly jarring, a harsh note grating on her nerves. Had she never sensed this before, or was she only now beginning to recognize it for what it was? He seemed full of benign arrogance, brimming over with the gentle tyranny of the one who always knows best. But her flash of anger was short-lived: as she looked at him sitting there, hunched over the coffee-pot, she felt an unaccustomed stab of pity. What she had seen as simply fatigue now appeared to her as more than that – his expression was sad, almost defeated. She felt suddenly frightened for him. He had always seemed so strong, and now, all at once, the serene, ordered pace of his life was changing and there were no more certainties. She had always seen James as rather plodding: a devoted family man, a good son and a thorough and methodical, rather than a brilliant, lecturer. Curiosity almost overcame her: she was dying to ask – is there someone else? Is Olive about to leave you, or are you, wonder of wonders, about to leave Olive? Wisely, she said nothing. Was she really behaving like an adult at last, complete with tact and understanding? She allowed the silence between them to deepen. He didn't seem to have noticed her momentary irritation. For the moment, she'd prefer to keep it like that.

'Why don't you light the fire inside and sit down? I'll go up and say a quick hello to Keith, and then I'm going to do some shopping. You could do with a break.'

'Yes,' he said. 'I could.'

'Go on, then.'

Beth handed him the newspaper and went upstairs, more and more surprised at the amount of emotion that could be fitted into less than twenty-four hours.

*

Beth moved around the bedroom, lighting the night-lights one by one. It already seemed like a long-established ritual, and she had to remind herself that only one full day had passed since she had left her other life behind. She felt as though she had inhabited this reality for years and years and the routine came easily to her now.

She had asked James earlier on in the evening to stay

until June left. She hadn't wanted to see her, to meet again with the nurse's unspoken disapproval.

'Only for tonight, please. I just don't want to have to deal with her attitude towards me.'

James had appeared surprised at her request.

'Why? What's wrong with her attitude towards you?'

Beth shrugged. 'She just makes me feel uncomfortable, that's all. I know that she thinks badly of me.'

'Why on earth would she think badly of you?'

There wasn't even a hint of challenge in James's tone – just amazement.

Beth was relieved that, no matter what June's motives were for disapproval, James certainly didn't share them.

'Trust me – she does. Probably because I didn't come home sooner. Anyway, I'll get over it; just not tonight.'

James had nodded, but Beth could see that he'd felt completely at a loss. They had both let the subject drop.

Now she settled herself back into the little chair, and waited until the room became used to her again. James had just left to go home with Keith, and she was glad to be back in the cocoon once more, surrounded by the flickering candlelight and the warm, still sense of being really *present* here, sharing her mother's company. And tomorrow, Dr Crowley would come. Beth had the absurd sense of having reclaimed some time for her mother. It was as though by making the phone call to the doctor, she had somehow helped to prolong Alice's life. She felt almost confident now that her mother could hang on through the low ebb hours of night. She was glad that she was alone in the house this evening; she felt full of eager anticipation, thinking about the next letter, lying waiting in the silky depths of soft, silent purple.

lumbering old-fashioned wardrobe, taking up almost all of one wall: old-fashioned even when Jack had bought it, and not yet old enough to have become fashionable again. And finally, the culprit – the mahogany desk that Jack had made, and which lay against the wall just inside the door. The bruise on Alice's hip this morning was at the exact level of its outer right-hand corner; she must have stumbled against it as she came through the door last night.

She pulled up the sash window now and let the warm breeze blow through the room; the patterned muslin curtain billowed and swam around her. The room was filled with the sudden, heady smell of cut grass. She remembered that Keith was coming tonight, probably under protest, to help her tidy her own garden and trim the hedge. She must remember to put a little something in an envelope for him. She fought back at the filmy material, beating it down, closing the window just a little to calm the stream of air. There was still a very faint smell of damp in this room, more from lack of use than anything else. Elizabeth hadn't been to stay in such a long time. The last person to use the bed had been Laura, almost eight months ago. She must make a note to herself to air it, soon. Alice smoothed the bed covers, patting them here and there, although there were no creases anywhere. Then she took the can of Pledge out of her apron pocket, and her yellow duster. She sprayed and polished the little desk, restoring the surface to its original soft lustre. She liked the clean, lemony smell: it dispelled all traces of neglect, and made her feel again like the meticulous housekeeper she had once been. She wiped the seat of the wooden chair, and dusted its fiddle-back. Finally, she turned round to face the wardrobe.

Three times that Alice could remember, she had found herself in this room, sitting on the floor beside the wardrobe. It puzzled her that her illness seemed to take her over so completely in the darkness, thieving in the night. During the day she was mostly clear-headed, aware of herself, becoming frustrated only occasionally as another word or two stole away from her and went into hiding. She had learned to live with all that long before her recent visit to the hospital. On the whole, her days had not changed; it was the nights that were stealing bits of her from herself. On one occasion, a month or so back, she had, while still asleep, opened the right-hand door of the wardrobe in Elizabeth's room and taken down one of Jack's photograph albums. Perhaps 'asleep' was not really the word for it – it had been more like a non-waking state, halfway between sleep and dreaming.

Sometimes when she went wandering, she knew, vaguely, what she was doing, where she was going: she felt semi-conscious, but no longer in control of herself. It was like seeing something out of the corner of her mind's eye, a fleeting image that she couldn't quite catch. She always felt compelled to obey the instinct that pushed her on, making her search towards something she believed long forgotten. Sometimes, when she sat, or stood silently, having reached her destination, it was like looking at a blurred photograph. She knew she was there, was aware of her own presence, but she couldn't quite get herself into focus. Other times, when she woke, she couldn't distinguish whether she'd been dreaming, or whether the dream was really a hazy memory. Either way, she had never hurt herself before; but last night she had been jolted into wakefulness, fully conscious to the danger of injury. It was as though she, and the bedroom, had suddenly sharpened into a shocked brightness, with all the fuzzy lines and images finally converging into one, clear picture. She was sure now that it was the stinging pain in her hip that had brought her to.

Later, making tea in the kitchen, she had decided that today, in the daylight, she would start sorting through all the personal belongings that she had stored at the top of the old wardrobe: it was now time. Perhaps if she did all she could do, to still the nagging little voice which drove her again and again into her daughter's room, she would be left alone. Maybe the night-time searchings would be over then, having served their purpose. She had no idea why anything stored in this room should be important to her now – it was mostly old stuff, snaps and documents from her commercial college days, her first paypacket, things like that. Nothing to do with either Elizabeth or James. Most of their photographs and souvenirs of childhood were all safely housed in leather-bound albums, on the bookshelves downstairs. Jack had always been very proud of his photographs, and Alice had made sure they'd all been properly looked after, pasted into his lovely old albums, stored safely out of the reach of childish sticky fingers.

She had decided to stay and use Elizabeth's desk. It

would be nice to spend time in this room, and she could leave things just as they were once she got tired: there would be no need to put everything away again. James never came upstairs, unless Alice asked him specifically to get something for her. She could be private here; she would not need to explain herself to anyone. James, she knew, would be suspicious if he caught her at anything like this: he would know at once why she was tidying up: getting ready to put her life away, to shelve herself and her memories.

Carefully, she lifted the boxes and albums one by one from the top three shelves. She was amazed that there were so many: the shelves were high and deep and she had forgotten how much they could hold. The desk was now littered with half-full cloth-bound photo albums and Cadbury's chocolate boxes overflowing with black and white memories. Alice sat down and began to turn each of the photos over, checking to see if anything was written there. She knew that she used to be very methodical, once upon a time: that she used to write the names and dates on the backs as soon as she got the photographs. But this whole box was a jumble – these had simply been looked at once, and then put away safely for some day in the future when she might have more time. Well, she had time now, however little of it was left to her. And now was the right time, too.

This was not the first occasion that Alice had been astonished at the sharpness of her memory when dealing with events that had happened forty or fifty years ago, while the whereabouts of her glasses, or her keys, or yesterday's shopping list were still a complete mystery.

She chose five or six photographs at random from the pile beside her, glancing at them quickly, delighting in her instant ability to name the people and the places she saw. She had been afraid that she would feel frustrated; she had fully expected to be. And so, her first glances were hesitant, prepared to move on at once if recognition did not come quickly. Instead, she was deluged by details of names and dates – it was as if her mind couldn't give her enough memory, as if it were trying to make up for the occasional cruel lack of connection which was now becoming part and parcel of her daily existence. It had only been two weeks since her hospital visit, two weeks since that first, all-important letter to Beth, and she had been amazed at how much of her past life she had relived in her memory since then. It was like watching a video speeding up, fast-forwarding with jerky, vivid images until it reached the point in the story where Alice suddenly wanted to linger, to look over her life once again, this time in slow motion.

She selected one of the albums that was almost empty, and laid it on the table beside her. Then she began writing on the backs of the pictures she'd selected, pinning down her knowledge, making it concrete before she bent each one of the photos very gently, easing them into the four little slits in the stiff, grey cardboard. There they were, anchored safely, for good. It didn't matter if no one ever looked at these again, if no one ever cared who Margaret Cooper was, or Bridgie Phelan, or Mary Byrne. *She* cared, and paying due regard to these memories was important, a way of finding her place in the past, and grounding herself there. It would be safe, a solid vantage-point from which to look back at the years which had since become her future. She turned again to the landslide of papers on her left and slid out one of the larger photos from the bottom of the pile. She knew what she was looking for now, she had her chronology established.

There was a circular stamp on the back of this one, barely distinguishable among the brown splotches on the off-white background. Just like liver spots, Alice thought. She held Jack's magnifying glass close to the printed words. *'Miss Rutherford's Secretarial College for Young Ladies. Class of 1944–1945'*. Alice exclaimed out loud with delight. She turned the photograph over; its surface was a little cracked with spidery white lines, but she was able to distinguish the twelve sepia-toned young faces that smiled out at her. She felt her breath catch. How many of these girls' names would she be able to remember? She was struck by how much the same they all looked – neat, hatted, gloved. It was strange to see her other self, sitting tall and proper, in the second row. She could remember in detail the costume she'd worn for the occasion, too – navy-blue linen with a fur collar, and a matching hat, its brim just tilted over one eyebrow. She had made her own outfit, cutting it down from a suit once worn by her mother; the collar had been on loan for the occasion of her graduation. Alice smoothed the photograph in front of her, and applied the magnifying glass more closely. She could match names to just five of the faces in front of her, and these she wrote on the back, at once, in case they slipped away from her again.

Margaret, Bridgie and Mary stood tall in the back row, as inseparable as they were in Alice's memory. Seated primly in the front row, gloved hands folded in her lap, was Ellen Smyth, a whizz at shorthand, and typing speeds of sixty words a minute; poor Ellie – she'd died of consumption within two years of leaving Miss Rutherford's in a blaze of glory. She'd got the cream of the crop of jobs that year, too – straight into the Civil Service typing pool. The pearl buttons on her gloves were still distinguishable; Alice remembered those gloves well: envy sharpens the mind. They were pale lilac, a perfect wrinkle-free fit, expensive. Beside her sat Bernie O'Rourke, whose large capable hands seemed even larger, distorted by the angle of the lens. She'd gone off to Boston immediately after graduation, with her new husband. Alice could still see her, frozen for ever in memory, on the day she'd left Dublin. Her face shining, she'd held on tight to Dominic's arm, gazing up at his handsome face, enraptured. Handsome is as handsome does, Alice thought grimly. Bernie had always been the innocent one. Alice moved along the rows, and could feel something stirring restlessly in the depths of old times, but nothing else surfaced. Reluctantly, she left the picture to one side, for now. She had learned that if she didn't strain too much, the memory of a face or name would suddenly come to her, like a tiny light exploding, illuminating the dusty corners of her mind. She wanted more than just the five names; but she could wait, she could be patient.

She pulled more photos from the bottom of the pile, tapping the sides of the unruly bundle into place, trying to even it up, to stop everything from sliding on to the floor. She recognized the first snap, straight away. Arthur Boyd and his wife, Millie. She was there, too, all three of them sitting on her rug, picnic bits spread out all around them. Alice had no memory of that particular day, although she tried hard to recall it. Its complete absence puzzled her. She could often date an occasion by whatever it was she was wearing: a handbag that Jack had given her for her twenty-first birthday, a particular hand-knitted cardigan with Swiss embroidery that dated from the first winter of her marriage, or the floral cotton skirts she had made on her mother's sewing-machine, the same year that she had perfected the smocking on Elizabeth's summer dresses. But there was nothing distinctive in this photo, just an ordinary home-made summer dress whose pattern was now indistinguishable.

Alice pulled the magnifying glass back a little: Dollymount or Bray? It was impossible to tell: all she could see was sand, and a few surprised tufts of coarse grass. Bray had been Arthur's favourite haunt, and Alice tried again, to see if she could recognize any landmarks, but there was nothing to help her. So who had taken the picture? It certainly hadn't been Jack – his photographs were always crystal clear, without even the slightest suspicion of shake or blur. He always said it was the Leica, that he couldn't go wrong. But Alice had often wondered. He should have been a painter – a real painter with oils and canvas – or maybe even a photographer. He had spent neither his money nor his talents wisely, Alice reflected. So much waste.

She shook her head impatiently, brushing the thought away, and went back to examining the photograph. This was no time for bitterness. Maybe Arthur's eldest had taken it, or a passer-by? Arthur had always had the happy knack of getting people to do things for him, even complete strangers. Charm the birds off the trees, she had once heard someone say of him, sourly. He was a good ten years older than Jack, had taken him under his wing within weeks of Jack's joining his family firm. They had become great friends, and Alice had grown quickly fond of Millie, a gentle, shy-eyed woman who was content to be forever in her husband's shadow. Already a mother of four when Alice met her, she'd been glad to have a younger, greener mother as a friend. She'd loved showing off her boys, who didn't mind at all their mother's public demonstrations of affection. The older ones had been kind to Elizabeth, too, and seemed to enjoy looking after her in the water when they were allowed to go swimming. The memory of all that shocked Alice now, and left her breathless. The day of that photo wasn't important, of course it wasn't. It was of no significance at all. It was *later* that mattered . . .

She hadn't thought about any of that in *years*. She'd never told anyone, not even James. Is this what had been prodding at her, nudging her, goading her in the direction of Elizabeth's bedroom? She stood up for a moment, and moved towards the window, breathing deeply, trying to calm herself. She'd stopped wondering, years ago, whether she'd made the right decision. How come all of it was flooding back now, picking at her, hurting like a sore that wouldn't heal? After all these years, Arthur's face was still vivid; she could still see his bright, lively blue eyes, the instant lure of his crooked grin. She went back to the desk again, and started to rummage through the pile of photos.

Something had suddenly become urgent inside her, as though her waking self were coming close to finding what her restlessness had been searching for. She now knew what she wanted from these photos heaped on the little desk. It should be easy to find: only a few of the photographs were studio ones, most of the others had been taken with Jack's 1934 Leica, a gift from his father, and his pride and joy. Alice could still see how he'd handled the tan leather case with reverence, folding the camera away neatly into its soft depths, securing it with a satisfying snap of its sturdy fastener. She pulled out three of the larger pictures from close to the bottom of the pile, ignoring the ones that avalanched noisily to the floor. She was too impatient even to sit down.

There it was: the standard family portrait. Arthur and Millie and their four boys. The photograph had been retouched: Millie's lips and hair had an unnatural orange tinge, and the six pairs of eyes that now regarded Alice were a bright, startled blue. She walked towards the window, holding the photo away from her, leaning into where the light was better. It was the youngest, Colm's, First Communion, and he sat in the centre of the frame, his parents on either side of him. Behind them, like gently graduated steps of stairs, stood the other three, hair slicked down, smiles wide and gap-toothed. Like all children then, they looked much older than their years, their jackets and short pants formal and ridiculous at the same time. Millie was smiling radiantly, looking right into Alice's eyes. She felt her breathing quicken.

She turned the photo over. In shaky, childish handwriting, she read: 'May, 1958. To my godparents, Uncle Jack and Auntie Alice, a souvenir of my First Holy Communion. Love from Colm.' She smiled. They weren't a real aunt and uncle, of course, at least not if these things were decided by blood. But they had loved the boy, and his brothers. Alice looked closely at Millie's face, trying to find some hint of the tragedy to come, some shadow in the eyes of the swift and brutal death less than a year after she'd smiled for the camera. Her baby, a little girl, hadn't made it either, and Alice saw again Arthur's body wracked by sobs as the four, suddenly smaller, figures stood beside him in the church, white and uncomprehending. She had held on tight to James and Elizabeth that day, while Jack, along with Arthur and his brothers, had heaved Millie's coffin onto his shoulders and made slow, dignified progress down the centre aisle of the church. That day, Alice had felt not only grief, that was natural, but a cold, clammy premonition that had clutched at her, somewhere near her centre.

No wonder she had put all of these away. There would be pictures of Jack here too, of their early days together. She'd have to take all of this very slowly. Alice sensed that something very strange was happening to her: she felt dislocated, no longer at the centre of her own life. The years seemed to be falling away all around her. The only reality was the one that faced her now, images captured by the camera in sepia and white-toned frozen moments. She felt disturbed by the intensity of the scenes that swam out at her from the grainy surfaces. Her chest began to tighten, and she could feel something like a sob forming just under her heart. She sat abruptly on Elizabeth's bed, her hand at her throat, trying to still the uncomfortable, fluttery sensation which was growing there.

'Stop it,' she said aloud. 'You're getting upset, and it's all far too long ago.'

She could feel her back hunching over, her shoulders collapsing forward. All of this was making her tired, very tired. Writing to James and Elizabeth was one thing, she had grown to look forward to that, but this onslaught of memory was quite another. In the last couple of weeks, whenever she'd sat quietly in the evenings to compose her letters, she'd felt in control. She could be careful of her own and her children's feelings then, choosing moments of significance from their lives to reassure them that she had done her best, always, that she had loved them. It was almost like imagining the story of their lives, something make-believe, where she, and she alone, could determine the final outcome. It was almost like giving each of them a gift of their own happy ending. She was able to filter the past through the kinder lens of her present wisdom and old age. Although Alice kept reminding herself that these letters were directed to adults, the pictures in her head were of two red-haired children, one calmly older than his years, the other troubled and ill at ease, ready to fight with the devil. She found it strange that they were children of the same parents, that each had been brought up by the same rules. Maybe that was the problem, she reflected now as she lay down on Elizabeth's bed, kicking off her shoes. Maybe the same rules didn't work for different people. In her new carefulness, Alice had decided that she wasn't being dishonest in what she wrote, just conscious of how her children might feel, reading her words after she was gone. The whole truth, as she had learned long ago, was not necessarily the best thing for children, at least not in its plain and unvarnished condition. Lying still on Elizabeth's bed, trying to calm the beating of her heart, Alice felt that maybe it wasn't the best thing, either, for forgetful old ladies well on their way to being eighty. She pulled the eiderdown over her, reacting to the sudden chill she felt in the bedroom air. She covered herself, right up to the chin, and closed her eyes.

'I'll just rest for a while,' she told herself. 'I'll be right as rain in an hour or so.'

But sleep would not come. Instead, she felt wakeful behind her closed eyes, surrounded by voices, presences, the ghosts of those she had locked away in her wardrobe all those years ago. It became difficult to distinguish whether the childish laughter she heard came from the back gardens outside her window, or from the air around her. And suddenly, there he was.

Arthur was standing in her front porch, his favourite battered fedora held in front of him like a shield, just as it had been on the night he'd arrived, unannounced, on her doorstep. She could see herself, too, that other, younger Alice in a green woollen dress, opening the door to him, puzzled by the familiarity of the outline through the glass, yet unable to guess who it was.

'Arthur!' she said aloud, surprised. Just the same tone as she'd used nearly forty years before.

'Hello, Alice,' he said, quietly. It was as though he were speaking to her again here, now, the same words, the same expression in his eyes, the crooked grin just a little less sure of itself than before.

She'd opened the door to him that evening, sensing unease in the way he handled his hat, and the way his back was so straight, suddenly upright. All the lazy stoop of comfort and familiarity was gone. His expression had confused her, too, that and the fact that he was on his own. No boys to soften his visit this time. She was aware of Mrs McGrath across the road, cutting her hedge just a little too diligently, clipping away with her shears at the same spot, over and over again. Her glasses glinted accusingly at Alice from over the immaculate privet, and with a flash of anger, Alice had opened the door even wider, almost pulling Arthur inside.

'Nosey old bitch!' she'd said. It was a useful anger; it covered the moment of surprise she'd felt when she opened the door to him, and the deeper, wordless instinct underneath. She felt certain she knew why he'd come.

His expression was so alarmed that Alice laughed, and ease was restored between them. She had laughed very little lately; the sound almost shocked her.

'Tea?' she asked, leading the way into the kitchen.

'Lovely,' he said, still holding on to his hat, following her.

'How are the boys?' she asked as she filled the kettle, keeping her back carefully to him.

'Fine, fine. And your two?'

'Grand. Peggy's taken them to Bray. They took a picnic. It's good for them to be with their cousins.'

She stopped. She always explained too much when she was nervous. She became busy instead, pulling out cups and saucers, filling the milk jug, rummaging in the press for biscuits.

'And you. How are you?'

His tone was gentle; he never seemed to pose this as a question. It was more like a statement, an opening for her to fill in the blanks.

'Oh, you know ... some days are better than others. It's not easy, but ...' and she shrugged. He should know, if anyone did, that it wasn't easy. After eleven months, she could still feel Jack's presence in the house. The suddenness of his death had left shattered pieces of him everywhere. There had been no time to prepare, to tidy up. He'd simply stopped breathing, sitting in the chair across from hers, the fire lighting between them. And although her mother had come at once, that same evening, and opened all the doors and windows, Alice felt that Jack's spirit had never really left her. She still came across things of his almost daily: a pipe that had made its way deep underneath the sofa cushions, bits of paper with the addresses of jobs scribbled on them, even his clothes which she hadn't been able to give away, although their empty presence hurt her. His old jacket still hung under the stairs, and sometimes the smell of pipe tobacco was so strong in their bedroom that she believed he really had come back to her.

Arthur was still talking. His voice was soothing, the words familiar. They had been over this ground many times before. She had learned to expect what he would say next.

'The first year is the worst – all the firsts are the worst. Once the anniversary is over, you should find things getting a bit easier.'

He was looking directly at her now. There was something underneath his words, something implicit in his certainty that he knew how she should be feeling, and Alice felt suddenly on edge again. She wasn't ready for this. She concentrated hard on pouring tea.

'Alice?'

She had to look up at him then. His large body was leaning over the table, inclining towards her. She noticed how odd his big hands looked, beside her delicate bone china cups. They were very different from Jack's; no speckles of paint peppered his knuckles, the nails were scrubbed, trimmed.

'I can make things easier for you, Alice.'

She didn't want him to go on. She put the teapot down carefully onto the table. Her hands were unsteady. She smoothed the skirt of her woollen dress, to have something to do other than meet his direct gaze.

'Please, don't say any more, Arthur. I don't want you to say any more.'

'You don't have to decide right now. I'm very fond of you, Alice, you know that.'

His words were slow, measured. There was none of the reckless charm that had made her cautious of him, when Millie was alive. His humour then had often been personal, jaunty, careless of wounding others, although he had always treated her and Jack with kindness. Jack had often spoken of his good fortune in finding, eventually, such a decent boss. Alice knew that he was sincere now, too: he had always been at ease in her company. But lately, she had been disturbed by his visits. He had helped her out after Jack's heart attack, becoming almost like family. But she had no answer to give him now. She glanced over at him, seeing that his eyes were bluer than ever. Appalled at herself, she fought the urge to reach out and touch his face, to caress the strong wrists that were visible under the immaculate white cuffs of his shirt. She saw at last, with a little shock of revelation, that he had dressed up for her. Dark suit, gleaming white shirt, a sober tie. No wonder he'd looked awkward at first: he was not one to wear his heart lightly on his sleeve. She had a great rush of shame that she could feel so drawn to this man while her husband was still present to her in so many ways, all around her. But he's dead, said a small voice inside her head. And you have two children.

'You're young, Alice. You deserve a second chance.'

He put his cup down gently onto the fluted saucer, as though afraid it would shatter in his hands.

'I'm asking you to marry me, Alice. Will you think about it?'

She nodded.

'Yes. I will think about it. But I don't know when I'll be able to give you an answer.'

He smiled.

'Don't worry. I'll wait until you're ready.'

Quietness filled the kitchen. Alice wished he would go. She needed to be on her own, to sort through the thoughts and feelings which had her as thoroughly tongue-tied as a young girl. She had known that this was coming, of course she had, but now that he had spoken, she felt thrown off balance, out of control, as giddy as a child. She could feel the silence between them beginning to grow dangerous. She could almost imagine herself blurting out *Yes, yes I will marry you,* just to break the tension between them. There was no young Colm or Elizabeth or James today to come in and out of the kitchen and break the spell, looking for food and reassurance, for knees to be bandaged or noses to be wiped. It was the first time they had ever been alone together, and the sudden charge of intimacy in the air was too much for her. She needed him to go, now. The visit was over. To her relief, he sensed too that it was time. He stood. She stood. Both pushed their chairs back awkwardly.

'I'd better be going,' he said, finally.

She nodded and smoothed her dress, again. She wished she had something kind to say to him, anything, to respond to his generosity. But the words wouldn't come until much later.

'I'll see you out,' she said.

On her way past, he reached out and touched her arm.

'I'm fifty-one, Alice. Don't make me wait too long.'

She hesitated for a moment, almost paralysed. Her arm was warm, tingling where he had touched her. Everything around her seemed to become slow and distant as he raised his hand to stroke her hair. She could feel her face begin to burn as he pulled her gently towards him, one large hand still on her hair, the other around her waist, pressing her to him. She felt the coarse material of his waistcoat scratching against her cheek until he released her, cupping her chin in his hand. He bent towards her, his face warm, pressed closely to hers. He kissed her lightly, once. Alice felt almost dizzy with delight until panic surged, making it difficult to breathe. *What am I doing?* She broke away from him abruptly, pulling her eyes away from his blue gaze; she wanted, needed to break the spell. He let her go.

She kept her eyes down, then, waiting for the pounding feeling in her chest to go away. He touched her shoulder once more, just as he was leaving.

'I'll see you very soon.'

His voice had gone quiet. She wondered what he was thinking. She nodded, wordlessly. She reached out and opened the door, her hand just a little shaky. She hoped he hadn't noticed.

He settled his hat as he stood in the porch, delaying. Mrs McGrath was sweeping up the clippings from her hedge, the last cut before the winter. Alice could see her curiosity, could almost discern the twitch in her ears as she listened for scandal. *And Jack Keating hardly cold in his grave.* Alice could imagine her satisfaction, her smug little triumph that she had finally detected unseemly behaviour on the street she regarded as her own.

'Good night, Arthur.'

She closed the door quietly behind him.

*

Alice heard the click of the bedroom door as the wind gusting through the window finally pushed it closed. She opened her eyes, suddenly wide awake. For a moment, she couldn't move; she knew where she was, instantly, and yet her surroundings felt unfamiliar, displaced. Arthur's presence in the room was so strong she had to hold her breath, afraid that any sudden movement would disturb him. After what seemed like a long time, the room began to lose its sense of otherness, and to settle itself around her again. She breathed more easily. He was almost gone.

'Silly old woman,' she grumbled aloud, her eyes fixed on the crack in the ceiling above her. 'It's a bit late to start believing in ghosts at your age.'

In one brisk movement, she pulled herself up to sitting. The wave of love she'd felt at Arthur's touch began to recede; she shrugged the remains of it off by straightening her shoulders and patting the back of her hair. She looked down, checking for any hairpins that might have come loose during sleep. But nothing had been disturbed. She plumped up the pillow, smoothing the lace edging. Now she felt refreshed, alert again. Even if she weren't resting properly at night, these brief afternoon naps seemed to make up for any loss. She glanced at her watch and was surprised to find it was almost six. She'd a couple of hours yet before Keith came. She sat up straighter, feeling the floor with the tips of her toes, looking for her shoes. All of her movements had become decisive, purposeful; no more nonsense. But as she closed the window of Elizabeth's bedroom, she had to fight the memory of the way Arthur had walked away, down the front path, lifting his hat to Mrs McGrath, stooping to open the door of his red Volkswagen. She paused by the window, letting the soft curtain material drift through her fingers. Physical movements alone were not enough to dispel him completely. Even her shoulder still felt tingly, warmed by his final touch. Her head was alive with the vivid images of sleep: at first, when she'd opened her eyes, she hadn't been sure whether it had all been dream or memory. It didn't really matter; there was no confusion, the pictures were bright and clear in her mind. That's the way it always was now when she revisited her other life. Confusion saved itself for the assaults it made from time to time on life lived in the *now*, a place from which she was beginning to feel more and more remote; all of her emotional energies were becoming refocused on the other Alice, the one who was still young, vital, with her grip on life and reality strong and assured. There was the growing sense of something deep and still having been disturbed within her. No wonder this was one of those things she had kept locked away, carefully, instinctively understanding its power to wound.

Arthur Boyd had been every bit as real to her this afternoon as he had been forty years before. His presence had touched her, stirring something that demanded to be heard, finally, to be felt and seen and tasted. Alice had never been one for regrets; her life had been far too busy, filled by her children and their needs. She'd always prided herself on her lack of sentimentality. But now, in the deceptive calm of these unbusy days, her mind had suddenly turned traitor. It was making her pick over the broken pieces of that part of her life she had thought long and safely buried. In her practical, no-nonsense daily existence, Alice had always known that most things could be mended – broken delph, fraying carpets, stuck door handles. And she had learned to cope with all of them, becoming gradually more and more familiar with the contents of Jack's toolbox. What she couldn't fix, whatever was beyond repair, she unceremoniously threw out, without sentiment, without nostalgia. *That's that.* But now it seemed that her memories weren't so accommodating. Of course she couldn't change what had happened between her and Arthur, nor could she mend it. But something was nagging at her to put the pieces back together again, just so that she could see the whole picture one more time, and become familiar with its contours. She felt helpless for a moment, wondering where to start. It was all such a long time ago and regret was such a wasted emotion. Suddenly, she knew that she wanted to tell Elizabeth about Arthur, felt sure that her daughter would understand what was only now forming into words inside her head.

The August evening was fine, the summer light still good. Alice decided she'd begin the letter straight away. She wanted to do something with the sudden surge of energy that had been released by Arthur's visit. She sat down at the little desk again, and pulled her writing paper towards her.

'Woodvale'
11th August 1999

My dearest Elizabeth,
I need to write to you again, this time from the little desk in your old bedroom. I've been spending a lot of time in the house in the past two weeks, tidying up, gathering together loose ends. I'm very careful that James doesn't see any of this, or he'd insist that I came to stay with him and Olive. He'd worry, and want to make sure he could keep a close eye on me. But I like this time on my own – I don't feel lonely and, strangely enough, I'm not frightened in the house any more, even though I'm waking at night much more frequently than before.

There is something inside that's been nagging at me recently to meet my old memories head on – I've woken up on three different nights now, standing beside the wardrobe in your old bedroom. Today, I decided to try and find out why, to discover whatever it is that seems to be drawing me back to the same place, again and again. So I've taken to spending time here, working at the desk your dad made for you. You used to do your homework at this desk – do you remember us fighting because you had Radio Caroline on at full volume? You insisted that the music helped you to concentrate. Music – how are you! Many's the time I threatened to throw that transistor in the bin. The more we fought, the louder you turned up the volume on the following night. Of course, we weren't fighting about music at all, but about much more important things. I belonged too much to the old school, I think, where children had to be seen and not heard. You certainly didn't seem to be aware of that piece of old wisdom – you fought very hard indeed for your right to be heard. You were, I think, that word which I rarely hear applied to children nowadays – wilful. I'm sure now that it wasn't right to try and bend that will as much as I did. You insisted on being yourself, and I think you were right to do so. My generation understood a lot about duty to others, and very little about duty to ourselves.

Alice stopped herself. This wasn't what she'd meant to write about at all. The last sentence took her somewhat by surprise. She, who had chided Elizabeth on so many occasions in the past about her duty and responsibility to others, now seemed to be questioning its value in relation to her own life. She must be rambling. She tapped her pen impatiently on the desk, and started again.

I've never really talked to you about the time after your dad died. The belief then was that children didn't really understand loss, that if we didn't talk about death, it would somehow go away. I know that even then I never really believed it, but at the time it was comforting: I didn't have the strength to deal with your grief as well as my own. I feel sad about that now, for you. When you got older, it became easier to talk about the times when your dad had been alive, and we did: you used to test your memories of him on me quite a lot. But we never talked about what it had been like to lose him, what life was like for each of us after he died.

I've been thinking about those days a lot as I've been going through the old photographs, the ones at the top of your wardrobe. It is, at times, quite painful. But I want to see it through to the end, because I'm learning things about myself, and beginning to feel more complete, somehow.

I don't think that I'm expressing myself very well – I've a tendency to stray from the point, these days. My dream will probably explain things better. I'm dreaming a lot more these nights, and sometimes in the afternoons, too. I usually take a little rest after lunch, and the dreams then can be especially vivid. I had a really strange one the other day: I was dressing up to go to a party. I knew it was me, because in a dream, you do – you just know these things, even though I couldn't see my own face, and when was the last time I went to a party! I was putting on Granny McKinney's pearls – you know the necklace I'm talking about, the single string with the little diamond-chip clasp? Your dad and I used to call it our insurance policy. Anyway, there I am in front of my dressing-table mirror, fastening the clasp, and suddenly, the string breaks. I feel shocked, paralysed in that awful, suffocating, dream-like way, when you can't even move your head or your arms. I watch as all the pearls scatter across the bedroom floor, bouncing on the wood, disappearing under the bed, hiding in the gaps between the floorboards. I am unable to move until all the scattering has stopped. Somehow, I know

how many pearls there should be – don't ask me
how, because I certainly don't know that in reality.
I start to pick them up, one by one, and the sense
of shock begins to get less. I remember feeling very
happy, very still inside, as a voice says to me, 'You
must gather together all the pieces of yourself to
become whole.' At this stage, I know I'm dreaming,
but I still can't wake up. The dream continued until
I had picked up every single pearl, and then I woke,
my head so full of what I had dreamt that it felt like
another reality. I remember thinking, 'What an
extraordinary dream!' The voice has stayed with me,
it was so real, so old-fashioned and formal, that it
was utterly convincing. I actually got out of bed and
took the pearls out to have a look at them, to check
and see if I was going mad, or what. (Remember
where they're hidden – in the last drawer of your
dad's wardrobe. They're for you and Laura.)

They were in one piece, of course, and I was
relieved to see that they were. The dream gradually
faded over the next few days, but the powerful
sensation of picking bits of myself up off the floor
has not gone away. That's the instinct that's been
disturbing my sleep and pushing me to look at old
photographs, even to write like this to you and
James. I feel that there are bits of me, fractured, all
over the place – after your dad died, I blocked out
so much of my life because it was too painful to
remember. But the memories have been refusing,
lately, to stay locked away. They are surfacing in all
sorts of surprising ways. Today, I spent all afternoon
remembering Arthur Boyd, a good friend of ours,
and your dad's employer. You might remember
Arthur's sons – you and James used to swim with

them on the Sundays when we all went to Bray together. After their mam died, they used to visit here quite a bit with their father. You would have been about six at the time. Their visits stopped just over a year after your dad died.

Around the time of Jack's first anniversary, Arthur asked me to marry him. I knew, instinctively, that he was going to, that day. I think I'd probably known for some time. I was tempted. He was handsome, kind and well-off. Any other woman would have given him hope, at least. But I couldn't. I felt guilty that I could even think about marrying him, less than a year after Jack died. It felt almost like being unfaithful. You see, I never really lost the sense of your dad's presence all around me in this house and particularly, when I stepped out into his beloved garden.

And then there was the money. I was broke, I had nothing. Arthur was wealthy, and he had always been a generous man. But I felt ashamed that I was now poor, that charity might be part of his motive for wanting to marry me. I was afraid, too, that I was the solution to his need for a housekeeper. He would have taken care of all of us, I know that. But that wasn't the point. I just couldn't do it. Part of me felt that I was being bought over, although I do believe that he was genuinely fond of me. I looked at his four sons – Colm, the youngest, was eight at that stage, Peter was eleven, the same age as James. David was fourteen and Arthur junior, sixteen. All I could see was my two children being swamped, swallowed up in a household where all of those boys came first. I agonized about it for a long time, and eventually I told Arthur no. I've never really known if I made the right decision. Years ago, I stopped wondering about it. I wouldn't even let myself think about it – but it's come back to haunt me – literally. Today, I felt the presence of Arthur so strongly that I could hardly breathe. He came back again to ask me to marry him, just exactly as he did forty years ago. It was like being given a second chance. I wanted to hold on to him, I could feel how warm and alive he was. The sense of him being there, beside me, was overwhelming. When I woke up, I was disappointed to find he had gone. I hardly dared move, I wanted to keep him with me a little bit longer. It should feel ridiculous and pathetic, but it doesn't. It feels like an enormous pool, a great deep well of loss, and I've nobody to blame but myself. I'm writing to you now in the aftermath of that dream, or vision, or whatever it was. As I write, I feel sadly conscious of a missed opportunity – a very important one in all our lives.

Should I have said yes? Wouldn't we all have been happier, less pressured as a family if I had agreed? Or is this just so much useless nostalgia? We were close, the three of us, weren't we? A real family? I wish I knew that I'd done the right thing by all of us. I wish I could feel it. I often felt guilty for refusing him – he was terribly hurt and disappointed the night I said no, finally. I almost changed my mind, seeing him sitting at the kitchen table, looking smaller, hunched in on himself, as though someone had let the air out of him. He'd brought flowers, and the water was seeping through the white paper, making a little puddle on the table, making the wrapping all grey and soggy. I'll always remember that. That was the last time I ever saw him; he was married less than a year later, to a much younger woman. I wrote to him, wishing them both happiness. But I never heard anything back. I suppose I must have been hurt, but everything seemed to ooze into numbness at that time of my life: I could hardly distinguish one feeling from another. I suppose I was too busy.

I've often asked myself did I love him. I really don't know. That whole year was so traumatic, so difficult in terms of money and grief and worry about the future, that I really don't know what I felt. Your dad hadn't been working long enough for Boyd and Sons to get any sort of a pension, but Arthur cashed in an insurance policy your dad had started once he joined the firm, and I got a few hundred pounds for that. It helped with the funeral, and afterwards. I've often wondered whether that policy really existed; I have my suspicions – I think Arthur was just being good to me. He was a good man, a very good man. And still, I turned him down. I know he fully expected me to say yes. But I couldn't shake the notion that his family would always come first, that you and James wouldn't get the attention you deserved. And maybe I wasn't ready to be a mother to six children. It was all I could manage to be a good enough mother for you two. I made the choice then to go it alone, and we've all lived with the consequences of that decision.

Anyway, once Arthur disappeared from our lives, there was never anyone else for me. I put my head down, earned my few pounds cleaning and cooking and, later on, sewing, and I brought you two up as best I could. And I'm very proud that you and

James got such a good education – I'd have to say that I'm proud of myself for making that happen. I never wanted to see my children cleaning other people's floors or preparing other people's food as I had to do. I wanted more for you, more than your dad and I had had. But it was hard. I know what it's like to be lonely, and to carry all the responsibility. That's why I worry about you. I suppose what I'm trying to say is, that if I had my time again, I might make a different decision. It's a long life, living it on your own. I'll probably never get the chance to talk to you like this, so I'm going to say what's on my mind: will you please try again with Tony? He's a good man and I'm sure he still wants you back, any fool could see that he never wanted to let you go in the first place. Years don't mean anything when that sort of strong feeling is there between two people. Don't give yourself something to regret when you're eighty.

I heard that Arthur died about ten years ago. I didn't go to the funeral. He was the mainstay of the family firm: once he retired, that would be almost twenty-five years ago now, his brother, Robert, let the business go to hell. He'd never been interested in it, not really, not in the same way that Arthur was. He basically drank it to death, and within a few short years, there was nothing left. You'd wonder what it's all for, sometimes, wouldn't you?

Alice stopped. A wave of depression flooded her as she looked at what she had written. What had her life been about, after all? She had left nothing of value behind her, her life had been of no significance to anyone other than her own immediate family. And her children's lives were no great shakes either, it seemed. James was just past fifty, happy only in the escape that his work offered him from the rest of his life. Alice knew that he and Olive were heading towards a much-postponed crisis; she didn't need a crystal ball to tell her how tense and angry things were between them and, against all her principles, she was beginning to believe that he would be better off on his own. Olive's incessant demands for him to be other than he was, to be different from the man she had, after all, freely chosen to marry, were finally wearing James down. He was nervous-looking these days, pale, almost bloodless, with those increasingly vulnerable blue eyes watching out for everyone else's welfare, everyone's except his own. And then there was Elizabeth. Her malcontent. Married to a thoroughly good and kind man, separated on a whim, it seemed to Alice, living apart for no good reason. Escaping again, as she had always done. Her daughter's reaction to everything and everyone that had ever challenged her, was to run. She'd been doing it all her life; she was still doing it now. Eventually, Tony would get fed up waiting for her to come back, if he hadn't already done so: ten years was a long time to be hanging around without hope – and then where would she and Laura be? Alice sighed. These depressing thoughts were doing her no good at all. It was time to stop. She went to glance at her watch and had to pull the tiny face back to where she could see it. It had moved around, sliding easily over her wristbone. She thought of Jack, of the way he'd proudly slipped this watch over her fingers, fastening it carefully and wishing her a happy Christmas, just a few months before they'd become engaged. She smiled at the memory.

Jack had loved tradition, loved to feel that his life was mapped out by others before him, so that his future was nothing more nor less than a well-worn path he had to follow. Even Alice's mother had made fun of his predictability. First the gold watch, then the ring; she had teased the young Alice over the family tea one Christmas evening, making her blush furiously, not knowing where to look. Yet, it was this same unshakable belief in the predictability of life that had made Jack into a man careless of the future. He had not thought of leaving a young family behind, and a wife who was ill-equipped to earn her own living. He had thought he'd go on for ever, see his children grown, bounce his grandchildren on his knee. Maybe we all do, reflected Alice, but life had taught her different. She could still feel the guilty rage that had consumed her after his death when she'd discovered that there was nothing left, nothing at all. No savings, no pension, no policies other than the one Arthur had cashed in for her, the one he insisted was hers. It had terrified her, how quickly that had been swallowed up. Money from the sale of the garden had been frittered away too, without her knowledge – lent, as she subsequently found out, to a ne'er-do-well cousin who had blown the lot on a sure thing at Punchestown races. She pulled the bracelet tight around her wrist: she must remember to have a link or two taken out of it. Her arms seemed to have shrunk lately. Half past seven. Keith would be here in half an hour. She pushed all thoughts of Jack away for now, pulling the sheet of writing paper towards her again, resting her elbows on the desk.

> I'm going to stop for now. I feel worn out, to be honest, and suddenly depressed. This is the first time in a long time I've felt so hopeless about what my life has meant, what it might continue to mean. I'm not just feeling sorry for myself, either – it's an entirely different feeling, as though I can see myself in terms of the vastness of the rest of the world. I feel very tiny and insignificant. It is rather a frightening feeling. Writing whenever I can to you and James has meant that I have managed to keep that feeling at bay lately, but sometimes, like now, it returns very fiercely, and I don't quite know what to do with myself. I must go now; Keith is coming soon to help me with the garden. He usually cheers me up, although I think he probably has much better things to be doing on a Friday night. I hope I'll be feeling more cheerful in my next letter!
> With much love,
> Alice.

And I hope that I'll have the time to write another one, Alice thought, as she wrote Elizabeth's name carefully on the envelope. She wanted to leave this room now, to go somewhere uncrowded and still, away from the pull of memory; she wanted to escape the grip of feeling that had been merciless in its intensity all day. The garden beckoned. Alice looked out of the bedroom window at all the beauty below her. Everything was bathed in warm westerly light. She knew that the old stone walls would have retained the heat of the day, and that she'd be safe there, sheltered from any evening breeze. She decided she would go and sit for a while on Jack's garden bench, placed among the wildflowers which were all in riotous bloom. Their lovely disorder appealed to her tonight. She'd had enough for now of thought and memory, times and dates. She wanted to lose herself in the wild safety of her husband's walled garden.

Keith would come and keep her company. The evening should pass swiftly enough. And with the extra exercise from the chores of weeding and sweeping, she should sleep well, maybe even right through the night. Then, she would see what tomorrow had in store for her.

*

Beth leaned forward and checked Alice's breathing one more time before she stood up. She smoothed the covers, patting her mother's hand as she stepped away from the side of the bed, no abrupt movements, and made her way towards the jewellery box on the dressing table. She was filled with a sense of expectation, of almost child-like excitement, as she wondered what her mother's second letter might hold. This almost-correspondence between them might be little and it might be late, but it had begun to fill Beth with a profound sense of gratitude. She felt that each letter would pull her closer and closer to a mother she had never really known. In their silent, unspoken conversation, mutual understanding had finally begun to grow. Her father had often taught her that wildflowers thrived best in thin, insubstantial soil: the rarest varieties established themselves where the ground was poorest. Beth remembered that now, and allowed herself to feel hopeful that communication between her and Alice might blossom in the same way. She knew instinctively that being home now was one of the most important things she had ever done with her life.

She leaned down, inserting the little key into its ornate keyhole. She was just about to turn it when she was sure she heard the front door close. She stopped what she was doing, puzzled, and straightened up at once. For a moment, she felt guilty, almost panicked, as though she had no right to be here, rummaging among her mother's things. She hadn't time to do anything other than open the bedroom door, as she heard James's heavy steps on the landing. Her relief was absurd. Who had she been expecting?

'Jesus, James, you gave me a fright . . .'

Then she saw his face.

'What is it? What's happened?'

From somewhere else, from another life, she remembered a saying about troubles coming not singly, but in battalions. James's face was grey, crumpled. For a moment, she wondered was he having a heart attack, was he going to die on her, too?

'I thought I'd come back and keep you company.'

He pushed past her and resumed his position at the bedside, as though he had never been away.

'What's happened? You look awful.'

She followed him uncertainly to his side of the bed and stood behind him, not knowing what to say or do next. She was aware that she was playing his part now, acting almost like a protector. She was struck by the absurdity of the situation. James took out his handkerchief and carefully polished the lenses of his glasses. Without them, his eyes looked sunken, old, lines etched deeply like the arid surface of an African river-bed. When he'd finished polishing, he held the glasses towards the candlelight, checking for smears.

'Olive's thrown me out.'

His voice was dry, cracked.

'Jesus.'

It was all Beth could think of to say, and yet she didn't feel shocked; she didn't feel anything. Was she suddenly becoming immune to ordinary feelings? She noticed that James's hands were shaking, ever so slightly. She rested one of hers on his shoulder.

'Do you want to talk about it, or do you want me to leave you alone?'

He smiled up at her, over his right shoulder. It was a tight, sad smile that never quite reached his eyes.

'Right now, I'd love you to make me a cuppa.'

She nodded.

'Of course I will. Back in a minute.'

She was glad to leave him alone, to escape, glad to bang things about in the kitchen. She slammed the cutlery drawer and kicked the pedal bin on her way past. How *dare* she! Talk about timing! Could she not have left him alone, at least until his mother died? Had she no decency, common or otherwise? Beth felt the hot, angry tears spilling over as she tried to push away the image of her brother's grey face. She felt his pain now, as suddenly as a physical hurt. She didn't know which emotion she felt more keenly: sadness for him, or rage at Olive. She rummaged furiously in the presses for cake, for Mikado biscuits, for any childlike comfort food she could offer him. She wanted to mind him, to look after him and keep him safe from any more wounds.

'Bitch!' she spat, as she closed the fridge door violently, shoving it with both hands so that the bottles inside rattled and clinked off each other. 'The fucking bitch!'

She wiped her eyes with the backs of her hands, hoping that James wouldn't notice anything amiss in the dim light of the bedroom. Then she made a pot of tea, picked up the tray and made her way calmly back up the stairs.

*

Almost an hour had passed since James had thanked her for the tea. They had sat together, for the most part in companionable silence, watching closely for any changes in Alice's breathing. All of them together like that was strangely comforting, and Beth had a strong sense of family: the three of them, always tightly knit, sometimes close, sometimes unravelling, but family nevertheless. She was torn between urgently wanting to know what had happened, and feeling content to wait until James was ready. Finally, he spoke.

'I'll make up the bed in the spare room in a few minutes. Then I think I'll call it a day.'

Beth nodded.

'Okay. There's plenty of sheets in the hot press – I noticed them yesterday. I hope the bed isn't damp.'

James shrugged.

'It'll be fine. I'll make sure the radiator is on full, tomorrow. And there's a spare electric blanket, somewhere. I gave it to Alice last Christmas, but I know she never used it. Didn't believe in them . . .'

He stopped suddenly, aware that he had just spoken of his mother in the past tense.

'Are you going to be all right?' Beth asked him quietly, ignoring his discomfort.

'Let me get through this, first, and then I'll tell you.'

'What happened tonight?'

James paused, and Beth could see the struggle written all over his face. Quiet, private, intensely loyal – she knew all the warring factions.

'It seems I'm not ambitious enough. I'm a stick-in-the-mud, content to let others walk all over me. I don't earn enough to keep my family, I'm a poor role model for my children. That's what happened tonight.'

Beth stared at him, uncomprehending. Olive's tone, even her voice, was instantly discernible in the words her brother now seemed to be speaking.

'Where has all of this come out of?'

James shifted on his seat, whether from agitation or discomfort, Beth couldn't tell.

'The Head of History is resigning in December and the post is being reorganized, restructured, redefined – whatever the current jargon is. The jockeying for position started way back, sometime in early January, I think, when the rumours started first. I hate all that manoeuvring and I've already been to more receptions than I can stomach. Olive has been pushing me to go for it ever since she heard of the vacancy. The applications are due in a week. Naturally, with all of this . . .' James waved his hand around the room, expressively . . . 'I've had other things on my mind. But even without it . . .' He paused, and Beth could see his face grow stony with anger. She was amazed. This was the second time in a couple of days she had seen her brother this angry; and the second time in forty-five years.

'*I don't want it.*'

He looked directly at Beth.

'I really don't want it. I'm fifty years of age, my house is paid for, my kids are set up. There's more than enough to see Keith and Gemma through university; the twins are like their mother – they make more in a month than I do in a year. And more luck to them. May the New York Stock Exchange be all they ever wish for from life.'

James stopped, his voice bitter. When he continued, he resumed in his old, gentle tone.

'I'm quite happy being a Senior Lecturer. I don't want to put my foot on the pedal. I've been dancing to everyone else's tune for the last thirty years. Now it's time to slow down. I feel like it's my turn. I want to do more research, travel for primary sources, enjoy the fact that my kids are adults. I don't want to have to watch my back at department meetings for the next fifteen years, wondering where the blade is coming from. I don't *want* to have to cover my arse until the day I retire. I want to live a little – nothing too extravagant, just owning the space inside my own head. If that makes me a failure as a husband and a father, then so be it. I'm a failure.'

It was a long speech, for James. Beth could see at once how Olive would have longed for her husband's promotion. Finally, James would have done something significant with his life, something *public* that other people would have to acknowledge. She'd have enthusiastically embraced her new role as the academic wife. She'd give dinner parties for all the right people and set the standard that all others would fail to reach. That, after all, was the whole point of standards. There'd be money and business success on her side, and, at last, prestige and *class* on his. The perfect partnership, worth all those years of waiting.

'That's a very odd definition of failure.'

James looked at her over the tops of his glasses.

'Well, it's the one that's currently on the table in my house and frankly, I've had enough of it for tonight.'

He blew his nose angrily. Beth leaned across the bed towards him. She could see by the set of his shoulders that he didn't want to talk any more.

'Why don't you go on to bed. It's nearly one o'clock. Try and get some sleep.'

He stood up and stretched, wincing as he did so.

'Bloody cramp in my calf.'

He limped his way past her, pausing to rest both hands on her shoulders. He kissed the top of her head, the same way he had comforted her, a hundred lifetimes ago, after a fall from her bike.

'I'm not avoiding the conversation, Sis. Just postponing it until after I've had a sleep. I'm absolutely exhausted.'

She nodded.

'I know. I'm not surprised. I'm only here two nights

and already it feels like at least a year. We'll talk tomorrow.'

He hesitated, his hand on the doorknob.

'I don't know what happened between you and Tony, but if it felt anything like this, I'm sorry I was no use to you.'

Beth smiled up at him.

'It's all a very long time ago – nearly ten years now. I'm over it. But thanks.'

He nodded, pulling nervously at his beard.

'Why don't I ask Keith to sit with Alice tomorrow evening, and let you and me go out for a bite? There's a good Italian just down the road, and Keith can contact us on your mobile if there's any change.'

'I'd like that. But don't forget Dr Crowley's coming tomorrow . . . If that's still okay.'

Somehow, in the midst of her brother's unhappiness, it felt less urgent to Beth that her dying mother be dragged back from the threshold of wherever she was to say goodbye. Look after the living. Alice would have approved of that.

'Yeah, of course it's still okay. All the more reason to go out afterwards, though . . . have a bit of a breather from all . . . this.' He hesitated, looking towards the bed. 'To be honest, she hardly feels like Alice any more. Pottering about the garden or making tea in the kitchen – that's Alice. But this . . . this is . . . something else.'

Beth looked at him, shocked. And then it struck her: how Alice was vividly alive to her, through the letter she had read last night and the others that now lay waiting for her. But James had no such lifeline. The last time he had felt his mother live and breathe was almost a week ago. His process of letting go had begun a long time before hers.

'I know,' she said quietly, looking at Alice's motionless figure. 'But it's all we've got.'

Beth glanced down at the little locker, guilty again at the secret they shared. Surely she should tell him? Surely he deserved to know? Why should the good and faithful son be denied the comfort of his mother's living words, while she, the prodigal daughter, be rewarded for all her past waywardness? She remembered from their youth that James had always been indignant about that particular moral fable, an apparent favourite of the Christian Brother who'd taught him religion. James had been outraged at what he'd seen as the injustice of it all. He'd always said how sorry he felt for the poor fucker who'd stayed at home. How come there was no fatted calf for him?

'I'll see you in the morning, Sis. Call me if you need me.'

'I will. Good night, sleep tight.'

'Don't let the bugs bite.'

They both smiled as he answered her in the tone of their childhood, bringing back a light-filled, summer memory: the silly rhyme, singing out across the landing once they were both in bed. And then he was gone.

Beth didn't move for some time. She kept seeing James's face, grey and vulnerable, and the shake in his hand as he'd held his glasses up to the light. She'd never liked Olive, but there was precious little comfort in that. Maybe they'd patch it up; even the worst of rows seemed to dissolve between couples married as long as they were. That, or people just learned to put their differences away, hiding them from view. They shelved the issues quietly, wrapped in tacit agreement, and continued their pursuit of a quiet life. Then they'd dust them off again and again as the same old conflicts repeated themselves, year in, year out. That had been her pattern, anyway, hers and Tony's, until she'd finally felt: enough. She was glad it had all been a long time ago. It had hurt then, and it hurt again now, seeing her own failures reflected in her brother's sad, wounded face.

She reached for Alice's hand, whispering to her.

'I wish you could hear me, Alice. I really need to talk to you about James. We have to help him.'

There was no answering pressure on her hand, no murmuring. Beth's need to hear and be heard was becoming desperate; she could feel the tears stinging the insides of her eyelids. She delayed reaching into the locker, although the suspense was becoming unbearable. She was terrified that James would come back into the room and catch her reading one of Alice's letters. He would see it as yet another betrayal of his trust. It wasn't fair: surely her mother wouldn't have wanted James's exclusion at a time like this? She, Beth, had promised to do as Alice had asked, but surely her own instinct as a sister, a daughter, a mother, an *adult* must count for something? As she glanced nervously from Alice's face to the locker door, Beth felt a sudden ripple of shock, a sharp twist of revelation, a new and profound understanding: she had never before felt like an adult in her mother's company. Alice and James had always been the grown-ups, the competent, reliable ones: she had been the badly behaved little girl, the troublesome child that everyone else had had to keep under control. The past twenty-four hours now felt like the last stages of an induction into adulthood. Like it or lump it, she was here, close to being an orphan, her brother's life in the sort of chaos she'd thought was reserved only for her own. She felt all the emotion of the previous few hours hardening suddenly into resolve.

Reaching into the locker, she let go of Alice's hand, placing it on the bedspread within easy reach of hers. Her fingers trembled a little as she pulled out her bundle of letters and undid the ribbon. She took out the next envelope. It was heavier than the first one had been, fatter. On a sudden impulse, she tucked the remaining envelope into the waistband of her jeans, shoving the piece of red ribbon into her back pocket.

'I'm sorry, Alice,' she whispered. 'I'm not going against you just for the sake of it. Right now, James needs all the help he can get.'

Then she pulled the drawstrings tight over the remaining bundle of letters, placed the silk bag as close to the edge of the locker shelf as possible, and pushed the door to. She left it unlocked, and left the little key there as a sign for James. He was, she knew, the least curious of men: there was no possibility of his coming upon these letters by chance. She would have to try and create a moment to send him off looking for lip-balm, handcream, a hairbrush – anything to make him stoop and search until he found what was meant for him.

Okay, so it was cheating; but sometimes people needed a push in the right direction. She didn't want Alice to die before James had had the chance to read her last words to him. She knew that that was important, now more than ever.

She sat back finally, relieved. She opened her own envelope carefully, not wanting to disturb the silence that had descended everywhere, once James's door had clicked to. Quickly, she skimmed the neat lines of her mother's handwriting, words and phrases here and there making her heart speed up. Ten pages. Somehow, she knew that this was going to be significant in a way that the first letter hadn't been. She glanced at her watch. Almost two. She pulled the bedside light closer.

FOUR

Abbotsford

'AUNTIE BETH?'

She jumped, startled by the sudden, deep voice. Keith poked his head round the kitchen door.

'Sorry – didn't mean to give you a fright.'

'Keith – come on in! It's good to see you. Sorry we didn't get a chance to talk the other day. How are you?'

Beth stood up to hug her nephew. He towered over her. She was glad to see him, relieved at the interruption. She'd been sitting at the kitchen table, the remains of a late breakfast all around her. The whole house seemed to have acquired a new stillness, the calm after the storm of James's late-night revelations. He had slept little, it seemed, and gone out as soon as Keith arrived. She'd heard his early step on the creaky floorboard just outside her bedroom door, and had woken instantly, holding her breath, expecting the worst. But there was nothing: he hadn't even come in. They'd passed each other briefly on the stairs a couple of hours ago.

'I went out for some fresh air,' he'd said, and handed her Saturday's *Irish Times*. 'Keith is with Alice. I'm going to lie down for an hour.'

The newspaper was now propped up against the

coffee-pot. But Beth couldn't concentrate. Her mind was restless; it kept jumping from James and Olive and their bitterness, to the real tenderness between Arthur Boyd and Alice – a tenderness that had been easy to discern between the careful lines of her mother's hand-writing. Ever since she'd read the letter, she'd been filled with images of Arthur, his dead wife and his almost love affair with her mother. In the early morning, she'd even dreamt about them during the few hours of fitful sleep she'd had after her night by Alice's bedside. Her mother's face had been real, vivid, but Arthur's presence had kept melting into Jack, then into James, finally becoming Tony. Beth had brushed the memory aside. She wasn't yet ready to meet that vision head-on: she needed time to revisit herself and Tony. Even her dream-self had refused to confront him: as soon as he had appeared before her, she had awoken hot and confused. Her eyes still felt tired and sandy, but she was nevertheless fully alert, all of her senses finely tuned, ready for whatever the day was to ask of them. She was beginning to wonder now was there any other way to live: she felt so completely taken over by this new routine. Even trying to do very ordinary things, like stoking the range or glancing at the newspaper head-lines, had been useless: the secrets of Alice's hidden life were much more absorbing.

'My God,' she laughed, looking up into her nephew's face. 'You've grown – again! What are you now, six one, six two?'

He returned her hug.

'Six three, actually,' and he grinned down at her.

'You look great,' she said, stepping back to look at him. 'Fancy a cup of tea?'

'Yeah, and I could eat somethin', too. I'm starvin'.'

Beth smiled back at him as she went over to the sink to fill the kettle.

'Some things never change.'

'Well, it *is* midday – a long time since breakfast.'

'So, how's College treating you these days?'

'All right.' He buttered a slice of cold toast, and folded it over. 'But I'm thinkin' of changin' courses.'

She looked at him in surprise. 'Can you do that, so soon?'

'Yeah. I've applied to transfer, through my tutor. I really don't like what I'm doin'.'

'Economics, isn't it?'

Beth took a large sliced loaf out of the freezer compartment.

He nodded.

'Mum wanted me to do Business Studies, Dad was kinda hopin' I'd do History, I think, so . . .' he shrugged. 'Economics seemed to be a good compromise. But it was a mistake. I hate it.'

Beth put two slices of bread into the toaster.

'So what are you transferring to?'

'To what I wanted to do in the first place – pure English.'

'Do your mum and dad know about this?'

'Yeah. I've discussed it with Dad. He's cool. Haven't told Mum yet, though.'

'Well, good for you. Changing to what you really want, I mean.' Beth moved on, hurriedly. It sounded as though she approved of his lack of discussion with his mother. 'You've always been a reader.'

'Yeah – should've stuck to my guns in the first place. Mum'll come round, I'm sure.'

Beth smiled to herself. She wouldn't feel so sure. She was constantly surprised at how each of the young people she knew took their parents' approval for granted, how they assumed that that was what parents were for. Maybe that was why they stayed at home so much longer these days, hanging around for bed and board well into their twenties. She knew several harassed mothers of her own age, all longing for a bit of peace and quiet after the hard years of child-rearing. Instead, they seemed doomed to step over long legs, endure loud music and satisfy enormous appetites well into their fifties. At Keith's age, she had already fled the nest, couldn't wait to be gone. She'd left in the midst of recriminations, disapproval, even outrage. But parents now, including herself, it seemed, tried to please their children. On balance, she supposed it was a good thing. Remembering James's face last night, she wondered now if all that were about to change for Keith and Gemma.

'How's Gran this morning?'

'There's nothing different, Keith, she's still exactly the same. June comes in to make her comfortable every evening, but there's no response. Your dad and I just sit with her while she sleeps.'

Keith poured himself a glass of milk.

'Do you think she'll ever come round?'

'No, no I don't think so.'

Beth was surprised to hear herself say that. She hadn't known that she felt that, so positively, until now. So where was all her earlier urgency about saying good-bye? She'd been obsessed by it, less than twenty-four hours ago. In some strange way, last night's letter, written months ago, had had all the immediacy of the intimacy that she'd been craving. It had brought Alice so much closer to her, and that, strangely, was making it easier for Beth to let her go.

'Is your dad with her now?'

Keith nodded, his eyes suddenly fixed on the table.

'Here, sit down. Would you like something else with your toast?'

He shook his head, looking away from her.

'I did the garden with her, all during the summer. She was . . . fine. Always full of stories.'

Beth was shocked to see his eyes fill.

'I know.' She rested her hand on his arm, as he shook the tears away. 'Keith – she really looked forward to your visits. She told me so. She really appreciated you helping out – particularly as you'd much better things to do on a Friday night!'

He wiped his eyes with his sleeve.

'She insisted I took money for it – I didn't want to. I feel really bad about that.'

Beth smiled at him.

'It gave her pleasure to give you something. She wasn't paying you, as such – it was just her way of giving you a present. Don't feel bad about it.'

He nodded, recovering himself. He looked embarrassed, ashamed of his tears. Beth poured more coffee for herself, giving him time. Eventually, he was able to look at her again.

'How's Laura?'

'She's fine. I spoke to her last night. Her dad is with her for this week. She's anxious to come over soon, but we'll wait and see what happens.' Beth paused. She didn't want to say 'when Alice dies'.

'Have you had enough?' she asked instead.

'Yeah, thanks. I think I'll go back up and give Dad a break. Can I help you with these?'

He gestured towards the dishes.

Beth shook her head.

'No, go on ahead. I'm going to make more toast and coffee. Send your dad down for some, will you? I don't think he's had any breakfast.'

'Okay. I'll see you later, then. Thanks.'

Beth watched him go. His long body looked suddenly childlike, vulnerable. So wrapped up in her own grief until last night, when James had shocked her out of it, she hadn't realized the endless ripples caused by Alice's final illness. James and Olive, herself, Keith, Gemma, Laura – their lives at least temporarily thrown up in the air, nobody knowing how all the pieces would settle when they eventually fell. Maybe her only child *should* be here, to share this with her cousins. On the other hand, Alice could continue in this stasis for a long time yet. Tony was probably right to keep Laura in her own routine. But still. Beth didn't know what to do, didn't know what the right thing was any more – she'd think about it later, after Dr Crowley's visit. At least it was one decision which could be postponed.

And she had never known time to pass so slowly. It was only Saturday – she'd arrived a mere thirty-six hours ago, and already it seemed like for ever. Trying to measure what was happening in terms of hours or minutes was meaningless; she no longer felt like the same woman who had almost killed herself by behaving stupidly in a hire car on an otherwise normal October evening.

She looked up as James came into the kitchen. He shook his head at her.

'Nothing. Not even a movement. I'm glad Ellen Crowley is coming tonight, I think Alice's breathing is becoming wheezy.'

Beth felt suddenly frightened.

'Pneumonia?'

He shrugged.

'I've no idea, but I think there's something going on.'

She tried to absorb the impact of his words. What had she expected? *Where there's life, there's hope*, her mother's voice said to the inside of her head. The voice was so clear, so direct that Beth was startled. She wondered for a mad moment whether James had heard it.

He was pouring coffee, oblivious. He was still withdrawn, silent. They were obviously not going to return to their conversation of the previous night. His face looked less ashen, but his eyes were still dull, tired behind his glasses.

'Should we book a table for tonight, seeing as it's Saturday?'

He nodded.

'I'll do that in a minute.'

He answered her curtly. Beth let the silence sit for a moment. Then she spoke quietly.

'I'm going to call Laura, and then I'm going to have a bath. The coffee's made, and there's more bread in the toaster.'

'Thanks. Take your time. Keith will stay as long as we need him.'

Beth stood up and pulled the belt of her dressing gown tighter. She felt suddenly tongue-tied in her brother's presence.

'Give Laura my love, won't you?' he said.

He barely glanced in Beth's direction. His evasiveness saddened her. She guessed that he was regretting his confidences of the night before.

'I'll do that.'

As she went to leave the kitchen, he picked up the newspaper, and became immediately absorbed. Beth hesitated briefly, feeling there was something more that needed to be said, something other than her awkward offerings of toast and coffee. She felt guilty, leaving him there on his own like that. But he had shut down: Beth knew all the signs. James had always demanded respect for his silences. He would come back to himself again soon; he always did. And she would just have to wait. Besides, last night's letter was pulling at her insistently, needing to be read again, demanding her full attention. Beth felt that her life had come full circle: Alice's words were now tugging at the skirts of her memory, goading and prodding until they got a response, the same way she remembered pestering her mother as a small child. As she climbed the stairs to her old room, she decided that she needed to find the time soon to rummage through the boxes of old photographs that her mother had mentioned. It was time to put at least some of the pieces of the jigsaw into their proper place.

She took Alice's second letter from under her pillow, folding it carefully into the pocket of her dressing gown. On her way to the bathroom, she stepped into her mother's room for a moment.

'All right, Keith?'

He nodded.

'Yeah. See you later.'

And he returned to his book.

She locked the bathroom door, and turned both taps on full, pouring bath salts into the old-fashioned tub, its enamel stained by a swathe of bright green under the cold tap, painted there, patiently, by years and years of leaky washers. As she waited for the bath to fill, she took out Alice's letter and read it through again in the undisturbed safety of the locked bathroom, one of her old childhood refuges.

Sinking into the warm, scented water, she became aware once more of the aches and pains she hadn't noticed since her arrival on Thursday night. Across her shoulder blades still hurt, and she winced as she lay back, resting her body against the grainy, sloping surface behind her. She touched the right-hand side of her jaw, gently. It still hurt. She closed her eyes. None of that mattered. All that mattered now was what her mother had written to her. She'd been deeply disturbed by Alice's direct request that she try again with Tony. It had shocked her, engulfed her in a flood of conflicting emotions, disturbed even her dreams. On waking, she had felt again the huge surge of ambivalence that she had thought long resolved. And now, it seemed that James and Olive's marriage was beyond repair, too. Everything seemed to be conspiring against her, prodding her to confront the decision which had come so easily, so naturally to her almost a decade ago. She and Alice had never spoken of her separation before, apart from Beth's announcement of it, some six months after the fact, when she and Laura had paid their usual visit home at Christmas.

She had arrived in full emotional battledress, alert, angry and on the offensive. Her communications with Alice had been abrupt, presenting her new situation as a *fait accompli*, and inviting no discussion. Even before she saw her, Beth had read her mother's mind, had sensed her unbending disapproval, or had felt she had. She wondered now, in the light of her new knowledge, what Alice had really thought. She'd probably never know, never understand the complexity of her mother's real feelings, and that saddened her. Anyway, it was all much too late for reconciliation: both her own and Tony's lives had moved on. She suspected that he had someone else, although he never said, and she was quite okay as she was. But her mother's words, and James's predicament, had stirred up all the old feelings again.

Sadness, regret for what she and Tony might have become, and the ever-present sense of failure.

She'd never learned to get on with Alice; she'd made a mess of things with Tony, and she'd been far too terrified to try again, in any serious way, with anyone else. Laura was her last hope for anything approaching a proper relationship. Mixed up with all these emotions was the growing ache of tenderness she now felt towards the young Alice as she imagined her sending her hopeful lover away. She had a moment of intense, searing loneliness as she realized the full impact of that decision on the rest of her mother's life. She had never imagined that Alice could have loved any other man after Jack died: had never even *thought* about it. Children everywhere, she supposed, thought of their parents as just that – parents; that is, if they thought about them at all. All through Beth's adolescence, Alice had been the mother who fought her, who tried to change her, who reminded her of everything that had been done for her. Beth used to rage silently against the whole notion of her mother's life being given up on her behalf. *I didn't ask to be born.* She had hated it whenever her mother reminded her of how fortunate she was. And now she was saddened by the enormity of the one, probably unnecessary, sacrifice which her mother had made and never mentioned – until now. Beth wondered how different all their lives might have been if Alice had married Arthur. She couldn't help being haunted by the phrase: *Don't give yourself something to regret when you're eighty.*

Last night, she had been startled to realize the similarities between her and Alice's lives. She, who had fought for so long to maintain and exaggerate their differences, had been forced to acknowledge the extent of their common ground. They had both been the same age giving birth to their daughters, and five years later, each of them had been on her own. Another ten years on and she, like Alice, was struggling along as a single parent. Her struggles were very different from her mother's, of course: her solitude was the result of choice, not of the blind, destructive hand of chance. Tony was a good father, a loving one, but it wasn't quite the same thing as *family*, as all of them living within the same four walls. Beth's recollection of her own father was clear, etched brightly against the dark background of his early death. Idly, she wondered what he had been like as a husband. She and James had simply accepted his absence, or so it seemed to her now – but then, they had had each other. Laura probably had the worst of both worlds: no constant fatherly presence, and no brother or sister to share that loss. For the first time in several years, Beth felt an overwhelming sorrow that she had driven Tony away. There was suddenly too much to feel guilty about, too much to make her sad. She had had no Arthur to offer her a second chance. Would she have taken it, anyway, even if she had?

She closed her eyes and allowed her mind to drift. She tried to let go of the sudden, powerful sense of mourning which had her in its grip. Instead, she wanted to concentrate on the comfort offered by warm water and silence. It was good to feel suspended like this, cherished by her surroundings, safe from the eyes of others. It was good to feel freed, just for a little while, from her own debt of vigilance. She wanted whatever was pulling at her memory to float to the surface. Almost immediately, she saw Granny Mac, standing at the door of *Abbotsford*, waving to the three of them as they approached her down the long gravel driveway. Even at that distance, Beth's young self could tell that she was smiling. It was early May, bright and clear, as all her memories were of being – what, eleven, twelve? – when bright blue skies seemed to last all summer long. The two red setters, Amber and Prince, came charging down towards the gates, Prince bounding along in his ridiculous sideways fashion, the way he always did when excited. The dogs' coats were gleaming, burnished in the sunshine. She was wearing her Confirmation clothes: patent-leather T-bar sandals, home-made blue coat, grey pleated dress and a pillbox hat. She'd slept all the previous night with rags in her hair, and now her head felt heavy with sausage-shaped ringlets, some held hotly, cruelly in place with hair-clips. She hated her hair: it was that insistent shade of red that went with pale skin and flat, dark freckles. She wanted to brush out all the stupid curls, and fling her sweaty hat high up into the clouds of circling, raucous rooks. Instead, she had to look downwards: she was terrified of scuffing the shiny surface of her new shoes on the unruly gravel.

Beth shifted her position in the bath, easing out her shoulder blades. She smiled to herself, eyes still closed.

'Jesus, Mother,' she said aloud, 'how did you ever let me out looking like that?'

She remembered walking carefully, wanting to pet the dogs, to throw the ball for them as she always did, and hug them as they returned to her, grinning their insane doggy smiles. She wanted to bury her face in the long warmth of their gleaming coats, but on that day, she'd been too terrified to move. She knew, that with the smallest sign of encouragement, they would jump up on her, snagging their long claws in the worsted wool coat her mother had spent many tense hours making, hunched over the Singer, her mouth even fuller of pins than usual. Beth could still feel the prickly sensation of the wool collar on her hot neck, as they all finally came to the end of the long, sweaty walk from the bus stop.

'Hello there!' called Granny Mac. 'Elizabeth, you look wonderful! James, you've grown at least another inch!'

Kisses all round as they reached the front door. By this time, Granny Mac had a firm hold of Prince's collar. Amber, as usual, was meekly back by her mistress's side, her long pink tongue dripping.

'Hello, love,' this to Alice, and a strong, one-armed hug. Beth could still see Granny Mac's sharp, inquisitive glances, rapid reconaissances from face to face, her eyes well versed in the tactics of family warfare. Then, 'Hello, James, Elizabeth,' a quick peck on each grandchild's cheek, and they were inside. Immediately, both dogs were banished to the back yard.

'Now, let me have a proper look at you!'

Granny Mac washed her hands quickly at the sink, and dried them on the blue towel hanging on a rail inside the back door. There was a faint doggy smell in the cramped scullery, but Granny Mac was, as ever, all brisk country elegance. She wore her good pearls, the ones she always said would be Beth's one day, and a mauve twinset of some light, deliciously fluffy wool. Her dark tweed skirt was sensible – but that would be changed for a nicer one if they went down to the village later for tea. Her green wellies stood just inside the back door, and she wore her favourite, gleaming lace-up shoes. She hugged Beth first, then held her away from her, at arm's length, admiring her hot and red-faced granddaughter. Beth remembered how cool the skin of her face and hands had felt, balm to an over-dressed, over-heated eleven-year-old on the day of her Confirmation. Granny Mac's dark eyes had danced with mischief.

'James, I'm sure you want no part of this fashion parade. Take the key to your grandad's study – it's on the shelf there. We'll be in the garden if you want to join us for ice cream. Otherwise, we'll give you a shout at tea-time.'

His eyes had lit up. It was a privilege to be allowed to choose from his grandad's bookcase, and bury himself in the over-sized green armchair, locked away from all distractions, surrounded by the old smells of pipe-smoke and soft leather. Now that he was sixteen years of age, it was a privilege granted to him more and more often.

'Thanks, Gran.'

He had taken the key and fled. The older woman then turned her attention back to Beth again.

'Don't you look grown up! Take off your coat, now, and show me this dress I've heard so much about!'

Beth unbuttoned the solid blue coat. The relief had been enormous. Granny Mac had taken it from her at once.

'I'll hang it under the stairs for you until you go home. It's got very warm all of a sudden.'

She smoothed the fabric as she folded the coat over her arm.

'Lovely material, Alice, you made a great job of it.'

Beth remembered glancing nervously at her mother. This coat had been a massive undertaking, and she wasn't even sure if it was proper to take it off. But Alice had smiled at her, a rare, warm smile that seemed to take in all three of them, standing in the damp, slightly chilly scullery of her old home. With a little shock of recognition, Beth realized that she had known, even as a child, that her mother had been really happy that day.

Granny Mac had returned from the cloakroom and bent down to test the quality of the fabric in Beth's grey pleats. She measured its fineness between thumb and forefinger, rubbing the soft material gently.

'Give us a twirl, there's a girl.'

Beth had obliged, feeling the slightly tickly material breeze out from her legs and settle back again to just below her knees.

'Perfect – it really suits you. That little touch of red braid at the cuffs and the waist cheers up the grey no end. Turn around again.'

Beth did as she was told.

'I think it's the best you've ever done, Alice. Elizabeth, you must be very proud of your mother.'

Beth remembered catching her mother's delighted smile and she'd been slightly puzzled by it. Why should she care what Granny Mac thought? Her mother was a *grown-up*. She was allowed to do as she liked, to make whatever she wanted. She didn't need anyone telling her she had done well.

Whether it was the relief of being rid of the coat, or the welcome thought of ice cream and lemonade in the shade of the garden, or perhaps simply Granny Mac's infectious generosity, Beth could still recall being filled with gratitude, a warm, real feeling of love and appreciation towards her mother.

'I am,' she'd said, feeling suddenly shy, feeling the usual blush creep up her cheeks.

There had been a tinge of sadness to her pride too, she remembered now, a child's pity for her mother and the suddenly realized harshness of her life. She had felt sorry that day for the prematurely grey head always bent over the sewing-machine, the rapid, high-pitched taka-taka-taka audible well into the night.

'Now.'

Granny Mac had paused for a moment, her expression that of someone musing over a complicated equation. She had had a habit of doing that; it never failed to get everyone's full attention.

'If we're going to go out into the garden, I'll have to let Prince and Amber loose, otherwise they'll drive us mad with their barking.'

She looked over at Alice, her sharp, pointy face full of concern.

'I don't want Elizabeth's outfit to come to any harm. Don't you think she should change out of it for a while?'

Alice had already started to fill the kettle. She turned to her mother, her face back to its permanent worried look. Beth remembered wishing she would smile again, remembered praying silently that she would say yes.

'Sure – but I didn't bring anything else with me.'

'You just leave that to us. Elizabeth, come with me.'

Alice had nodded over at her daughter, smiling.

'Go on; off you go with Granny.'

Beth had followed her grandmother up the wide, gentle staircase, her feet now beginning to hurt in her new shoes. She felt a small flutter of excitement at the ghost of conspiracy which Granny Mac had conjured up between the two of them – she knew that she was up to something. They went into her bedroom, a large, airy room at the front of the house, and Beth had held her breath as her grandmother pulled open the heavy doors of her old wardrobe. As a child, she had always liked the feel of the cool cut-glass handles that adorned the dark mahogany doors.

'Try this for size.'

Smiling broadly, Granny Mac handed her a cotton dress of a deep, rich green, with tiny sprigs of vivid yellow flowers crowding its smooth background. Beth had recognized its shape instantly.

'Oh!' she gasped. 'It's a *tent*-dress!'

Quickly, she slipped out of her grey wool and pulled the cool cotton over her head. It slid gratefully over the satiny surface of her new slip. She felt transformed. A little uncertainly, she looked at her grandmother.

'Is this really for me?'

Granny Mac stooped and hugged her.

'Just for you,' she whispered. 'I made it last week when your cousin Clare told me they were all the rage. This shade is just beautiful with your hair. I thought you'd like it for the summer.'

Beth hugged her back.

'I love it! Thanks, Granny Mac. Can I wear it now – are you sure?'

'Yes, you can. I'd hate you to get your new clothes dirty.'

She had stroked Beth's hair, and seemed about to say something. Instead, she kissed her granddaughter on the forehead rather briskly and straightened up. She became suddenly busy, her back turned. She began fussing over the Confirmation dress, hanging it up on a special padded hanger, smoothing the pleats of the skirt into place.

'Now, off you go downstairs. I'll be with you in a minute.'

Beth ran all the way back down to the hallway, full of excitement. Just before she opened the scullery door, she stopped for a moment, running her hands over the yards and yards of light cotton. Some instinct had quieted her happiness and stopped her from bursting into the room to show off her new dress. Instead, she entered the scullery silently. Her mother's back was to the door. She was standing at the window, unmoving, and she seemed to be looking out into the orchard, at something invisible among the neat rows of apple and pear trees, heavy with blossoms.

'Mam?' she said, suddenly scared. Her mother had never been one to stand still.

But as she turned around, Alice's face had lit up with pleasure.

'Oh, Elizabeth! What a lovely dress! You look much cooler!'

It had seemed the natural thing to do, and Beth remembered moving towards her mother without even thinking about it. She had wound both arms around her neck and, surprised by sudden, guilty tears, had said:

'But I love my Confirmation dress, too.'

She wondered now if that had been the last spontaneous hug on her part for several years. She had been just on the threshold of adolescence then, just before all the shit between them really began in earnest.

Her mother had hugged her back, and laughed.

'I know you do, you silly goose! You can change back into it again before we go home. That's much more sensible for the garden.'

'Now, then.'

They both turned around.

Granny Mac was already sweeping through the scullery into the big old kitchen which she used very little, even in those days. That the house was now much too big for an old lady on her own was a familiar topic of conversation whenever they came to visit.

'Come on, let's go and sit outside.'

She began opening presses, pulling out bowls, spoons, glasses.

'We'll bring out lemonade and ice cream, and I'll make some tea for us, Alice – that all right with you?'

Of course, Beth remembered that she hadn't actually *sat* in the garden, not for a minute, unless you count the time it takes to shovel down two bowls of ice cream and three glasses of cream soda. James had mysteriously reappeared at the same time as the ice cream emerged from Granny Mac's proud new fridge, and if Beth's memory served her right, he'd stayed with her for most of the afternoon, playing with the dogs. The sticks and balls they threw were retrieved tirelessly, the two dogs panting and barking, competing with each other madly. Eventually, Granny Mac had sent both her grand-children off to fill the dogs' bowls with water from the huge, green pump that dominated the back yard.

'You do it, Sis. I'm going back to Grandad's study.'

Before she could protest, James had disappeared through the back door and she was left standing on her own in the cool, mossy shadows. Right in front of her, carpeted here and there by dank green growth, was the trough her grandad used to fill with water to clean the potatoes. Bucket after bucketful, clay-lumped and earth-smelling, just dug from the field beyond the orchard, he would pour them into the clear water, watching as they splashed and tumbled to the bottom. Beth used to look on in fascination as the water became immediately cloudy, grainy with dirt, as Grandad scrubbed the watery mound of potatoes with a large, stiffly bristled yard-brush. No other potatoes since had ever tasted as good, she thought now. Small as marbles, big as sods of turf – she could see them still, and the way Grandad had scrubbed vigorously until their skins were a delicate fawn colour, peeling back sometimes to show the bone-whiteness underneath. The young Beth had known by its greeny, mossy interior that no one had filled the trough with water in a long time. She shivered; she missed Grandad and it was suddenly cold where she stood. Granny Mac said that the sun never got to that bit of the garden. That's why she had planted ivy and hosta and grasses everywhere, great big urns filled with them. Even the dogs knew not to go near them. Beth had filled the two cracked bowls with water from the giant pump, and then she'd followed James into the house, pulling the back door quickly closed behind her, hoping Prince and Amber wouldn't start barking. She was curious as to the attractions of her grandad's study. James spent hours in there, whenever they came to visit. While she had never really minded before, she'd felt a little excluded that day. After all, Confirmation day was supposed to be something special.

She'd stretched out her hand to the wooden door handle, a solid carved piece, comfortable inside your fingers; its swirly design always reminded her of a bowl of freshly poured custard. She was just about to turn it when she heard a loud, rasping laugh from outside. She stopped for a moment, puzzled, and listened.

Beth reflected now that she seemed to have acquired a lifetime habit of opening doors at inopportune moments. She topped up the bath-water, goose-pimples beginning to rise on her arms; the skin on her fingers was beginning to wrinkle. She'd have to get out soon.

Her mother's laugh had been such an unaccustomed sound that she had felt doubly curious. What could she be laughing at? Granny Mac seemed to be silent. She made her way cautiously towards the front of the house, ducking into the large, high-ceilinged front room which had been used as a dining room when Grandad was alive. But shortly after his death, it was used only to store boxes and old furniture that Granny Mac no longer had any need for. Her heart thumping, she moved silently to the big sash window, standing just behind the faded red velvet curtain. She could see that its furry surface had acted as a trap for a thin coating of whitish dust. Granny Mac's passion for airing the house meant that the window was raised just enough from the sill to make audible the conversation of the two women sitting together in the front garden.

'There, now, dry your eyes,' Granny Mac was saying, handing her daughter one of the big men's handkerchiefs she always carried up her sleeve. Beth could still feel how the shock had rooted her to the floor, paralysed her, made her incapable of thought.

Her mother? Crying?

When she spoke, her tone was unmistakable. It had that strangled, sobbing, hurting sound that everyone shared when they cried really hard.

'I'm sorry, Mam. It's just that on days like this I still really miss him. It's so difficult doing it all on your own, you know? And James is sixteen – he really needs a father.'

Then she had cried again, not so much this time, and blew her nose.

'And I still feel so guilty when I get furious at him for leaving us without a penny.'

'I know, love. The last six years have been tough. And I wish I could have helped you more. But since your dad died, this place has been riddled with debt.'

'That's not what I meant, Mam – you've always done all you could, and so did Dad, when he was alive. I'm grateful, really I am. No, I'd have been fine if Jack had just been more careful, if he'd looked after us properly . . .'

'There's no point in going down that road again, Alice.'

Granny Mac's voice had been a little sharp. After a moment, she'd continued in a softer tone.

'He was a lovely man, was Jack, but useless at managing money. And he was a sure bet for every hard-luck story there ever was. There's no point now in crying over spilt milk.'

There was a long quietness.

'I know. I just sometimes get tired of working so hard.'

The two women had fallen silent, then, both gazing away in front of them, eyes roving over the lush Meath countryside. Beth had known that now was the time to go, to sneak back through the hallway past the study, through the kitchen, out the scullery door. The dogs would be waiting for her. They'd be bound to start barking any second now; they hated being cooped up.

Beth pulled herself, with difficulty, back to the

present. The bathroom was filled with steam, her head full of ghosts. Poor Alice. Everything had started to break up, soon after that. Her Confirmation day was the last day she could recall when the old order had still remained, when everything to do with her grandmother, on the surface at least, had been solid and unchanged. The reality, of course, must have been very different. Beth knew, from somewhere, someone, that Granny Mac had been cheated and lied to by various farm managers ever since her husband's death. *Abbotsford* – the house and the lands had to have been on the point of collapse for some time. It seemed that very shortly after that day in May, Granny Mac had sold up everything, finally admitting defeat, and gone to live with her sister Sally in Wicklow. There had been precious little left: Beth could still remember Alice's bitterness that her mother had received virtually nothing for the lovely old farmhouse. She'd been tight-lipped and angry at the relentless loop of history that seemed to repeat itself from generation to generation, reaching from the past into the future and back again.

Beth dried herself vigorously and remembered the oil lamps, the Singer sewing-machine and the big kitchen table that had come to their house after the auction. She felt suddenly glad that, financially at least, she had been luckier than either her mother or her grandmother.

'Beth?'

There was a soft tapping at the bathroom door.

'Yes?'

'I think you'd better come quickly.'

James's voice was muffled, but the panic was unmistakable. Jesus, was this it? Beth threw on her dressing gown, dragging her wet hair back from her forehead. She felt everything around her speed up again; her chest was tight, her mind racing. Should they call an ambulance? Did undertakers work on a Saturday? Dear God, would Alice already be gone?

She wrenched open the bathroom door and ran straight to her mother's bedside. James was standing in his usual place, his expression lost, haunted. He didn't seem to know what to do with his hands. Keith's face was a blank sheet, white and stretched.

Alice's mouth was open wide; each breath taken was hoarse and gravelly.

Beth looked down at her, surprised at her own sudden calm. She could see nothing different. She checked her mother's colour and the rise and fall of her chest. She didn't seem to be having any difficulty breathing. Then, suddenly, it struck her. She started to laugh. She couldn't help it. James and Keith stared at her: two sets of eyes, of an almost uniform, piercing blue. Are you mad? their gaze asked her.

'I'm sorry!' she gasped. 'It's just that she's – she's snoring!'

Keith began to grin, his features relaxing back into familiarity again. James looked at her.

'Are you sure?'

She nodded, biting her lip to keep from exploding. The last minute's laughter right now felt suspiciously like hysteria. Suddenly, Alice's head turned slightly to one side. Her eyes flickered open, and abruptly, the harsh breathing was stilled. She murmured something, and again closed her eyes. It seemed as though the room held its breath. Beth reached down for her mother's wrist and felt for a pulse. There it was, faint but steady. Keith snorted once; he was grinning hugely.

'I'm sorry,' he said. 'It's like being at Mass and knowing you can't laugh.'

James sat down abruptly. He looked suddenly several sizes smaller.

'Jesus Christ, that scared the living daylights out of me.'

He took his mother's other hand in his.

'Maybe we should stay in tonight – just in case.'

Beth saw the helpless way he looked at her, saw that, for now, it was pointless to argue with him. She didn't even know whether she wanted to argue. This uncertainty was driving both of them to the point where the thin thread of connection between them and ordinary life was stretched almost beyond breaking point. Living inside this death was now their only existence. If there were any way of knowing how long Alice's half-life would go on for – a day, a week, a month – they could manage. They would learn to cope. It was this constant see-saw between hope and hope against hope that set everything around them on edge. There were apparently two roles to be played out in this drama – the part of the strong and the part of the vulnerable one. She and James seemed to keep on exchanging roles, so that she never knew when it was her turn to be the rock.

She smiled at him.

'Let's talk to Dr Crowley this evening, and decide then.'

He nodded.

'Okay.'

'I'm going inside to clean the bath, all right?'

He looked at her stupidly.

'Keith, will you stay with your dad until I get dressed? I won't be long.'

'Sure.'

She left both of them, sitting side by side. She locked herself into the bathroom again, and sat down on the floor, her knees no longer able to hold her up. She dabbed at the back of her neck with a towel, trying to catch the drips from her hair. Suddenly she wanted to weep. The hysterical bubble at the base of her throat had deflated now, and she felt flat, useless. After a few minutes, while she waited for the beating of her heart to subside, she pulled herself up into a kneeling position and began to scrub the bath with a violence that left her sweaty and breathless. God, she needed to do something *normal*, something that felt real. She needed to think about everyday things, even the things that usually bored her senseless. She would go shopping; there was bread and milk to be bought, at the very least. Surely Alice's sheets should be changed again – she must ask June tonight. And she needed a walk; even dank October air would be welcome. Besides, there was nothing to make for dinner . . . She laid her forehead on the side of the bath and let the tears rise and heave from nowhere, filling her eyes and her throat and her ears with the same harsh choking sobs she had heard through the window in County Meath, all those years ago.

*

'Dr Crowley. Come in, please.'

Beth took the vast umbrella that Ellen Crowley was struggling to keep above her head in the gale which had kept everyone housebound since early afternoon. The noise of the wind howling down the old chimneys and setting off house alarms nearby had had Beth's teeth on edge all evening. She'd called the Garda Station three times already, to complain. Bloody neighbours were probably away in the Canaries or somewhere, sunning themselves, while she . . . Beth stopped herself. She knew she was being unreasonable; she just needed someone to be angry at.

Ellen Crowley grinned at her.

'Hello, Beth. Welcome home. Let's dispense with the formalities, shall we?'

She handed Beth her coat and scarf, and peeled her leather gloves off carefully, finger by finger. Beth returned her smile.

'I was so used to calling your father "Dr Crowley" that I've just transferred the name to you.' Beth busied herself, hanging up the coat, placing the dripping umbrella in the stand. 'How are you?'

'Fine, thanks, and you? How are you holding up?'

Beth shrugged. 'You'd need to ask me that on an hourly basis – I hardly know, myself. I'm glad to see you, though. Thanks for coming.'

'No problem. How is Alice today?'

Beth gestured in the direction of the kitchen.

'No change, as far as we can see. Come on inside. James is here. We'd like to talk to you together; there are lots of things I need to ask you, and I know James has some questions, too. Keith will stay with Alice until you're ready to see her.'

Beth opened the door into the kitchen, and James stood up at once. He shook hands warmly.

'Ellen. Good to see you. Would you like a cup of tea?'

'That would be lovely; thanks.'

Now that she was here, Beth felt suddenly at a loss. The issue of sedation no longer seemed important. All that mattered to her now was Alice's comfort. She knew that Ellen couldn't give her the answer she was looking for, the reassurance of known boundaries for herself and James. But she wanted to ask the question anyway: how long?

'Has the nurse been to your mother yet today?'

Beth was relieved. A perfect opening. She looked over at James, who was refilling his cup, his eyes down, concentrating on what he was doing.

'No, not yet. June usually comes about half nine or ten. She's been great, and she's given James as much information as she can, but . . .'

James placed his spoon carefully in the saucer. The little ping of metal against china sounded to Beth like a punctuation mark, and a disapproving one at that. What was wrong with him? Did he suddenly not want to talk about this, or was he still hoping for some sort of miracle cure? Not for the first time since she'd come home, Beth felt angry at him. She was finally growing resentful of his air of superiority, of propriety, almost, where Alice was concerned. He had agreed to this meeting, and now he was distancing himself from any of the hard questions that she felt the need to ask. She suddenly hated him for his air of detachment from her, at a time like this. She turned away from him.

'I know that my mother has suffered a massive stroke, and I think I understand all the implications of that. But – I also think she's still *present* in herself. She spoke to me on Thursday night, the night I arrived, and she seemed quite lucid. She pressed my hand, and was definitely trying to tell me something. And today, she opened her eyes again, very briefly. I – we need to know what's going on.'

Ellen sipped at her tea, and looked at Beth with interest. Her eyes were bright, intelligent. Beth was reassured by her obvious alertness. Her mother was in good hands.

'How lucid was she? Did she make sense?'

Beth began to feel uncomfortable. Her secret was now such a guilty one: talk about a skeleton in the cupboard. How was she going to get through this without lying, without deliberately keeping James in the dark about their mother's letters? She tried to be careful.

'Well, that's just the thing. Her eyes were lucid, if you know what I mean – she definitely knew it was me. I could see that she recognized me. But before she could finish whatever it was she wanted to say, she drifted off again. I've no idea if she wanted something, or if there was something pressing on her mind, or what.'

Ellen nodded.

'Let me explain to you exactly what has happened to your mother. Then I'll be as clear and precise as I can about how she is right now. After that, we can discuss the future, what's likely to happen over the next little while.'

Beth nodded, startled at the effect of the doctor's 'little while'. Was it not going to go on for ever, then?

James intervened quietly.

'We asked you to meet us today, Ellen, because we both want to do what's best for Alice.' He paused. 'And because we think it's important for all of us to be able to say our goodbyes. I know my mother would want that. We thought that perhaps, if her sedation was reduced a little, we might be able to speak to her again. But neither of us wants her to suffer.'

Beth felt her eyes sting, and she was glad she didn't have to answer James. All her anger deflated as suddenly as a child's balloon and she looked over at him gratefully.

'Right. I understand. This is the picture.'

Ellen Crowley's voice became softer, and she paused frequently, looking from Beth to James for confirmation that they had both understood her.

'Alice had suffered a series of small strokes before she went to the hospital in July. That process is known as multi-infarct dementia, and it's characterized by sudden bouts of confusion, or dizziness. The memory becomes less trustworthy, and physically the patient begins to slow down, to become more hesitant, feeling weak and tired much more easily than before. In the past three months, your mother has had some episodes of confusion, some little difficulties with language and short-term memory. However, she's a fighter, and she held on to everything that was important to her, right up until last week. With some patients, the symptoms can go on for years, but most commonly, a major stroke or some other illness intervenes, as it did in Alice's case. Her stroke occurred in the left side of her brain – that's why the opposite side of her face, the right side, is affected. It's called aphasia, which means the loss of the power of expression, although comprehension tends to remain reasonably intact.'

Ellen stopped for a moment. Beth thought she was weighing her words very carefully.

'Alice's most recent stroke was a very serious one, and it resulted in coma. I don't need to go into detail about all the possible complications here: in her case, the cause of death will most likely be pneumonia. Coma is the perfect ally for the microbes that cause pneumonia: Alice has no resistance, she doesn't even have the reflex to cough. Eventually, the oxygen levels drop below the critical point, and the heart will stop. That's why we're keeping her sedated. She can't recover, her breathing will become laboured and we want to make sure she dies in her sleep.'

Beth looked directly at her. She had heard these words before, during James's first telephone call, but her body had responded to them then with a numbness, a sense of unreality, and the feeling that this was all happening to someone else. She now felt their impact fully, almost as an electrical shock. She placed her elbows carefully on the table in front of her, making herself feel more grounded. Almost at once, she began to feel calmer. She could cope with this. No matter how awful it was to think about, it would all be over soon, and she would see it through. She had a real sense of being filled by her own strength, at last.

'The only reason they let her home,' continued Ellen, 'is because she had always insisted to me, in the strongest possible terms, that she didn't want to die in hospital. I told her that I'd do my best to make sure she didn't. However,' and here she looked from Beth to James, 'I also promised her I'd make sure she suffered as little as possible.'

'Then it would be cruel to deprive her of sedation. There's no question of it.'

Beth spoke quietly; a certainty, finally. One less option, one less possibility to be considered. She felt immediately guilty. Everything kept shifting: this awfulness was now easier for her than it was for James. She had her mother's words, her mother's voice, waiting for her. He had nothing to help him, nothing that he knew of. God, she hoped he'd hurry up and find his letters soon. She had always found obedience difficult, but she was determined to keep her silent promise to Alice for as long as she could.

'If it was my mother, I wouldn't want it. But that doesn't mean that Alice won't come to again, on her own. She was physically very strong before all this, and she has a will of iron. My guess is she still retains some level of comprehension. Stay close to her; you may well get to say your goodbyes.'

Beth nodded.

'Thank you, Ellen. I understand better now.'

She couldn't stop her eyes from filling.

Ellen's voice was still gentle, but its note of almost professional compassion had faded, and her warmth was genuine, personal.

'Please call on me, whenever you want. I'll always have the time to talk to you.'

She stood, and placed her hand on Beth's arm.

'It will mean a great deal to your mother to know that you're both here, even if she can't tell you herself.'

Beth nodded.

'Thanks. Do you have any idea, any idea at all, how long . . .'

Ellen looked at both of them carefully.

'When I was here on Thursday morning, there were some definite signs of a chest infection. I'll examine her again now, and we should get a more complete picture. Either way, we're talking days, certainly not weeks.'

Beth felt a stab of relief. It *was* all nearly over, then.

'Would you like to come with me while I examine her?'

Beth shook her head. Right now, she wanted to keep the old, energetic Alice alive for a little longer in her mind's eye. She didn't want to see the skeletal frame that she knew must now exist under the comfortable burden of blankets and bed-jackets.

'I think I'll just stay here.'

Ellen turned to James.

'Perhaps you could come with me, James? I may need some help.'

'Of course.'

They both left the kitchen quietly, and Beth heard the doctor's words, over and over again. Now it felt as though they were testing her, measuring her strength, seeing how much she could take. She waited, almost breathlessly, for collapse, for tears, for the old familiar sensation of wanting to run away. But it didn't come. Instead, she felt a gathering stillness inside her, a sureness that this was right, this was where she should be, this was what she should be doing. The words might not be new: what was new was this almost tangible sense of peace. She no longer wanted to escape, to flee mindlessly from something that made her unhappy. And it was as though a reward waited for her upstairs, the third, unopened letter, waiting to speak to her. She would read it tonight, now that she knew how swiftly they were running out of time.

Beth rested her forehead on her folded arms. She didn't move until James came back into the kitchen.

'You okay?'

She nodded, smiling at him. He seemed to have returned to his old self; his aloofness had vanished and his eyes met hers without difficulty.

'Yeah, fine. Is Ellen gone?'

'Just now. She said to say goodbye; she didn't want to disturb you. She'll drop in again after her rounds on Monday. There's been no real change since Thursday.'

Beth nodded. A reprieve, perhaps.

'Are *you* okay?' she asked him.

'As well as can be expected,' and he grinned his old grin at her. He started ticking off a list on his fingers, one by one. 'My mother's dying, my wife's just fucked me out, I've no chance of promotion and I've a pile of bills waiting to be paid. Why wouldn't I be okay?'

'Well, that's just fine, then. God's in his Heaven and all's right with the world.'

They both laughed.

'Come on, you. I could eat a lorry-load of pasta.'

Beth looked at him in surprise.

'Are we still going out?'

'Yeah, why not? Whatever's going to happen isn't likely to happen tonight. Anyway, I think we've both got cabin fever.'

Beth was relieved, almost joyful.

'Great – I could really murder a bottle of wine. I'll just go and get my mobile, in case Keith wants us.'

She stood up from the table and went to open the kitchen door.

'Beth?'

She turned.

'Yeah?'

'I'm really glad you're here.'

'Me too.'

She ran all the way up to her bedroom. She felt ridiculously light and free, as though someone had just taken the steel bar from across her shoulders. She and James were okay again. He needed her. Her mother needed her.

She must be doing something right.

*

James poured the last of the remaining wine into Beth's glass.

'Dessert?' he asked her.

'God, no; I couldn't. That was absolutely delicious. Amazing how much better it tastes when you don't have to cook it yourself.'

He grinned over at her.

'Still not a fan of the kitchen, eh?'

Beth shook her head exaggeratedly.

'Now less than ever. Laura's good, though. She makes sure we don't suffer from malnutrition.'

'Gemma's the cook in our house. She's good, too, but there's always a row about the washing-up.'

James fell silent. He began to fidget, pushing at his wineglass restlessly.

'How is she?' Beth asked, suddenly.

He paused for a moment while the waiter placed their coffees in front of them. He studied his cup, not meeting her eyes.

'Unhappy. She senses what's going on between me and Olive, much more than Keith does. She goes very quiet from time to time. Spends a lot of time alone in her room, too.'

He sipped at his coffee thoughtfully.

'I don't quite know what to do with her. I don't know how much is due to Alice, and how much to Olive and me. I'm afraid to think about it, to be honest.'

'Would it help if I talked to her?'

His face brightened a little.

'I think it might. She's very fond of you. Always says she wishes Laura was her sister.'

Beth smiled.

'How much does she know?'

James shrugged.

'We've told her nothing formally: she doesn't know that I've moved out, as such. As far as she's concerned, this is just a convenient arrangement while ... for looking after Alice.'

Beth looked at him in dismay.

'Then what can I tell her? I can't be the one to break that sort of news to her.'

He hesitated, looking at her over the tops of his glasses.

'Actually, she's been asking lately why you and Tony split up. Apparently she and Laura were talking about it last time Laura was over. And now, for obvious reasons, the subject has come up again.'

'Ah,' said Beth. She was surprised at the sudden stab of betrayal she felt at Laura's confidence to Gemma. But why shouldn't they discuss it? Laura had a perfect right to wonder about her parents. So why, thought Beth, didn't she ask me? She, Beth, had never refused to talk about the separation; she'd always given the same carefully agreed, politically correct version of the truth. A truth tailored, perhaps, more to the needs of a five-year-old than a teenager, but it had always seemed enough to say, that no matter what, Mum and Dad will always love you. At fifteen, obviously, such comic-strip formulas wouldn't do any more. Laura hadn't asked her the question because she'd known she'd never get a real answer. Beth felt herself shiver. Was this the beginning of another Gulf of Misunderstanding? One to match the muddy waters that she and Alice had been longing to bridge for at least twenty-five years? Is this how it would happen between her and her own daughter – an evasion here, a half-truth there, a refusal to unravel with hard honesty the knotty complexities of the ties between men and women?

'Beth? Are you okay? You look very tired all of a sudden.'

'Yeah, I'm fine. Someone just walked over my grave, that's all.'

She hugged her arms close to her, warding off the chill winds of a guilty conscience. She didn't want to meet James's eyes.

'Do you want to go?'

'Yeah. I think I'm ready now. Are you?'

He nodded.

'I'll fix up the bill. You stay here.'

Waiting for him to come back, Beth felt the return of the same old sadness that had recently, suddenly, begun to plague her again. How could she possibly explain to Laura, to Gemma, to anyone, why she had sent Tony away? How could you possibly say that the reason for the end of your marriage was that your husband watched television every night and washed the car on Sundays? Like balm for a bruised soul, Tony had drawn her to him in the first place with the eloquent promise of ease and stability. After twelve years of the hectic pace of life in London, she'd been tired, her emotions ragged and discordant. She'd felt the need for peace and ordinariness.

Friends had introduced her to Tony just as she'd

begun looking for somewhere to settle, for someone to still the creeping, insistent ticking of her biological clock. He had seemed like the perfect answer: solid, dependable, predictable. It had been a mistake; she'd married him under false pretences. And then, she'd sent him away for precisely the same reasons that she'd married him. It was her fault, all of it. And yet, they had made each other happy enough for more than five years, until her old, fractious restlessness began to surface again. All the unfulfilled expectations of her whole life seemed to come home to roost in her marriage, nagging at her, driving her away. She didn't know where this irresistible urge to *move on* kept coming from, all her life. *Running away, again: as soon as things get tough.* Alice's voice, hard-edged, tight-lipped, was clear and direct inside her head. And perhaps there was more truth to that than she was prepared to admit.

Things had changed after Laura's arrival – not that she'd ever have been without her baby daughter, not even for a moment. But life had become tougher in so many, indefinable ways: family ties had become more fixed, more complex, somehow. Beth could still remember the feelings of panic that had assaulted her in the early years of her daughter's life. She'd felt almost suffocated, trapped by the needs of this little human being, her life changed for ever, the same for ever. She could see her entire future mapped out inexorably in front of her, while Tony settled into the blissful domesticity which she had never craved. Panic had tightened its grip. The only time she'd felt really alive was when she fought with him. She'd sought conflict, upping the

FIVE

Jack

ALICE PULLED HER bedroom window closed, and locked it. It was only the middle of August, but already the change in the evenings was perceptible. Or maybe she was just feeling the cold more than she used to. She had suddenly, unexpectedly, begun to shiver. The heavy afternoon rain had released the scent of stock and jasmine in the front garden, just below her window, and she had been standing there for some time, inhaling the freshness all around her, enjoying the bite in the air produced by the early autumn showers. And the gardens, front and back, were looking lovely. Some of their colours were dying back, to be sure, but enough of the greenness and lushness were left to be a tonic for the eye. She thought gratefully of Keith, and how he had taken the hardship out of Jack's gardens for her. His swift eye and endless energy had restored them to her again as a place where she could just *be*. She had reclaimed Jack's seat at the end of the back garden, too, and the sense of peace that went within the high walls, a stillness she could not remember having had since the children were very small.

But now it was time to lock up for the night. Over

the past few days, she had started to write messages to herself, little yellow reminders of the ordinary daily tasks that had lately started to slip from her fingers. She was forgetting to close windows and lock doors, and recently, she had gone to bed without switching on the house alarm. So now she spoke aloud to herself more and more often, reminding herself of all the things that had to be done, rehearsing their order in her nightly scheme of things. It was becoming like a game to her – she tried to remember which small ritual came next, before consulting the yellow flags that adorned the mirror in her bedroom, the kitchen tiles behind the kettle and the bit of bathroom wall just above her toothbrush. The same messages, repeated in three different locations, just in case.

She was tired tonight. Her sister Peggy had called for tea, with Clare, and Katie, Clare's youngest teenager. Alice had felt slightly weary at the thought of their visit, and had had the good grace to be immediately ashamed of herself. But no matter how hard she tried not to, she always saw Clare, her oldest niece, as a rebuke for the mess she, Alice, seemed to have made in bringing up her own daughter. Beth and Clare had always been chalk and cheese. Even as children, they had maintained an indifferent distance from each other. They hadn't even cared enough to fight. And now, every time she saw Clare, gentle, soft-spoken, conscientious in visiting her elderly aunt, she was overtaken by a perverse instinct to boast about Beth, her high-flying London life, the success of her business. The truth was, Clare reminded Alice all too sorely of the daughter she thought she'd have liked better: one who'd stayed close to home, who'd minded her children herself, and who'd had the good sense to stay married. After they'd gone, Alice had cleaned up the dishes in the kitchen, missing Beth and Laura so keenly she thought she would cry. She'd felt guilty, too, hoping that none of her visitors had sensed any lack of welcome on her part; Peggy had been very good to her and the children after Jack died.

And that was just the point, wasn't it? A part of her had always resented having to be grateful to those who were kind to the poor widow; Jack was the one who should have looked after them. Alice sighed, pulling her curtains impatiently. It was wrong of her still to feel angry at Jack, wrong of her to keep on feeding this bitterness which surged unexpectedly to the surface more and more often these days. He'd always been a good man; he'd always done his best. It wasn't his fault that he hadn't foreseen his own early, catastrophic death. She hadn't seen it coming, either.

Alice squeezed some cream into her palm and began to massage it methodically into her hands. It was another of her nightly rituals, made necessary now by the increasing dryness of her skin. She sat on the padded stool in front of her dressing table and pulled the hairpins out of her bun, letting the fine white hair fall loosely to her shoulders. She should probably have it cut. Was it just an old woman's ridiculous vanity that made her wear it long, a pale wispy reminder of its former glory?

And could that face in the mirror really belong to her? She looked at it closely, so closely that the reflection began to distort, and she thought she could recognize something of the young woman who had so happily, so easily fallen in love with Jack Keating. She wanted to remember those early days again, to share them with James and Beth – her children deserved a memory of their father that was not wedded to poverty and hardship. And she, she deserved to relive the warmth and joy of their early relationship, to feel its substance fully, unshadowed by death and all the later disappointments.

She began to brush her hair gently, with her mother's tortoiseshell hairbrush. She was much too tired to write to either Beth or James tonight, but she was in just the right frame of mind for remembering. Once she got into bed, her mind would begin to drift, as it usually did, between sleep and waking. The trouble was, this drifting state was now a lot more real to Alice than her present life: she could feel *that* marching away from her inexorably, every footfall of her own mortality measured out in yellow Post-It notes.

'Just let me finish my business with my children, that's all I ask.'

Startled, Alice realized that she had spoken out loud. She sighed. This was all getting to be very difficult. Perhaps she shouldn't be so stubborn. Perhaps she should take James up on his often-repeated offer to move her in with his family, to be taken care of. Tomorrow. Like Scarlett O'Hara, she'd think about it all tomorrow. For tonight, all she had to do was remember to switch on the landing light, so that at least if she went wandering and woke up suddenly, she wouldn't have to feel quite so terrified in the clutching, vulnerable darkness.

Alice left her bedroom door wide open and slipped in between cool sheets. When had she changed them last?

'Stop vexing yourself,' she said crossly. 'Just lie down and be good.'

She closed her eyes, breathing deeply. Sometimes, the rhythm of her own heartbeat frightened her. Would she know, with some sixth sense, when it was about to stop? Should she really be alone when it did? But now, the breathing was easy, effortless. She felt as though she could go on for ever. This was going to be one of the good nights.

Sure enough, Jack was waiting for her.

She knew, just by the look on his face, that tonight he had brought the ring with him. She never wanted to forget that chill Sunday evening in late April, when she'd watched him from the top of the stairs at *Abbotsford*. She had reached the top landing just as her mother was closing the front door. It was too late to turn back, useless to pretend that she hadn't been waiting for him. Some instinct had made him look up, immediately he entered the hall, and their eyes had met instantly.

'Alice?' her mother called. 'Jack's here.' She followed his gaze up to the landing. 'Oh, there you are.'

'Thanks, Mrs McKinney.'

'You're welcome, Jack.' Then, over her shoulder, as the older woman made her way back to the kitchen: 'The fire's lit in the front sitting room.'

'Thanks, Mam,' Alice called, suddenly nervous.

She was acutely conscious of Jack's gaze as she made her way down the long, elegant staircase. She kept her own eyes down, focused carefully on her new strappy shoes. The last thing she wanted to do was trip, and she wasn't completely used to the height of these heels yet. He was waiting for her at the bottom step, smiling up at her.

'Hello, Alice,' he said quietly. 'You look lovely.'

'Thanks,' she smiled. It was a good job he'd never know the rush she and her mother had just had to finish that dress: good quality, peach-coloured cotton, the first welcome sign that the shortages of the War years were finally coming to an end. Her mother had chosen the material for her, and together they had spent hours the previous morning rustling through the fat envelopes of Vogue patterns in Clery's until they'd found just the one to flatter Alice's slim waist and full hips.

Home again, they'd bent together at once over the long kitchen table, pinning the whispers of tissue paper pattern onto the folded material. Mouths full of pins, neither woman had felt the need to speak. The only sounds were the rustle of paper, the hiss of tailor's chalk on soft cotton and, finally, the clean, deep echo of scissors slicing through fabric, resounding against the wooden surface underneath. At five o'clock the following evening, several impatient fittings later, Alice had begun to panic. It would never be finished in time.

'Stop fussing, Alice, and stand still!' her mother had said sharply. 'This is the last time you'll have to try it on – all you've got to do now is the hem. I'll press it for you while you have your bath.'

And of course, it had been ready in time – just. Alice reflected sadly how the rituals of dressmaking had never made her draw any closer to Beth: with her own mother, it had been a common interest, a real expression of their shared femininity. But it seemed only to have made Beth more angry, more resolute than ever to break free of the ties that bound them. Maybe it was just the difference in generations, but it had sorely disappointed Alice nevertheless. She had had such high hopes for herself and her only daughter.

She remembered her own mother's pride as she'd smoothed the full skirt of Alice's new dress, tugging at the hem a little, settling the shoulder pads, tucking in the facing. They'd stood in front of the full-length mirror in the main bedroom, admiring their handiwork, adjusting Alice's dark, wavy hair, waiting for the front doorbell to ring.

'You look perfect,' her mother had whispered, squeezing her daughter's shoulders as she went past on her way downstairs to let Jack in.

And now he was here and they were alone together, standing awkwardly in the wide hallway.

'This way,' she said as she opened the door to the smaller of the downstairs sitting rooms. But he had already taken her hand, lacing his warm fingers through hers. He closed the door behind them quickly and immediately took Alice in his arms. He buried his face in her hair, kissed her mouth, the bottom of her ear, the side of her neck.

She was startled. He had never been so bold before, never so demonstrative, not even when he'd given her the gold watch last Christmas. There was a new air of excitement about him, a new sureness of her and of himself. She held him closely, clasping her hands together at the back of his neck. Even with her high heels, she had to reach up to him.

Finally, he stepped back from her, still holding on to both of her hands.

'I've brought something for you,' he said, his face almost immediately recovering its familiar, shy expression. Then she knew for sure. She felt a thrill of excitement; she had wanted this, expected this for so long. She and her mother had spoken of nothing else all afternoon. Was this really it, at last? Her mam had said it would be, and Alice had felt almost too delighted, too nervous for words. Apprehension and anticipation had combined to produce a delicious ache inside her. She wondered would the evening ever come.

'Are you sure he's the one you want?' her mother had asked her earlier, as she pressed the seams of Alice's new dress, her daughter standing by with the pinking shears.

Alice had looked at her in surprise.

'Of course. He's lovely! You and Dad have said all along what a good man he is.'

She was puzzled by the way her mother kept focusing on the pointed nose of the iron, as she eased it in and out of the channels of soft peach-coloured fabric.

'He is. He's a very good man, but he doesn't care

too much about the future. You'll never be rich, Alice.'
She paused, still concentrating hard on her ironing. 'I
like him very much, but you won't have it as easy as
Peggy.'

Alice shrugged. She really didn't care. She'd never
wanted to be like Peggy, anyway. And money didn't
bother her.

'It doesn't matter. As long as we have enough.'

Her mother had nodded and expertly turned the
dress right way out as she pulled it off the ironing board.

She'd smiled at her daughter then, patting her cheek
gently.

'Well, he won't be able to resist you in this.'

Jack guided her over to the small sofa now, and sat
her down. Grinning broadly, bashful as a small boy, he
knelt on the fireside rug in front of her. The flames
licked up and down, shadowing his face, making his
eyes shine. Never taking his bright gaze from her face,
he put one hand into his jacket pocket and pulled out a
small, midnight-blue velvet box. He showed it to her,
nestled in the palm of his hand. Immediately, Alice
could feel her cheeks begin to burn.

'Open it,' he said softly.

Carefully, she lifted the hinged lid. Inside was a
delicate, thoroughly modern three-stone engagement
ring. Even though she had been preparing herself for
this, Alice gasped out loud. It was even lovelier than she
had wanted it to be.

Her eyes filled and she threw her arms around him,
feeling the heat of the fire on his skin. He drew back

then and took the ring carefully between his thumb and forefinger. Solemnly, he reached for her left hand, the ring poised just over the third finger.

'Will you marry me, Alice?'

His blue eyes were vivid, dancing.

'Yes, yes I will!'

She was almost sobbing now, overcome with love and delight and the astonishing promise of being a married woman soon, with her own husband, her own home, children. It was almost too much to take in.

They admired the ring together.

'If it's not what you want, we can change it.'

'No, no, it is what I want, it's just beautiful! I don't want to change anything!'

That night, Jack Keating had been perfect in her eyes. Tender, a bit shy, full of extraordinary plans and ambitions, all of which included her.

Alice shifted in the bed, trying to get comfortable. Her neck and shoulders had ached today, during and after the rain. The onset of autumn dampness always spelled trouble. She tried to ease herself back into her pillows.

Dear Jack. He'd been so proud that night, so delighted she'd said yes, although he couldn't have had any serious doubts about that. Alice had suspected quite early on that *both* sets of parents had been scheming away quietly in the background for some time. That had puzzled her, at first. The Keatings had moved from farming to the city years before; she was surprised that the friendship between the two families had run so long and so deep. Sometimes, she had thought that the older

Peggy might have been the preferred sister initially – she was gentle and docile, much more biddable than she, Alice, had ever been. But when Peggy married very young in '42, or was it '43? – anyway, Jack's occasional visits to *Abbotsford* had not stopped, but continued as normal, as though nothing unexpected had happened. Evidently, neither he nor Peggy had broken the other's heart. When Alice left to do her commercial course in Miss Rutherford's, it was with strict instructions to get in touch, and stay in touch, with the Keatings. She had known, even then, what her parents were up to, but had acquiesced willingly. This was what young girls did, wasn't it? Marriage was a highly desirable career, much more desirable than the typing pool in Cremin's Insurance Company. Your own home, your own chores, your own boss. It had to be better than rattling out endless top copies full of incomprehensible small print, with four smudgy carbons underneath: all of them just waiting for you to make a spelling mistake. And besides, Alice had been a little jealous of the status and freedom that Peggy now seemed to be enjoying. All the young people appeared determined to enjoy themselves, to kick over the traces now that the spectre of the War had finally disappeared.

She had dragged Jack down the passageway to the kitchen that night, bursting the door open with her enthusiasm.

'Mam, Dad, Jack and I would like to tell you something.'

Her mother's quick frown told Alice that she was doing something wrong. Confused, Alice stopped just inside the door, letting the play on the radio fill the sudden silence. Her father turned down the volume, and looked at both of them questioningly, his eyes finally resting on Jack. The fire crackled in the background.

'Yes? What is it, young man?'

Alice wanted to bite her tongue. Of course, this was Jack's role: he should be the one to announce the good news, or rather, to ask permission for there to *be* any good news.

'I . . . Mr McKinney, sir, I've asked Alice to be my wife, and she's said yes. I . . . we . . . wanted to tell you, and to make sure that it's all right with you. Sir.'

Alice wanted to giggle. It was a bit late to be asking for permission. A well-directed glance from her mother silenced her.

Her father's face broke into a broad smile.

'That's the best news I've heard in a long time – do you mean to tell me she's finally off my hands?'

Alice remembered shouting 'Dad!' at that point, and then everyone was laughing at once, hugging, kissing. The engagement ring was examined and pronounced perfect.

A couple of innocents, Alice reflected now, but without rancour. The glow of love had seemed to spread out way beyond them that night, into their future, and Alice had been happy to think of herself as a very lucky girl. That had been one of the best times, and she could still relive the thrill of moving in, as husband and wife, to Jack's old home in Dublin, in the summer of '48. She'd been determined to make it up to him for having lost both his parents within six months of each other. With no brothers or sisters of his own, Alice knew that it was now up to her to be all of Jack's family. She wanted to be everything to him.

And the house. She'd loved this house from the first day she'd stepped inside the gleaming hallway, and now it was theirs. She'd wanted to change nothing, out of respect for Jack's recent losses.

'Everything should stay,' she'd told him, 'we don't need to throw anything out. Let's just paint it, as it is, together.'

She'd been so happy during those first months, opening her wedding presents, building her nest, playing house, that she had hardly noticed. For Alice, it had seemed normal never to go short. She'd been puzzled, rather than worried, to discover one evening that 'The Bank' was empty a lot sooner than it should have been. She knew that Jack would have a good explanation.

'I've decided to go out on my own,' he told her over dinner. 'There's lots of work out there: I can earn far more by myself than working for Jimmy Power.'

She had felt a slight stab of misgiving, even then. But, as her mother would have advised her, she kept her powder dry. Jack had looked unusually determined, and she knew him well enough by now to realize that 'I've decided to' really meant 'I've already done it'. She wanted to believe in him, she really did, but she was secretly worried that things could go horribly wrong. Everything was beginning to pick up again after the War, even she knew that, but there had been many weeks when Jack brought home only a flat wage. She liked the security of Thursday's brown envelope, no matter what it contained, and she was proud of how well she managed. On the good weeks, she could even tuck something away for a rainy day. It was amazing, too, how much it cost to keep up old, draughty houses. Even though she loved her home dearly, she had recently had some sneaking, guilty thoughts about how much easier one of the new houses would have been: there were modern bungalows and neat three-bedroom terraced houses springing up in nice estates all over Dublin, ever since the end of the War. Peggy and Joe had just moved into one, and Alice had envied her sister the bright, shiny newness of her endlessly pretty home. She could never have told Jack that, of course; he would have been hurt, and she'd have felt like a traitor.

'Are you sure?' she'd asked instead. 'Don't you need someone like Jimmy Power to find you the work, first?'

He'd shaken his head.

'No. People know my work, they know it's good. Trust me, Alice, I know what I'm doing.'

And in a way, he'd been right. He'd never been busier. He left the house each morning at half past six, not returning until after seven o'clock most evenings. He grew short-tempered and turned greyer and greyer in the face until Alice became frightened. The work kept growing, and with it, the amount of money that Jack was owed. It took Alice time to learn that although Jack could scrape, sand, paint, wallpaper and finish the tricky bits to perfection, he was unable to demand, or even ask for, what was his. He felt it was indelicate – he preferred to trust to his clients' honour. Whenever she tried to speak to him about collecting some of what was due, he became short with her. He knew what he was doing, she should leave all of that to him. There was no need to worry herself into a state over money. But worry she did. And still no one paid him. She began to grow desperate. With all of this going on, how was she going to find a way to tell him they were going to have a baby?

She finally broke, the day the half-ton of coal was delivered. Standing by her kitchen window, she watched as two grime-encrusted men with peaked caps and filthy dungarees hoisted bag after bag of coal onto their shoulders, and made dusty progress through her side entrance to the coal-shed. Finally, one of them tapped on her back door.

'That's four pounds, missus,' he said, his face completely black except for the startling white gleam of his eyes. The glowing end of a cigarette was held delicately to his lips by dirty thumb and forefinger.

'Just a minute,' she said, turning confidently towards her willow-patterned teapot on the dresser. She put her fingers inside, expecting to grasp the four single pound notes, rolled into a tube, that she had put there last night, in readiness. There was nothing. Disbelieving, she turned the teapot upside down, and shook it. Nothing. She checked the spout. Frantic now, she ran her hand along the dresser shelves, took the lids off all the jars and dishes arrayed there. There was nothing: the money was gone.

Stupidly, she checked again. Had she been dreaming? Had the money never been there in the first place?

She looked around her wildly. Had they been burgled, then? She checked her handbag, resting as usual on the hall-stand. A ten shilling note, half a crown and a threepenny bit: just what had been there yesterday. So no burglar, then.

There must be some explanation.

She went back into the kitchen, ready to confront the coal man. She pulled open the door again.

'I'm sorry,' she said. 'My husband seems to have forgotten to leave me the money. It's not in the usual place. Can you come back for it tomorrow?'

The coal man regarded her steadily. He squeezed the lighted top off his cigarette, and placed the butt carefully behind his ear. Then, he turned to one side and spat, almost apologetically, on to the grass. Alice felt mortified. It was an insolent gesture, calculated to offend. He might just as well have dropped his trousers in front of her.

'Well, now, missus, I'm afraid we can't do that.'

He scratched his chin thoughtfully.

'Next delivery round here isn't until the end of the week.'

He stood, gazing at her.

'I'll bring the money into your office tomorrow – tomorrow morning, for sure,' Alice said.

She could hear her own voice rising. And underneath all the humiliation was a white-hot anger. Jack must have taken the four pounds – without even telling her.

The coal man shook his head.

'Sorry, missus. No can do.'

And he put two fingers to his lips and blew a long,

piercing whistle. The younger man reappeared immediately, although nothing at all had been said, with folded, empty sacks under his arm.

Alice looked at them in horror, her eyes darting from one to the other.

'You can't!' she gasped. 'You can't take it back!'

'Them's our orders, missus. Sorry.'

He turned away, and both men moved towards the coal shed. Alice slammed the kitchen door shut and locked it, hot, angry tears coursing down her face. How could he? How could he do that to her? And now everyone would see – Mrs McGrath, who missed nothing, perched by her front window for most of the day, Mrs Collins at the corner – the whole street would know, soon. Unable to bear watching, or even listening to the scrape of shovel against concrete, Alice ran upstairs and threw herself on her bed, weeping uncontrollably.

When Jack came in, he found her lying down, listless, the eiderdown pulled up to her chin. Her face was turned to the wall.

'Hello, love,' he said.

There was no reply. He spoke again, into the silence.

'What's wrong? Aren't you feeling all right?'

She couldn't answer.

'Alice?' his voice was growing alarmed.

'Did you take the four pounds from the teapot this morning? The money I'd put away for the coal man?'

There was a pause.

'Yeah. I had to borrow it. I was running short of paint for the new job.'

'Did you get paid for the last one yet?'

'No, not yet. But it's early days.'

'Or the one before that?'

He began to fidget. This was a new Alice, one he had never seen before. She knew that she was making him uncomfortable. She continued, still keeping her face turned away from him.

'Or even the two big houses, the neighbours on Griffith Avenue, that you finished over two months ago?'

He was silenced.

Then she turned to look at him, her eyes swollen, face streaked with tears. He started when he saw her.

'Alice . . . ?'

'Don't you "Alice" me! Do you know what happened to me this afternoon?'

She could still feel the molten anger that had filled her that day, right to her fingertips. She had screamed at him, hurling her hurt pride at him, wanting to wound. And then, for the final blow, the *coup de grâce*, she told him about the baby.

They'd made up, of course; he'd been chastened and remorseful, said he'd forgotten all about the coal delivery. He'd promised to go after the money owing to him, to have things under control before the baby came. Alice couldn't quite remember the sequence of events after that – whether he'd gone to Jimmy Power and asked for his old job back before, or just after, James's birth. It had been within a few months of that day, anyway, and she had taken careful ownership of the weekly brown envelope ever since. She'd never told her mother about the coal man, but had often wondered at the irony of her parents' choice for her. They had wanted a man who was steady and reliable, a man who was not a drinker: someone who would be good to her and look after her. Well, he wasn't a drinker, and he did love her, but it was Alice who'd done most of the looking after. She'd also wondered that her mother hadn't warned her more about money: that day at the ironing board hardly counted, it had hardly been a warning at all, just a gentle little piece of advice on the day of her engagement, not to try and be like Peggy. It had taken Alice years to realize that, just like her own daughter, no matter what warnings Granny Mac might have given, she, Alice, would have listened to none of them.

But they'd been good together, really, she reflected now. They'd grown close and happy after that. She knew it couldn't have been easy for him to go back to Power, cap in hand, begging, as Jack would have seen it, to be taken on again. But he'd swallowed his pride, insisting that Alice and the baby came first. She smiled to herself in the darkness now as she remembered what a doting father he'd been. There was none of the detachment she'd often seen in other men, who left all the child-rearing to their wives. Jack had been very modern in that sense, a father involved in everything to do with his children's lives, a father who knew how to have fun. She felt a sudden sweep of sadness now for the little souls who hadn't made it: Jack had been every bit as devastated as she was when three miscarriages followed, one relentlessly after the other, in the years following James's birth. They had named those babies together, planted shrubs in their memory. Alice still thought about them, fleetingly, all the anguish finally assuaged by the birth of Elizabeth and the swift passage of years since then. That little girl had never known just how precious she was.

Alice pulled herself up onto one elbow and switched on her bedside lamp. She squinted at her watch. Three. She was hardly going to sleep now. Dawn would be breaking in another couple of hours. She might as well read. She pulled an old magazine from the top of her bedside locker. James had given her a book recently, some biography of Lady something or other that he'd said she'd enjoy. She hadn't had the heart to tell him that she could retain nothing, not even a single thread of thought from one paragraph to the next. With any luck, the load of old nonsense they wrote in these magazines would soon make her nod off. She'd write to Beth and James in the morning. Now that she had clear, urgent ideas about what she wanted to say.

*

'Everything all right, Keith?'

'Yeah, fine. She's hardly moved since you left. How was your meal?'

'Fine,' Beth and James said together, and grinned at each other.

'You both look half-pissed,' said Keith, bluntly.

James tugged at his beard and looked at his son, quizzically.

'I wouldn't pursue that line, if I were you. Not after last Friday night.'

Keith grinned. 'Point taken.'

'Now off you go home. Beth and I'll take over.'

Each of them had taken up their position by the bed, automatically.

''Night, Dad. 'Night, Beth. See you tomorrow, then.'

''Night, Keith.'

Beth settled herself into the bo-bo-dee. The room gradually became quiet again. She was actually glad to be back: the restaurant had felt peculiarly artificial, detached somehow, as though real life were going on somewhere else. They had both been anxious to get home, back to where they belonged. She reached for Alice's wrist, checking her pulse. The old woman's breathing was still regular, steady. She noticed that June had changed the sheets, or perhaps James had done it, during Dr Crowley's visit. She looked comfortable, safe, held in place securely by the neat blankets. Keith was right: the wine had gone straight to her head, and she could hardly keep her eyes open. But she didn't want to miss anything, didn't want not to be there in case her mother needed her ... Suddenly, her head jerked forward and she realized that she had fallen asleep, just for an instant. She had had a nightmare flash of wet road, leaves swirling, a car hurtling into the solid darkness. Even her chin hurt again at the memory.

James was watching her.

'Go to bed,' he said, 'even for a couple of hours. I'll call you at three, I promise. Wine keeps me awake, and there's no need for both of us to be here.'

'Are you sure? I'm really sorry about this – I just feel

suddenly wrecked. I think it's the first time I've felt relaxed in a week.'

'Positive. And don't worry, I'll definitely call you at three. I'm not into self-sacrifice any more.'

*

When James came in to call her, Beth was already awake. She pulled her dressing gown on over her pyjamas, conscious of the next letter buried deep in the towelling pocket.

'She's been a bit restless for the last hour or so,' he said, 'but I think she's settled again. Call me if you even think you need me.'

He rubbed his eyes vigorously.

'I will. Sleep tight.'

Beth kissed him lightly. His face was worried again, deep lines of anxiety creasing his forehead, pulling down the corners of his eyes. She wished that Olive would at least ring.

She tucked in Alice's blankets, turned up the radiator a little and began lighting the night-lights she had dotted around the room. On their way to the restaurant, she and James had stopped off to buy a couple of little burners, and she filled them now from the jug on the dressing table, sprinkling oil of lavender across the water's surface. Lavender was a soothing oil, the woman in the shop had told her, and Beth liked the way the scent immediately filled the room. It reminded her instantly of Granny Mac, who had always placed little pillows full of dried lavender into her clothes drawers, and hung them around her woollens in the wardrobe. It kept the moths away, she'd said. Better than camphor. It was a pleasing, old-fashioned smell.

Beth pushed the bedroom door closed, once she'd checked that James's light had been switched off. She still felt guilty about this small subterfuge, but her hunger to read the next letter was almost overpowering. She held Alice's hand for a moment, making sure she was warm enough. Then she eased the envelope open, her heart thudding.

'Woodvale'
18th August 1999

Dearest Elizabeth,
This is getting to be quite a habit – and one I look forward to more and more. I can feel myself growing much closer to you, and I have a real need to fill in what I consider to be the 'blanks' between us. I feel very bright and alert this morning, which is rather strange, as I hardly slept at all last night. I've begun to notice that the early morning is my best time, and that things start to cloud over a bit by late afternoon.

I was reminded of something in the early hours of this morning, just before I fell asleep for a while. I know I slept, finally, because my lamp was still switched on at seven o'clock, although it was already bright outside. I don't even remember closing my eyes.

I have been feeling sad recently that you, particularly, will have such few memories of your dad. At least James was of an age to understand, and to hold on to the moments which were important to him. But you were so young when Jack died that you have the right to feel more or less abandoned. And so, I've tried to gather together some memories for you. Of course, they won't be yours at first, but maybe you can add them to the ones you've already got, and that way, they can become yours. Am I making sense? I've put aside a little bundle of photographs for you, at the top of your wardrobe, and one for James, too. I don't have too many pictures of us together as a family, but those I've found, I've divided carefully between the two of you, and made notes on the back – that is, if I could remember anything significant to write.

I have one really clear picture in my mind of a time when the four of us were together, happy. You had just had your third birthday, and James would have been almost eight. Of course there were many other times, too, but this is the one I keep coming back to, or rather, that keeps coming back to me. You'll find the photo of this day right at the top of your bundle – it has 'Phoenix Park, May 1957' written on the back.

We took the bus into town, and then the number 10 to the Park. You were really excited at being upstairs on the bus, and you chattered away to everyone around you. You took a real shine to the conductor, who gave you a blank roll from his ticket machine to play with. Have you any memory of playing buses with James for weeks afterwards, tearing a little scrap off the roll and handing him his ticket every time he 'boarded'? Your bus was made out of two kitchen chairs lying on their sides on the floor. You used to sit between the legs, James in the same position behind you. Sometimes you played at being the driver and sometimes the conductor.

Occasionally, you were both at the same time – but you were never the passenger. That ticket-roll never left your sticky little hands, not even for a moment! Your dad really enjoyed your chatter and your games – he couldn't get enough of you.

What you won't be able to see from the photo is the colour of the jumpers that all three of you are wearing that day. They were bright red, and my first attempt at serious knitting. I'd always been good at sewing and mending, but I'd never really tried to knit before that. Your dad had found several hanks of wool stored in a box in the attic when he went up to fix the roof – his mother, the granny you never knew, had been a marvellous knitter: Aran sweaters, Fairisle, the most complicated patterns – nothing was too hard for her. Anyway, that winter, Jack and I spent several evenings by the fire in the sitting room, winding those hanks into balls so that I could start using them. He was very patient – he would sit for hours on end with the wool stretched between his arms, moving them up and down, up and down, so that I could wind the yarn more easily.

Eventually, I had more than enough for two jumpers. In fact, I had more than enough for three, but I knitted your dad's one secretly, when he was working late, and I used one of the patterns that had belonged to his mother. He was very touched by that.

I finished all three jumpers in time for the visit to the Phoenix Park. I was delighted that you took to yours immediately. If ever you took a turn against something, there was no way on this earth I could get you to wear it. But you loved this little jumper, and I felt very proud of my first knitted creation. If you look carefully, you'll see the three little wooden buttons I used at the neck – you were intrigued by those buttons: you even used to suck the top one until you were told to stop!

Our day out was in May, and mind you, it was still quite cold. I was glad we'd wrapped you both up warmly. You spent most of that day up on your dad's shoulders, surveying the world. It was a Sunday, so there were plenty of people to look at, and most, like ourselves, had brought a picnic.

But first, we brought you to see the deer. You were enthralled – I think it was the first time we had ever seen you so quiet. Your dad took you by the hand and you both walked very slowly, very quietly, up to where the deer were grazing. James and I followed in your footsteps. We could see the deer's huge dark eyes rolling from time to time – they were very nervous creatures. But you were great: you did nothing to frighten them. You did exactly as your dad did, and eventually, you were both standing almost eye to eye with this huge, shivering, brown and white animal with enormous antlers.

I could hear what your dad was saying, and he told me afterwards that your eyes had been like saucers.

'This is Rudolph,' he said softly, 'Santa's favourite deer. The reason his nose isn't red any more is because he's in Ireland now, and it's not as cold here as it is in the North Pole. This is Rudolph's holiday – he'll be going back to Santa soon to help him get ready for next Christmas. Do you want to tell him what you'd like Santa to bring you?'

You did. You nodded your head very slowly.

Your dad said you whispered something, never taking your eyes off the deer, which had stopped grazing at that instant and turned to look at you, before moving off to rejoin the rest of the herd.

'Big Teddy,' was what he'd heard you say, and you never changed your mind, you never forgot – you held on to that wish for the rest of the year. I was fascinated – both your dad and I were. You were only three, but you never wavered for an instant. You told us, several times that winter, what Santa was going to bring you, and of course, you were right!

You were very quiet for the rest of the morning, and you kept looking over your shoulder for 'Rudolph'. Eventually, you seemed to forget about it, and you and James played on the grass together all afternoon. We'd brought the little tartan rug from your bedroom with us, and we all sat on it for our picnic. We didn't bring you to the Zoo that day, because it was too expensive, but we did rise to two ice-cream cones with chocolate flakes: weren't they called '99's? and you each seemed to be happy with that. Your dad and I had great fun with you for weeks afterwards, wondering how 'Rudolph' was getting on – we built a whole fantasy life for him. Anyway, it was lovely for us to be able to make your dream come true at Christmas: I've never seen a Teddy showered with such love. And, if you're interested, 'Dolph' is wrapped up in tissue paper behind the box of photographs. Take him home with you – he may be a rather ancient bear, slightly the worse for wear, and for having had his right ear sucked, but I'd like to think of you taking a piece of that day back with you.

I think you slept on the bus on the way home – you were adorable, sticky with ice cream, grubby from playing in the grass and completely and perfectly innocent. That was a magical day.

It feels that the years since then have gone by in a flash – and I always see you and James as you were then. They're precious years – think about Laura as a toddler, and how protective you felt towards her. That's how I felt about you. And close, as though you were still part of me. I've always found it hard to let go. But I've loved you just as much as a teenager and as a grown woman – the problem is, I only seem to be good at showing it with small children. Still, all of this writing is helping – I feel that in some strange way, you are already listening to me, and there's great comfort in that. I know I'm running out of time, and I don't want to leave anger and guilt behind me – I know how destructive that can be.

I think if your dad had lived, I might have found being a mother easier. As it was, it was often terribly difficult being on my own with two children. He adored both of you, you were his life. You, in particular, he had a special feeling for – I've seen it with other fathers and daughters. He didn't love you more, or less, than James, that's not what I mean – it was just a different sort of love. He'd have been very proud of you and Laura, just as I am.

That night, after the visit to the Phoenix Park, we put both you and James into the bath together, and the pair of you squealed and splashed for well over an hour. James was always such a serious little boy, but with you, at times like that, he was free and funny and silly. We had to take you out when your fingers looked like prunes. We ran downstairs with you – you in my arms, James in your dad's – and dried you by the fire. I remember that you each got a story – you loved *The Ugly Duckling*, and I've forgotten for the moment what James's one was – some 'Biggles' adventure, I think. Your dad used to read you *The Ugly Duckling* over and over again, and you would never let him skip even one word. You knew the whole thing by heart – you even knew when it was time to turn the pages.

I've often thought it was quite an appropriate story, too – now don't get cross. You were rather a gawky teenager, but you turned into such a lovely young woman. You're still lovely. I wish you peace of mind to go with it.

Now that that day isn't pulling at my memory any longer, I'm sure that lots of other times will come flooding back – this is what is happening to me now every night, usually just before I sleep. I've decided to leave a notebook and pen beside the bed now, so that I can make a note of the things I want to talk to you and James about. I know that there is so much to say, and I have so little time.

All my love,
Alice.

Almost at once, Beth could see the day her mother was writing about. The deer, the Phoenix Park, the picnic on the grass – these were all details etched deeply into the glass of her memory. Or had Alice's letter just made it seem that way? Maybe her mother was right: maybe she was just adding the details of this day to all the others stored in her memory-bank. It didn't matter;

either way, she had now reclaimed that day, and it was hers for good. She could see the scene unfold before her mind's eye, could feel herself almost becoming that three-year-old again. Her eyes filled over and over as she imagined the four of them, as distant and remote as the inhabitants of some foreign country.

She reached for Alice's hand once more, and began to speak to her, gradually raising her voice from a whisper to the tone of a normal conversation. Why not? Who was to say that her mother couldn't hear her? It was much more comforting to think of her as a seeing, hearing, sentient being, even if illness had made a prisoner of her will to respond.

'I do remember that red jumper, Alice: I absolutely loved it. And you're right, the little toggle buttons used to fascinate me. I remember when I was older, holding the hanks of yarn for you too, and grumbling that it made my arms tired!'

Beth noticed how dry and flaky her mother's hands had become. Still talking, she stood and walked over to the dressing table, looking for the tube of cream that Alice had always kept there.

'Was I really only three when I got Dolph for Christmas? It's funny, I can remember that really vividly, too. I have the impression of being just about the same size as the teddy bear, and he had a glorious red ribbon around his neck. Which I took off, of course, because I wanted to wear it in my hair.'

She began to massage the old hands gently, exerting pressure from time to time, varying the rhythm. Her mother had always taken very good care of her hands.

Even now, there were the traces of clear polish on the neat, rounded fingernails.

'I know you were trying to give me back my dad in this letter, but I have lots of good memories of him, stored away somewhere safe. What I really want . . .'

Beth paused for a moment. Alice seemed to have sighed, and her head had moved its position slightly. She leaned closer.

'Alice? Can you hear me?'

Alice's eyelids flickered, she moaned softly once and then settled again, her head resuming its former position.

Beth realized that she'd been holding her breath. Still staying close, she started to speak again, this time more softly.

'What I really want, Mother, is for the two of us to have good memories of each other. I don't want you to die thinking I'm angry at you, or that I hate you. These letters are the most precious things you've ever given me, because you've given me back yourself.'

Silence. Nothing. But it didn't matter, not any more. This letter, and the others, had begun to form the most complete picture Beth had ever had of herself, as a daughter, a sister, part of a family. Warts and all, she'd begun to know herself, to understand what had made her into the woman she was. With a powerful sense of realization, Beth knew now that she'd spent most of her adult life missing her mother. Alice's constant physical presence had made the emotional distance between them all the more immense. She had always felt remote, once she, Beth, had crossed the threshold of the childhood years. It was as though Alice had stayed behind, imprisoned by her longing for the little tendernesses she'd once shared with her baby daughter, dismayed that the ugly duckling had somehow managed to escape the nest, and had flown away with all the others. Her most dramatic flight, at eighteen, still hovered between them: neither of them had ever forgiven the other for that. Neither of them had ever even spoken of it to the other: Beth still felt it as a dead weight between them. She wished she could make that time all right again – for both of them – before it was too late.

She had missed her father too, of course, but in a different way – his presence had been so complete while he was alive that he'd left no shattered pieces for her to pick up after he died. Alice was right, she *had* found it hard to let her daughter go.

Leaving home the way she had had been inevitable, Beth reflected now, in the light of all that had gone before. But she had been too cruel, much too heartless. She could only hope that Laura would not make her suffer in the same way. Alice's shocked face, the tight angry line of her mouth, the blaze of disappointment between them – she could feel it all still, could even see the little white china jug with the gold rim sitting on the kitchen table, full of cold water, while her mother made pastry for an apple tart.

'Don't be ridiculous,' Alice was saying. 'How do you plan to earn your living when you've no qualifications to do anything? I've never heard of anything so daft in all my life.'

She'd rolled the pastry emphatically, banging the rolling pin onto the wooden table-top as though to beat

Beth's words into submission. The whole kitchen was bright with anger.

'I've made up my mind. I'm going to London for the summer. I can stay with friends until I find something. There's lots of work in London.'

'What friends?'

Alice cored an apple viciously.

'Pete's brother has a flat there; he's said we can stay with him.'

Such naked defiance had stopped Alice's knife in its tracks.

'You're going to London with *him*?'

'Yes. Why not? I'm eighteen; you can't stop me.'

'Well.'

Alice placed the pie plate on the table and wiped her hands on her apron.

'If you've no respect for yourself, then I suppose I can't expect any better from him.'

'What's *that* supposed to mean?'

They were glaring at each other now, furious.

'You know exactly what I mean. Go ahead, ruin your life. Throw it away, why don't you, and never mind the sacrifices that were made for your education.'

'I've no intention of throwing my life away. I'm talking about a summer, for God's sake! And I don't *need* reminding about *all* the sacrifices that were made for me – I've heard about them often enough already.'

Even then, Beth had known she was going too far, but she couldn't help herself. The words were out, curling like blue smoke into the atmosphere around them, trailing devastation in their wake.

'Go ahead, then!' Alice had shouted after her. 'I never thought I'd see any daughter of mine carry on like this! Don't expect me to pick up the pieces when your precious friends let you down!'

There had been more, too, much more, although Beth was now hazy on the details. It was all so long ago – well over twenty-five years. But if she couldn't remember the words, she could certainly recall the hurt; it had haunted her daily for months. That same scene in the kitchen had stayed with her all summer, and for many years afterwards, making it impossible for her to find any firm ground between herself and her mother. It had been quicksand, all the way.

Poor Alice! If only she'd known! If she'd been terrified about sexual shenanigans, she needn't have worried. Pete and herself barely survived the mail boat to Holyhead. They fought for the entire journey, arriving at Euston station at six a.m., gritty-eyed and fractious. They fought, too, for the whole week they stayed in Brian's flat, until he threatened to throw them both out, her and his brother.

In the end, it was Pete who moved out first, finding work for the summer on the building sites in Cricklewood, and entering with terrified bravado into the hard-working, hard-drinking Irish navvy community there – always knowing he was going home in September to the safety of university.

'What are you going to do?' Brian had asked her, shortly after Pete left.

'I don't know,' she'd said, thoroughly miserable and broke.

'Can you type?'

'Yeah, we did a course in school, in fifth year. But I'm a bit rusty.'

'That doesn't matter. There's lots of work for temps. That's what Annie, my girlfriend, did for the first year. You'll get your speeds up with a bit of practice.'

'Do you think so?' Beth had brightened immediately, seeing the prospect of having to go home with her tail between her legs slowly beginning to recede.

'Get yourself dressed up and go round all the agencies tomorrow. You can stay here for a couple of weeks, until Annie comes back. After that, I'm sorry, but you'll have to go.'

A couple of weeks was just what she wanted, just enough to prove to Alice, and to herself, that she knew what she was doing. She'd walked everywhere, saving Tube fares whenever she could. The agency windows had been full of ads, and she'd been prepared to lie. As a result, she got work straight away as a dictaphone typist in an engineering firm. Clutching her *A to Z*, she'd found her way, terrified, to her first placement. She'd been supposed to stay for a fortnight, and ended up there for five months. The money was good, the work was dull but easy, and her confidence grew daily. These people treated her like a grown-up. She remembered writing stiff little postcards home, ostensibly to James, but knowing that Alice would see them and be hurt.

She stroked her mother's forehead, still leaning close to her.

'Do you know, I was so homesick in London that it

was like a physical pain? But I was too stubborn to come home, and you were too stubborn to write to me. Do you remember the postcard I sent James with my new address on it? It was just before Christmas, and I'd got my own place, sharing with Angela. You remember Angela, the girl I'd met in the hostel? I really wanted you to write to me then and invite me home for Christmas. I willed you to send me a letter, a card, anything. I'd have been home in a flash.'

The shine had gone off London for her by that stage, Beth reflected now. All her wages seemed to be eaten up by the astoundingly high ransom demanded by landlords and London Transport. And she was getting sick of typing. There had to be more to life. Three years at university in Dublin was beginning to feel like a much more attractive option. The only problem was having to go home, having to admit defeat. She'd have to sit it out with her mother, who would claim to have known this would happen, would insist that she'd been right all along.

'But you sent James to get me, didn't you?'

Beth smiled at the memory. Twenty-three years old, already looking as grave and responsible as a man well into his forties, James had sat on the floor outside her flat, waiting for her, late one wet December evening. There was just one week to go before Christmas.

By then, she'd had no pride left. She'd burst into tears, hugging James as though there were no tomorrow.

'It's all right, Sis. I'm here to take you home. Don't cry.'

And it could have worked. She'd been so lonely that any welcome from Alice would have been enough.

'But you couldn't forgive me, and I couldn't forgive you. Even now, we can barely talk about it. You've said nothing at all in your letters about London, and here am I, feeling that it's already too late. That Christmas was a disaster. We kept flaring up at each other: I took everything you said as a criticism, you took everything I said as an insolence.'

Poor James had been stuck in the middle. He'd tried to act as the diplomat, tried to fix things between them. But nothing had worked. She and Alice had made their way around each other warily, when they were not fighting, like reluctant partners in some slow and circular dance, locked into repeating the same steps over and over again, standing on each other's toes, going nowhere.

He'd come into her room on St Stephen's day to find her packing her rucksack.

'It's hopeless, James. She won't even try to see my point of view. There's just no talking to her.'

He'd looked at her, helplessly.

'Maybe if I . . .'

Beth remembered that she'd cut him off, rudely.

'No – we've tried all that. Forget it. I'm going back. I don't know why she sent you to bring me home in the first place.'

That first Christmas had set the pattern for many years to come, until Laura.

Suddenly, Beth felt that there was something

different about the room. The quality of the air had changed, something imperceptible had shifted. She glanced around her, quickly. All the night-lights were burning, the door was still closed, there was no sense of a chill in the air – but something had altered. Quickly, she stuffed the letter back into her pocket. Terrified, she looked down into Alice's face. Her skin suddenly looked smoother, somehow, more stretched across her cheek-bones. There was no longer such an obvious pull on the left-hand side of her mouth: it was as though all of Alice's features were suddenly merging into anonymity, the last traces of personality rapidly disappearing. The slight rustle of old breathing had stilled. Her chest no longer rose and fell.

Beth shook her, almost roughly, panic rising from the pit of her stomach.

'Alice? Alice? Can you hear me?'

At that moment, Alice's head turned towards her. Her mouth opened and she breathed one long, guttural breath. Then there was silence.

Frantically, Beth reached for her pulse. Nothing. She laid her head down on the thin chest. Silence.

'Oh God, oh God, oh God – James! Come quickly! James!'

She flung open the bedroom door, screaming for her brother, turning back to Alice again, running from one part of the room to another, like someone demented. After everything they'd been through, was this it? No balm of resolution, no kind ending?

He was there instantly, his eyes wide and shocked, vulnerable without his glasses.

'I think she's gone, I think she's gone!'

Beth was now weeping uncontrollably, great gasping sobs that rose up on tides of anguish from somewhere deep inside her.

James stepped over to the bed and took his mother's hand in his.

'Ah, Jesus,' he said softly.

The compassion in his voice told Beth that it was all over.

Tenderly, he held Alice's mouth closed for a few moments and folded her hands carefully across her chest. After what seemed like a very long while, he leaned over to Beth.

'Here,' he said gently, 'this is for you.'

Beth wiped her eyes and took the wedding ring he handed her, sobbing once more as she put the ring onto her own finger, rocking back and forwards in her grief, trying to dull the pain with constant movement. The choking voice she heard somewhere in the room bore no resemblance to her own. James came and put his arms around her then, his warm hands pressing against her back once more.

She leaned against him, gratefully, remembering the sudden sting of her mother's hand against her kneecaps and the bright, painful vision of a greying head bent low over the black and gold Singer sewing-machine.

*

'What should we do now?'

Beth wiped her eyes and looked up at her brother, who still had his arms wound tightly around her. They had stayed like that for several minutes, neither wanting to move away from the warmth of the other. Time stood all around them, still and silent.

'What time is it?'

She looked at her watch.

'Ten to four.'

James touched Alice's forehead and was surprised at the coldness there.

'There's no point in calling anyone at this hour. Let's wait until the morning. I'd like to sit with her for a while.'

Beth nodded.

'I can't believe she's gone. So quickly! All over in what – nine, ten days?'

James didn't answer her at once.

'I feel very guilty that I didn't tell you sooner, Beth – Alice didn't want me to let you know. She had a mild stroke a few weeks ago – a sort of dress-rehearsal for the real thing, I suppose. I only found out recently myself that she'd seen this coming since July.'

Beth looked at him blankly. Why was he telling her this? Of course, he didn't know that she already knew all that from the letters.

'She made me promise to keep it a secret. She said something about telling you one, too, and that we could both swap secrets once she was dead.'

He shrugged.

'I don't know if she was raving, or what. She'd just had the first stroke, the mild one, at that stage. I didn't pay too much attention. But I am sorry for not telling you. She had this awful bloody knack of making me do exactly as she wanted.'

He looked towards the bed, shaking his head, his eyes full.

Beth stood up immediately.

'Don't be sorry. She made me do exactly the same thing.'

He looked at her, startled.

'What do you mean?'

She walked over towards the bedside locker.

'First time in my life I ever did as she asked me, without question. You've no idea how many times I was tempted, how many hints I tried to leave you.'

James just looked at her, his mouth slightly open, eyes blue and confused.

Beth pulled open the locker door, dug her hand into the silky depths of the cosmetic bag, and handed him his bundle of letters.

'I found these the night I arrived. I'm sorry, too, James, I probably should have told you. But it was really important to me that I didn't let her down, just this once.'

His face had paled.

Beth hunched beside him, uncertainly. God, she hoped he wouldn't be angry with her over this. She couldn't bear it if he punished her now with one of his silences. He turned the letters over and over, as though he couldn't quite believe in them.

Finally, he looked at her.

'She'd have been proud of you,' he said quietly.

Beth straightened up, tearful.

'I don't know about that – all I know is that I had to do as she asked for once in my life, without question or qualification, even if it was too late to make any difference.'

She paused for a moment, looking at the still figure in the bed. It helped that she no longer looked like Alice. That's not my mother, Beth thought suddenly. Not really. She's everywhere else in this house, but that's not her lying there. Suddenly, she remembered something from way back, something that Alice had said that had struck her forcibly at the time.

'Alice had one superstition that I know of,' she said to James. 'Do you remember when Granny McKinney died?'

He nodded.

'And we all went down to Sally's?'

'Yes.'

'I asked Alice why the bedroom window was wide open. She looked at me, all surprised. "That's to let her spirit free," she said. "You must always do that when someone dies."'

James looked at Alice, then nodded to Beth.

'Go ahead, then.'

Beth pulled the curtains back and opened the window wide. James stood, his hands in his pockets. Both of them waited until the room grew cold. Beth shut the window again, feeling slightly foolish.

He had sat down by the bed again, back to his usual place.

'I'm going to stay here until morning. Why don't you get some rest?'

Beth hesitated. Then she saw the way he was holding on to his letters. He wanted her to go.

'Will you call me if you change your mind?'

He nodded.

'I will. Try and sleep. We've a busy few days ahead.'

'Good night then – I'll see you in a couple of hours.'

He waited until she had almost left the room.

'Beth?'

'Yes?'

'We did everything we could, didn't we?'

It was half-question, half-statement.

'Yes,' she said, really believing it. No guilt, no 'if onlys'. They had done everything they could. 'We did.'

*

Beth tried to cry quietly. She didn't want to disturb James: God alone knew what he was having to read, right now. She hoped he'd tell her; she'd like to sit up all night with him soon, and pool her memories with his. She had the sense that Alice hadn't quite finished with her, that there would have been more letters, had she had the time. But it was enough: her mother had left her with more than enough.

And Laura's birth *had* made a difference between them: Beth knew that she had still remained hostile, long after Laura's arrival, always on the lookout for any slip-up on Alice's part. She had brought her baby home for the first time proudly, defensively, waiting for a sign, any sign, that she was not a good enough mother. Even at the time, she had had to admit that Alice had behaved impeccably. Struggling to breastfeed Laura, Beth had watched her mother button her lip, over and over again. Not once did she voice what Beth could see her thinking: *That child's hungry, give her a bottle.* Like all her generation, she had believed in science rather than nature. It was a comfortable belief: baring the breast was at best distasteful, at worst – well – somehow, indefinably, immoral. Almost defiantly, Beth had fed her baby in front of Alice in the most public place she could find: Bewley's café in Grafton Street. She could still remember the look on Alice's face as she had unbuttoned her blouse. Seated in the discreet, red velvet booth, she had been conscious of a desire to shock, to provoke a reaction of some kind, to continue the fight that had begun between them when she was twelve or thirteen.

Alice, on the other hand, sipped her coffee and buttered her cherry bun, smiling and nodding as though she'd been watching this all her life. At first, she looked around her rather nervously. They had the booth to themselves, and nobody else seemed to be taking any notice. Even the girl who cleaned the table, sweeping the crumbs on to the floor, clattering plates and cutlery on to a tray already piled mountainously high – even she never as much as looked up. Alice watched baby Laura latch on to feed, saw the way Elizabeth stroked the little head, and kissed the tiny fist, remembering with a shock how she, too, had caressed and kissed the grown woman sitting in front of her. Her eyes filled. Time was such a monster: she'd give anything to have those days back again. If she couldn't have them, then she was damned sure she wasn't going to make the same mistakes again. She made a tremendous effort to regain control, concentrating hard on her cherry bun and the cup of scalding coffee.

Beth looked up, surprised to see Alice's eyes glinting with tears. Or was it a trick of the light? The next time she put down her coffee-cup and looked across at her daughter, her eyes were normal again.

'She's such a lovely baby,' she heard her mother say. 'Just like you were – although I don't remember you or James being as strong as Laura is. I can't believe the way she's holding her head up already.'

Beth felt the warm glow of her mother's approval. She began to relax, to feel her hostility begin to melt, although it was always just below the surface, on the lookout for any slight, any criticism, overt or implied, any hint of disapproval.

Alice saw her daughter's shoulders suddenly relax, her face clear. This is it, she thought to herself. This is how I get her back. She leaned across the table and laid her hand on the soft, downy hair at the back of her granddaughter's head.

'You're doing a wonderful job, Elizabeth. She's such a happy baby. Anyone can see how she's thriving. I'm looking forward to her first smile.'

Beth looked at her then, interested.

'When does that happen – can you remember?'

'I certainly can. James was exactly six weeks old, you were just five weeks, and your first smile was for your father – a real broad, beaming grin. He was delighted.'

And Alice herself smiled broadly at the memory.

Maybe this will be okay, Beth thought. Her mother had not interfered, had not fought with her, not even once on this visit. Filled with sudden generosity, Beth felt sorry for her mother, sorry for all the wounds each had inflicted on the other.

'Why don't you come over next month and stay with us for a few days? We'd love to have you.'

It was almost painful to see the way her mother's face lit up with pleasure.

'I'd love to,' she said, without hesitation.

And it had gone well, all the visits had, until the separation. Even now, as she clutched her pillow, sobbing as silently as she could, Beth knew that the last ten years had been her fault. Too full of anger at the world, she hadn't even given Alice a chance. It hadn't helped that Tony had always been her mother's ally – not that Alice had ever known that, of course. He'd always got on well with her, treated her gently, with perfect, old-fashioned, English courtesy. He had charmed Alice from their first meeting, and she had been nobody's fool.

'You're lucky to have found him,' was what she'd said – but quietly, not squaring up for a fight, no criticism of Beth implicit in the compliment to her husband.

Suddenly, Beth missed Tony with a violence that took her completely by surprise. Why had she let him go? This was just the time of their lives, with Laura grown, when they could really have enjoyed each other: if only she'd stuck it out. Life held enough surprises as it was, surely, without her constant longing for something different, her restless searching after novelty. Wasn't what she had done to Tony every bit as bad as what Olive was now doing to James? Beth felt deeply ashamed at the suddenly perceived similarities between herself and her sister-in-law. Maybe that was why she disliked Olive so much: she saw too much of herself in the woman whose shallowness she despised. Quiet nights at home and the occasional Sunday lunch out: they *could* be okay, as long as you were with the one you loved. Couldn't they? She wanted him to hold her again, to make her laugh at herself, to love her as he once had. She had never missed him like this before, not even once in ten years: this physical ache that seemed all mixed up with love and loss and yearning.

'It's grief talking,' she whispered to herself in the darkness. She would see things differently in the morning.

Shock did strange things to people, at a time like this.

SIX

Leavetaking

ALICE WOKE EARLY, the rain heavy against the front windows of the house. September again; the evenings were already beginning to shorten. In just a few weeks, the clock would go back and winter would be here for real: long dark evenings, without even the possibility of a walk. The thought depressed her. She pulled the curtains back and looked down into the front garden. The grass was already covered with a light blanket of leaves, swirling around the shrubs and rose trees as she watched. She must give Keith a ring; he'd help her rake them up and dump them in the compost heap out the back.

She turned to take her dressing gown off the hook behind the door and suddenly froze. What was she doing here? For several moments, Alice's mind became completely blank. She was conscious of nothing, other than standing there, looking down at her feet. The floor seemed to be swimming away from her, racing off into the distance, the way the sand had pulled at her toes one day when she'd stood by the water's edge in Laytown. The waves had crashed around her feet, drawing her with them, the hideous pull of the water too strong to resist. She'd screamed and her dad had come running, but not before she'd landed flat on her face, nose and mouth breathing in grit and saltiness. She'd howled in terror.

'You silly goose!' he'd said, wrapping her in the big white towel. 'You got dizzy and lost your balance, that's all!'

But she'd cried and cried, still feeling the icy fingers of water clutch malevolently at her ankles.

'I couldn't stand! I couldn't stand!' Alice wailed, clutching the towel around herself warmly. But there was no towel, and she was on her hands and knees in her bedroom, face wet from weeping, palms stinging from her hard fall onto floorboards.

'Jesus, Mary and Joseph,' she whispered. 'What's happening to me?'

Shakily, she pulled herself up to standing, and shuffled uneasily over to her bed. She sat on the edge and waited for the trembling to cease. She examined her hands and knees. No obvious damage. She looked at her watch. It was only a few minutes after nine, so that was okay, then. She wasn't missing hours – whatever had happened to her had taken only a couple of minutes, no more. She felt fine again, now; her head was clear. She'd been going to reach for her dressing gown. Well, she'd be damned if she'd let this, whatever its fancy Latin title was, ruin what was left of her life. Grimly, she stood up and pulled the gown off its hook. She wrapped it around her slowly, making sure the belt was tight, that there was no danger of her tripping on the hem. She wriggled her feet into her slippers, wincing as she did so. Her shoulders had already begun to ache from the impact of the fall.

She made an effort to talk herself through her routine for the day, testing that everything was still in place, that her mind wasn't playing tricks. She began to tremble, shocked by the violence of the vision in her bedroom. She must hold on to the daily, the mundane, she must make sure her grip stayed tight. Today was Sunday, she was going to Mass at twelve and then to James's for a late lunch. Before that, she had to put on the washing machine. And right now, it was time for breakfast.

After two cups of tea, Alice began to feel less frightened. The trembling had stopped, and her mind was sharp. She began to feel optimistic again: back to her usual capable self. The return to clarity reassured her, made her feel more philosophical. After all, this was what she'd been expecting for the past two months: what she had known was bound to happen, eventually. The only question now was one of timing. This morning had been very different from all the other little absences – finding herself sitting on the bathroom floor or rummaging uselessly in a wardrobe were one thing, but falling was quite another.

Perhaps it really was time to tell James. She'd decide today, after lunch, and tell him when he took her home.

*

'All right, Gran?'

Keith kissed her cheek and helped her out of her raincoat.

'Hello, Alice.' Olive came out into the hall, immaculate in a jade-green linen dress. Alice felt the familiar prickle of irritation when she looked at her daughter-in-law. Olive was the only woman she had ever known who managed to wear linen and not crease it.

'Olive,' Alice murmured, obediently kissing her on both cheeks, as had become the younger woman's custom. Much too sweet to be wholesome, she thought, crossly. The kitchen door crashed open, and there was Gemma, flushed, untidy, smelling of roast meat. Almost at once, Olive pushed past her daughter, closing the kitchen door firmly behind her.

'Hiya, Gran!'

Gemma kissed Alice warmly, and Alice hugged her tight, tears springing suddenly to her eyes. She was almost exactly half of James and half of Beth, in looks, in personality, in mannerisms. Alice was glad that Gemma had so little of her mother in her.

'Hello, pet.'

'Come on into the dining room – Eoin and Shea are here, along with Cindy and Jackie.'

She made a comical face, and would have whispered something to Alice except that James suddenly appeared in the hallway behind them.

'Your mother needs you, Gemma,' he said, shortly.

Alice's heart sank. She hoped that Olive wasn't in one of her moods. By the look on James's face, there was something going on. Alice hoped it had nothing to do with her – she'd felt, often, that her presence was an imposition on Olive, that she somehow intruded into her family. It was a long time since she'd made her feel really welcome. Alice reflected briefly, bitterly, that she'd been welcome enough during all the years of free babysitting.

Stop it, she told herself severely, and went resolutely forward, to greet her grandsons and their American girlfriends.

*

'That was a wonderful meal, Olive, thank you.'

Alice tried to keep her voice warm, and grateful. Olive inclined her head, graciously, to the chorus of assenting voices.

'You're all very welcome,' she said, pouring the remains of the dessert wine into Alice's glass. It *had* been a wonderful meal – credit where credit was due. Alice wondered briefly how much of the real work had been done by Gemma.

'What do you think of these two young men, Alice, and their potential to become the family's first millionaires?'

James leaned towards her, jerking his thumb over at his twin sons at the other side of the table.

'I think they're wonderful,' said Alice honestly, 'and I hope all their dreams come true.'

There was a cheer and everyone raised their glasses to Alice's toast. She sat back, then, and observed all the different faces around the table as they became involved in loud, intense, conversations. The wine had made her a little sleepy, and she was content to watch and listen. She felt curiously disconnected from the scene around her, as though she had suddenly dropped in from elsewhere, and all these people were strangers to her. She had a sudden, strong sense of not belonging – a rush of feeling that told her her time was nearly up. The slow crawl of the past couple of months had distorted everything, including her sense of time. It shocked her for an instant to realize that she had loved, and cared for *as babies*, five of the grown adults around this table.

She felt utterly at a loss, too, as to what to make of Cindy and Jackie: first of all, which was which? She couldn't tell them apart, even by the end of the evening. There was a strange sameness to them: long blonde hair, garishly painted fingernails, impossibly tight blue jeans. Alice was careful never to address them by name, in case she got it insultingly wrong. Anyway, they weren't interested in talking to her. Their eyes were only for their men, and they preened themselves constantly, tossing their hair out of their eyes, crossing and uncrossing their legs, smoking. Alice was astonished at the amount they smoked. She'd thought that it was no longer fashionable among young, educated people.

'More coffee?' James asked her.

Startled, she shook her head.

'No, thanks, I'm fine. More than one cup and I'll never sleep.'

He leaned towards her again, concerned.

'You look tired: are you okay?'

She nodded, grateful.

'Fine for another little while. Maybe you could run me home in an hour or so?'

'Of course – just give me the nod.'

Alice sat back again, retreating into herself with

relief. Perhaps it was her new, strange sense of detachment, or perhaps it was obvious to everyone else as well, but Alice suddenly realized that Olive and James had not exchanged a single word during the whole meal. She was sure it wasn't just her imagination. Carefully, she watched them, while pretending to be absorbed in one of Gemma's long, outrageous stories about her first summer job in a London recording studio.

There was a careful physical distance between the two of them, that neither had breached during the course of the long meal. It was only now that Alice noticed how drawn James's face was looking, how quiet he was among his chattering family. He watched his children as they spoke; from time to time, his expression became fond, indulgent. But Alice saw his eyes follow his wife as she left the room to refill the water-jug, and she was suddenly frightened for him. She'd never taken to her son's wife, but that was neither here nor there. James had brought Olive home to meet his mother in the very early stages of their relationship, and Alice had known, instantly, that this was it. His quiet devotion to his girlfriend had reawakened all of Alice's memories of the young Jack. The same old-fashioned constancy, the same single-minded pursuit of what he wanted – but, Alice had thought ruefully, without his father's mischievous sense of humour. She had tried to warm to Olive, tried to treat her as a daughter: a difficult enough feat in itself. But the younger woman had always maintained a cool, impersonal demeanour and Alice had had to become resigned to the wide distances between them.

It was easy to see, too, what had attracted James to

her in the first place, although Alice had been surprised that he had fallen for poise, elegance and ambition; she'd always felt that he would have looked more for warmth and a shared intelligence. Pushy, was what Alice had called Olive to herself, right from the very start. She had bitten her tongue on more than one occasion: James would brook no interference in his life. She could see at once that her son's vanity had been flattered by the depths of his girlfriend's ambition for him. That had made Alice uneasy. But she knew her place. James was an adult; he would make his own adult choices. All she could do was stand on the sidelines and hope that he wouldn't spend the rest of his life picking up the pieces. And they had seemed happy enough up to recently. Alice had to admit that Olive had always been a super-efficient, super-competent mother: it was something James had really loved and admired her for. But now their life together seemed to be turning sour. Alice tried to think back, to remember when she had first seen the signs of danger between them. James had always been a good provider, they had raised children, kept house, gone on holidays together. But now there was something significantly different between them. What had appeared to Alice before as shadows, irritations, occasional out-bursts of exasperation, now took on a definable presence between them. Once she became conscious of that, it seemed to her that she could see it everywhere, all around her. It was like an electrical charge in the atmosphere, a cold blue cloud that hovered over and between them.

'Fanciful old woman!' she said to the mirror crossly,

as she dried her hands in the upstairs bathroom. But she couldn't shake the fancy, and right now she wanted James to take her home. She didn't want to see any more of it, not tonight. And there was certainly no longer any question of her moving in with James, not into an atmosphere like that.

'Ready?' he asked, smiling at her from the hallway. Shocked, she saw Jack's face looking up at her, the same piercing blue of the eyes, the same slightly quizzical expression, head on one side. It was a fleeting familiarity only, and it had already disappeared by the time she reached the bottom step.

'Yes. I'll just pop my head in and say goodbye.'

*

She was happy to be home at last, in the comfort of her own, pared-down nightly rituals. James had been quiet in the car on the way back, and she hadn't liked to disturb him. But she'd felt angry at Olive, nevertheless, feeling the hurt of her own child keenly, even though he was now a middle-aged man. She felt sure that Olive's coldness had something to do with money; she'd place a bet on it. She'd always been an acquisitive woman – nothing wrong with that, in itself, she supposed. But she'd married James because he was different, after all: because she'd enjoyed his other-worldliness, his almost absent-minded attitude towards all things practical. And surely they had enough, anyway? Olive's business seemed to be very successful, although Alice had never quite understood what it was that she did. Something to do with computers. And James's job was steady, secure: the perfect combination. They'd been a good team, as far as Alice could tell. But there was poison in that woman: she could almost smell it. She'd be damned if she'd sit by and let her destroy her son's life. Maybe James wouldn't want to hear what an old woman had to say, but she was going to find a way to say it anyway.

And Beth. All those young people today had disturbed Alice – they all seemed to be in such control of their own lives. They were independent, sure of themselves, self-sufficient – or, at least, that's how they appeared on the surface, and Alice suspected that enough of it was true to be real. It was time she apologized to her daughter for holding on too tight, for making hoops of steel out of bonds of love. Mothers and daughters needed ties that would give a little, would bend and stretch with generosity, not break and unravel at the first tugs of defiance and misunderstanding. She should not have pulled those ties so tight. She had been wrong.

She settled herself once more at Beth's desk, the curtains closed, radiator on low. James had made sure she'd locked the doors and the downstairs windows, had set the alarm himself on his way out. The hug he'd given his mother had been brief, distracted, and had made Alice's heart sore. But there was nothing she could do for him, nothing except shield him for as long as possible from what was happening to her right now. She'd have to be very careful with what she wrote, too. There was a line between loving concern and interference, and she wasn't sure she'd always got it right in the past. She didn't want to cross it now: all she wanted to leave to her children was her unconditional love. She could only hope that they would understand, as she herself had finally done after a long and difficult lifetime, that everyone has choices.

She made an attempt to tidy a space for herself at Beth's desk. As usual, there were photographs strewn all around her. She was getting close to the end of them, though, little by little. She pulled her writing paper towards her, and unscrewed the top of her fountain pen. She would write until she felt too tired to go on. She might as well; she was hardly sleeping at all, these nights.

And if this morning's fall was any indication of how things were going to be, she no longer had even a minute to waste. Although the last several weeks had passed slowly, sometimes painfully so, she could feel her own internal clock speeding up. Time was now clutching at her ankles in the same way as the cold water on Laytown beach over seventy years before.

*

Surely, sleep would come now. Alice had kept writing until well after midnight, inviting exhaustion. She had kept going until her mind had felt stiff, like her fingers. Even her eyes had refused to cooperate, changing her words into blurry, spidery strokes on the blue page, making them swim away from her, into the cloudy distance. She sealed the last envelope and spread her letters out on the desk in front of her. She made two little bundles out of them, one for Beth, one for James, making sure that each envelope was clearly marked.

Then she rummaged in her sewing basket, kept on the bottom shelf of her daughter's wardrobe, and pulled out a length of red ribbon. She used to use this to decorate Christmas cakes; now it had a more lasting purpose. At the last minute, she pulled one envelope from the bottom of the first pile, and put it to one side. Then she tied the ribbon firmly around the two neat bundles, and brought them with her into her bedroom. Stooping, she put them safely into her purple silk cosmetic bag and placed it right at the back of her bedside locker. Almost as an afterthought, she locked the little door, placing the key when she'd finished into her jewellery box. Just in case.

Now she longed for oblivion, for the healing darkness of long, restful sleep. She wanted to cheat her wakefulness: to creep up on pleasant dreams, to steal away with them before they noticed her.

But as soon as she lay down with the light off, the nightly parade of memories started all over again. Tonight, particularly, it frustrated Alice. Now that she needed all of her faculties to survive in the present, it seemed that some perverse old instinct was pulling at her, dragging her back to live in the past. Choosing her memories of and for her children had purpose – but these endless journeys back sixty or seventy years were not welcome; they were beginning to distress her. Sometimes, they took her to places where she had no desire to go. She closed her eyes firmly, breathing deeply as Ellen Crowley had shown her. Gradually, she began to grow still. It was as though she became conscious of falling asleep behind her own eyelids. Her body grew heavy, there was the welcome approach of darkness. She slept.

*

The insistent ringing of the phone finally woke her. She stretched out her right hand and lifted the receiver, feeling a strange weight across her chest as she did so.

'Hello?'

'Alice? Are you all right?'

'Fine, love. Just waking up.'

She took her time with each word: they seemed to want to rush, one into the other, as she spoke.

'You slept well, then? We were worried, you looked very tired yesterday evening.'

'I'm fine; I'll be grand. Really.'

'Sorry – didn't mean to wake you. I'll call you later, all right?'

'Thanks, love. 'Bye.'

Alice hung up carefully. The strange weight on her chest turned out to be her left arm, pressing down on her heavily. As she tried to move it, the numbness turned to tingling. She tried to rub it with her other hand. This felt a lot more serious than pins and needles, but she was too exhausted to work out why. The inside of her head felt strange and very, very tired. She'd just close her eyes again and sleep for another little while.

*

It was late afternoon when Alice finally woke. She looked around her in amazement. Where was she? Gradually, the bedroom came into focus. She could see bright sunlight behind her heavy curtains; there were the sounds of children playing on the street. There was something urgent she had to do, something pressing. Of course – it was Keith's christening tomorrow. She had to put the finishing touches to the cake. And Beth was home. She must put on the coffee for Beth's breakfast.

Alice pulled herself, with difficulty, over to the side of the bed. She shrugged away the useless feeling which seemed to have gathered all down her left side. Barefoot, she went downstairs to the hall, standing for a moment in the flood of sunshine that washed through the stained-glass windows. She smiled with pleasure, feeling her feet grow warm, soaking up deep pools of brightness from the polished floorboards.

Beth must be waiting for her in the kitchen. And she must remember to tread carefully with her prickly daughter; the last thing she wanted to do was make her angry. She would listen very closely to her, too, so that she'd know the right things to say when she told Peggy about all of Beth's successes. Peggy wasn't the only one who could have daughters that did well for themselves.

'It's called a franchise, Mother. It means I own the business, but I rent the name from a more established company, so that I can cash in on their reputation.'

They were sitting together at the kitchen table, drinking tea. Alice's cup and saucer were in front of her, and so was the little gold and white china jug, half-full of milk. Beth was sipping her tea out of a mug. That was one of the things she had to be careful about: she must not mention the mug. Alice was relieved that she had remembered in time.

Beth was still speaking.

'And the business is growing very nicely. It's the same employment agency I got work with almost eight years ago, when I went to London first.'

She sipped at her tea again. Alice was silent, waiting. There was something about London, too, but she couldn't quite put her finger on it.

'Anyway, they made me manager three years ago, and I bought out the franchise last January. I've got four people working for me, now.'

Alice nodded. That was a good thing, wasn't it?

There was a wallet containing photographs on the table, just in front of Beth. Alice watched as her daughter pushed them towards her.

'These are of my new house, in Greenwich. I live right beside the common, where the Observatory is. Take a look.'

Now Alice felt comfortable. This was something she could understand, something she could be enthusiastic about. A house! A good investment, so much better than throwing your money away on one of those rented places. Flats were such a silly idea – good money after bad, she always said. She pulled the glossy photos out of their wallet, and pored over them, one by one. Beth was smiling, but Alice felt her disappointment grow, picture after picture. She had to remember to be extra-careful here, not to criticize, not to exclaim over the bad condition of the floors, the problem with damp, the tangle of briars and undergrowth which her daughter called a *garden*. But she couldn't help herself. She remembered all the natty little terraced houses that she'd hankered after, at the end of the War, hankered after even still, if the truth be told. Surely there must be lots of those in London?

'Would it not have been easier to buy a new house? That looks like an awful lot of work to me.'

The sunshine in the kitchen was abruptly shattered, and Beth, tight-lipped, was stuffing the photographs back into the wallet. She took her mug immediately over to the sink.

Alice continued hurriedly.

'I'm sure it will be lovely when you've finished – what do you plan to do first?'

But she was already too late. Beth was looking at her watch.

'I haven't decided. Look, I'd better be getting over to James's. I promised Olive I'd pick up the wine for tomorrow. I'll probably be back by tea-time.'

She dried the mug briskly. Alice was afraid to tell her that that was the hand-towel, not the tea-towel. She'd wash the mug again after Beth left.

'Do you want anything from the shops?'

'No thank you, dear.'

And then she was gone. Alice was puzzled. Her cup and saucer seemed to have been whisked away into thin air, just when she was about to sip at her tea. And she hadn't heard the back door slam, either. How come she was still sitting at the table in her nightdress? She never did that – she rarely even came downstairs in her dressing gown, unless to bring a cup of tea back up to bed. And her feet were cold. Where were her slippers? Suddenly, James was beside her. Confused, she looked around her. There were no signs of Beth. Was this some sort of test? Was James a trick of the light?

He was kneeling by her chair, had taken her cold hands in his.

'Alice? Are you all right?'

She squeezed his hands. They were warm, real. And there was a different quality to James's presence now, a reassuring solidity which Beth's had somehow lacked. She thought carefully for a moment. This seemed right; it couldn't be Keith's christening tomorrow – she'd just seen him recently, and he was a man, one who raked her garden, held her coat for her, drank tea with her.

'James?' she said cautiously, expecting him to disappear in a puff of smoke.

'Yes – it's me,' he said, rubbing her hands. Even she could hear the relief in his voice.

'I think,' she said carefully, 'that I've had a little turn.'

She tested the words on herself; they sounded right, too. It meant that she could still understand, still follow what seemed to have happened to her.

'I think you're right. Come on, let's get you back upstairs. You're freezing.'

Tucked up in bed again, there were still gaps she needed to understand.

'How did you know?' she asked, almost shyly, hoping that there wasn't some fearfully simple answer that everyone but she would automatically know.

'Mrs McGrath called me. She was worried that she hadn't seen you at Mass or at the shops this morning. And you didn't answer when the vegetable man called.

When your curtains were still closed at four, she phoned me.'

Alice nodded. Yes, all of that made sense. Vegetable man meant Mondays; Sunday she had been at James's.

'Did you speak to me this morning?'

He nodded.

'Yes. We'd all been worried to see you looking so tired yesterday. I phoned around ten, but you sounded groggy.'

So that was all right, then. It was all adding up. Things had only been funny since this morning.

'What time is it now?' she asked suddenly.

'Half past four. Ellen Crowley is on her way – and I want no arguments.'

He poured her a glass of water, which she took, and sipped at meekly.

'You'll get none,' she said.

*

'So, what's the diagnosis?'

'I'll want to check you out more thoroughly when you feel up to it, but for now, I think I can safely say that you've had a very *mild* stroke, but a stroke nevertheless.'

Ellen was packing her blood pressure gauge into her doctor's bag. Alice spoke to her quietly.

'This is what we discussed after the hospital in July, isn't it?'

Ellen nodded.

'Yes, it is. You're going to have to take things very easy, Alice, and I want blood tests done as soon as

247

possible. We may need to put you on to blood-thinning medication to avoid the possibility of another attack. Also, it's probably better for you not to be on your own so much.'

'I don't want to go to hospital.'

Ellen smiled at her.

'That's not necessary right now. But you do need to let someone know you're all right, on a regular basis. And perhaps your grandchildren could take it in turns to stay over at night.'

Alice nodded.

'I'll be sensible, I promise. But I really don't want to give up my independence.'

Besides, she was feeling clear-headed again. Exhausted, certainly, but no longer confused. She'd take her future a day at a time.

Ellen nodded.

'I know. And I know you'll be sensible. And you know where I am if you need me. It'll take me a couple of days to arrange for your tests, but I'll call you before the end of the week.'

'Thanks, Ellen.'

She could hear the lowered voices outside her bedroom door. She was grateful to James for not intruding: he could have insisted on being present, on taking charge, stealing her autonomy from her – all for her own good, of course. But he'd chosen to respect her privacy instead, had treated her as a competent human being, not as a helpless, stricken victim.

He came back into her bedroom after Ellen had gone.

'I'm staying tonight, in my old room. You can shout if you need me. We'll talk tomorrow about whatever needs to be done.'

He bent down and kissed her forehead.

'Right now, I'm going to make you some chicken soup.'

He smiled at her, and made his way towards the bedroom door.

'James?'

'Yes?'

'Please don't tell Beth, not yet.'

He came back and sat down on the side of her bed.

'Alice, I can't do that. It's just not fair.'

'Please, James. I need the time without everyone fussing over me. Tell you what, you keep this secret, and I'll tell Beth one, too. Then you can both swap secrets after I'm gone.'

He smiled at her childlike tone.

'I can't promise that.'

'Give me a week – let's decide from week to week. Please.'

He sighed.

'All right – you can have one week. But I still don't feel right about it.'

Satisfied, Alice lay back, sinking into the grateful softness of her pillows. She felt sleep approach, almost at once. Surprised, she allowed herself to be carried away on the first wave. She'd just rest for a little while; James was sure to wake her for her soup.

*

She opened her eyes to find him standing by her bedside.

'Have you got my soup?' she asked, not liking him to think that she'd nodded off, that she hadn't waited for him.

He grinned at her.

'It's a bit cold after fourteen hours sitting in the kitchen, but I'll heat it up for breakfast if you like.'

Fourteen hours! She hadn't slept that long a stretch since she was an infant.

'Is it really morning again?'

'It sure is. What would Madam like for breakfast, apart from cold chicken soup?'

'I'd like to come down to the kitchen. I want to see how steady I am on my pins, while you're here.'

He nodded.

'Good idea.'

To her surprise, she pulled on her dressing gown with relative ease, the heaviness in her left arm having become a tingling sensation, more like the warm aftermath of night-time cramp. She negotiated the stairs without difficulty, aware all the time of James, of his eyes on her, watching. She filled the kettle by resting it in the sink and turning on the tap with her right hand: her left seemed to have lost most of its strength. She saw James glance at all the yellow notes stuck to the tiles.

'That's how I manage to cope with being forgetful,' she said firmly. 'And I'm quite happy to write as many as you want, and to keep in touch as often as you want. But I'm not leaving my home.'

He took the teapot off the dresser.

every day until term started. There was something else, too, something she wanted to do on her own: the sheets needed changing, that was it. It would be a good test, good therapy for her, to see how long this familiar job took, now that she was feeling strong again. She was looking forward to the challenge: she must never give up, must not turn her face to the wall.

Full of purpose now, she padded out in bare feet to the hot-press on the landing. She chose the warm winter sheets, blue flannelette with an all-over pattern of little pink sprigged flowers. She felt awkward as she reached up to the second shelf, surprised that she needed her left arm so much – she'd thought it would have been more of a silent partner. It was strange to miss it. Dragging the old sheets off her bed made her pause for breath several times. Her left arm seemed to increase in useless-ness just when she needed it most. Once she had the mattress stripped, she had to lie down for several min-utes, waiting for her heartbeat to return to normal. She could barely face the rest of the task on her own. She'd have to ask for help to smooth the new sheets into place, to plump up the pillows. But pride suddenly gave her strength. Bit by bit, she eased the clean sheets on to the bed, leaving the tucking-in part until later. The whole thing had taken her almost two hours; she was exhausted by it and she knew she should stop. It would be reasonable to ask for help with the blankets, they were heavy at the best of times. Alice felt that the more competent she appeared, the less likely James would be to tell Beth. And she wasn't ready for Beth, not just yet. There were too many things she had to tidy up in her

own head, first. She had so much to do, and so little
energy available to her. And now, there was no question
of her leaving the house today. She'd missed Mass,
anyway, and was much too tired to think of shopping.
She was going to have to consider her limitations,
instead, and how she was going to cope with them.

Downstairs in the silent kitchen, she made herself a
promise. If asking for help was the ironic price of
holding on to her independence for as long as possible,
then so be it. It was astonishing to think of all that she
had been able to do, even up to a couple of weeks ago,
but that way madness lay. This was the new normal,
this failing physical strength was what she had to get
used to. As long as she could hold on to her *self*, then it
didn't really matter if she could make up her bed on her
own or not.

The doorbell rang suddenly and Alice jumped. Now
who could that be? She made her way to the front door,
unable to make out the figure standing in her porch.
She opened the door cautiously.

'Mrs McGrath!' she said in surprise.

Her neighbour was standing there, a small bunch of
delicious-smelling freesias in one hand, a brown-paper
bag in the other. She was smiling a little nervously, as
though she didn't quite know what to expect.

'Mrs Keating – I hope I'm not disturbing you. I
didn't see you out this morning, and I was concerned.
I was speaking to James the other day, and he said you
were feeling a little better.'

She spoke in a rush: Alice could see that she was
embarrassed, that she didn't quite know the etiquette of

this new situation. How on earth did you explain to your neighbour that you'd thought she was dead, but were now quite pleased to see her standing in her hallway?

'Please, come in.' Alice held the door wide open. It suddenly amused her to think that this woman had been her neighbour for over fifty years, and yet neither of them had ever crossed the other's threshold before now. She had always regarded Mrs McGrath as nosey, and she had learned over the years that Mrs McGrath had always thought of her as uppity. They had spoken from time to time when the children were young, but each of them had chosen to keep her distance from the other. Now Alice was genuinely grateful to her – without Mrs McGrath's sharp eye a few weeks ago, she, Alice, could have wandered around the house on her own, ill and lonely, for an awful lot longer than she had. Now that they were both nearly eighty, 'nosey' and 'uppity' were hardly such mortal sins any more. There were much more important things to worry about.

Mrs McGrath hesitated to come inside: fifty years of formality would have to be overcome in a single step. It was quite a jump.

'I've got the kettle on,' offered Alice, and that seemed to do the trick. More tea, her neighbour's warm brown scones, and Alice's genuine effort to be welcoming made the rest of the morning disappear. Mrs McGrath only got up to leave when she heard James's key in the front door.

'Don't forget, now,' she said. 'You know I go to ten Mass every morning, like yourself. If you don't feel like going out, just give me a ring. I'll be glad to pick up whatever you want at the shops.'

'Thank you,' said Alice, touched by her simple kindness. She felt suddenly warm and cared for: tea with Mrs McGrath, lunch with James and then Gemma this afternoon, once school was over. This was a rhythm she could get used to. It was life at a very different pace, to be sure, but life none the less. If this was as bad as it got, she could learn to be content.

*

'Gran?'

'In here, love.'

Alice was sitting in her favourite armchair, with the tartan rug tucked around her. She was having increasing difficulty in keeping her feet and hands warm. James had lit the fire before he left, the late-September afternoon grown damp and chill. And no matter what he did, this old house continued to be draughty. Pulling the heavy curtains helped, but Alice liked to postpone that for as long as possible. She didn't like shutting out the natural daylight before she had to; besides, the green sweep of the grass soothed her, and she liked the orange and red frenzy of the swirling leaves.

Gemma burst into the room, breathless, trailing her usual cloud of energy with her. She knelt at once beside Alice's chair.

'How're you today, Gran – good?'

'All the better for seeing you,' Alice replied, kissing the young cheek made cold and ruddy by the sudden east wind.

'I'd better be careful, then – that's what Little Red Riding Hood's granny said – and she turned out to be a wolf!'

Alice laughed.

'Haven't you seen what big teeth I've got?'

Gemma threw her school coat onto the other fireside chair, and sat on the rug, spreading her hands towards the blaze.

'Cuppa?' she asked.

'No thanks, not yet. There's something I want to do upstairs, and I need your help. I'd like us to do it now, before we get distracted by anything else.'

Alice had made careful note of this task, sitting at Beth's little desk upstairs. She was ticking off her list, night after night, making sure each item on it was completed in the right order. She wanted to leave no loose ends for others to tidy up, wanted no quarrels or dissension after she died.

Gemma scrambled to her feet.

'Okay – let's go.'

Arm in arm they went upstairs to her bedroom. Alice was a little breathless when she reached the top, and had a moment of confusion when she felt Elizabeth's hand on her arm, and had been about to turn to her daughter in surprise. Just then, Gemma spoke, and the spell was broken.

'Here we are.'

'Sit down on the bed there,' said Alice, and went over to her dressing table. She opened the jewellery box that James had given her, and pulled out three pieces wrapped in tissue-paper. She sat down beside Gemma, and took her granddaughter's hand.

'I want you to choose one of these pieces of jewellery for yourself . . .'

Alice got no further with her speech. Gemma suddenly erupted into tears, and drew her hands quickly away from Alice's.

'No! I know just what you're doing and I don't want to! I don't want you to die! You're the only one I can really talk to!'

It seemed for an instant that she would get up off the bed and run for the door, but instead, she flung her arms around her grandmother's neck and sobbed. Alice held her close until the storm of tears had abated. They had been close these last few years, with Gemma coming to her more and more as Olive put increasing pressure on her only daughter to be different, to be other than she was. Alice was old enough to appreciate the irony.

'Sweetheart, I hope to be around for a long time yet,' Alice lied, 'but my memory isn't what it used to be. I really want you to have something precious that once belonged to me – I can't do that if you won't help me.'

Gemma wiped her eyes with the backs of her hands. Alice smiled at the gesture. It reminded her so much of Beth on the rare occasions when she had cried – she used to make the same angry gesture, furious at herself for her tears, for showing weakness in the face of the enemy.

'I just want you to put your name on it, so that I

can be happy, knowing it's gone to the right person. Once you've chosen, I'm going to put it away – the other pieces are for Laura and your mother.'

Alice unwrapped the delicate paper. Gemma watched, fascinated despite herself.

'These are very old pieces – they belonged to your grandad's mother, so they've been around for well over a hundred years. I don't know what they're worth, but that's not the point. They're of huge sentimental value to me, and I want you to have the one you like best.'

Alice stroked her granddaughter's hair, and watched as the young eyes filled again. She was such a little softie that Alice felt a sudden stab of anxiety for her. She hoped that life would treat her kindly.

'Can you tell me something about where they came from?' said Gemma, gesturing to the pieces on the bedspread. Alice unwrapped the first tissue-paper parcel, a gold locket on a heavy chain. She'd polished it recently until it gleamed. She pressed the little catch and the locket sprang open, revealing two tiny photographs of a dark-haired man and a fragile, pretty woman.

'These are your great-grandparents, on the Keating side, John and Margaret. They were married in 1918, just after the First World War. He'd been a soldier in the British Army, and apparently he'd never talk about his experiences. Your grandad Jack always believed he'd died young because of what had happened to him in France. He'd been with . . . let me see, I have it written down here somewhere . . . yes. He'd been part of the Dublin Fusiliers, the sixteenth Irish Division. They'd fought at the Somme and at Messines. Your grandad

Jack said it had been an absolute massacre. His father was not the same man when he came back from France. I think that James has done a lot of research on this period – you should ask him.'

Gemma's eyes were wide, fascinated.

'I will ... He has talked about it, but I never realized ... I mean, this makes it all seem so much closer.'

Alice smiled. She could remember exactly the same expression on James's face, probably thirty-five years before, when he'd come across old photographs and a campaign medal belonging to his grandfather. She'd liked the thought of another link forged between the generations. She'd been pleased then at James's obvious interest, and she was pleased again now. Something else for him and Gemma to enjoy; another thread of shared history to pull them closer together. Perhaps it would be something to hold on to amidst the wreckage of their own family, which Alice knew was fast approaching. She continued.

'Anyway, John Keating had a farm near ours in County Meath, his family's land, and his family had lived and worked there for donkey's years. But something happened to him and he had to give it up – Jack said his father had got so the silence of the countryside unnerved him completely. Now this was several years later, long after the War, but poor John kept waiting for explosions – even walking the fields terrified him; so they sold up and moved to Dublin. They were lovely people; Margaret was a pet. I was very fond of both of them.

'I cut these pictures out of a copy I had made of an old wedding photo of theirs, so that you could see what they looked like. They were both only in their mid-fifties when they died. Margaret died first, of a heart attack, and then John, only six months later. He just gave up living without her.'

Alice paused, surprised at the strong feelings she'd stirred up, talking like this to Gemma. She remembered the awful yawning emptiness after Jack died, in a senseless repetition of his own parents' untimely deaths. She wondered how long she, Alice, would have lasted if Beth and James hadn't dragged her back to life again, hadn't demanded that she put them first.

'It was a pity that neither of them lived to see their grandchildren – I've been so much luckier.'

Gemma managed a smile. She picked up the next piece.

'And this?'

It was a tiny solitaire.

'That's Margaret's engagement ring. She had very small hands, as you can see.'

'Were they happy, her and John?'

'Yes, I think so – when he got ill, I think things were very hard, but yes, they'd been happy together.'

'And you and Grandad, were you happy?'

Gemma was twirling the ring around, her eyes fixed on it. Alice thought she knew where these questions were coming from. She'd have to be very careful with what she said.

'Yes, we were. Not every minute of every day, you can't be happy like that, not all the time. And every marriage has its ups and downs, some years are better than others. But yes, I loved him, and I am glad I married him.'

Gemma nodded.

'Did you fight over money?'

'Yes,' said Alice honestly, 'we did, particularly at first. Your grandad was a hopeless case when it came to managing money, and in the early days we were often hard up. He'd give it away to anyone who asked him, without realizing that there wasn't enough to go round. It's not a happy way to be.'

'But when you *did* have enough, did you still fight?' Gemma persisted.

Alice could feel herself begin to sweat. This couldn't wait for another letter – she'd have to find some way, soon, to tell James of his daughter's distress.

'I don't remember ever having enough – but don't forget your grandad died very young. I had to struggle along on very little money on my own.'

It wasn't an answer, and it probably wasn't even completely honest, but it was the best Alice felt she could do, for now.

'And this?'

Gemma had picked up the third piece, a simple gold bangle, most of the engraving worn away by time. But still visible on the inside, were the words 'Margaret from John, 10th March 1920'.

'That's a gift from John to your great-grandmother, to mark your grandad Jack's birth. He was an only child, you know. There were no brothers and sisters.'

Gemma nodded.

'They're all beautiful. But I really like the locket best – I like feeling part of their story.'

Alice smiled. She had hoped that Gemma would say that.

'Maybe you might get round to tracing the Keating family history, one day. Now that you know some of the background.'

'Can you do that?' Gemma asked in surprise. 'I'd love to do something like that.'

Alice wrapped the three pieces and put them back in her jewellery box. As soon as Gemma went, she'd make sure to put the locket in a little box, with her name on it. It wouldn't be right to do it in front of her. The child seemed to be upset enough, as it was. Maybe she wouldn't give a piece to Olive, after all. She'd been right; that woman was causing trouble, more trouble than she might be able to handle.

She turned to her granddaughter, and smiled at her.

'Let's see if we can find any more photographs to help the new family historian. The Genealogy Office will help you do the rest. What about that, and a cup of tea?'

*

She was exhausted after Gemma left. This business with James and Olive was obviously very serious. How was she going to broach the subject without James going all stiff and silent on her?

She closed her eyes. She really couldn't think about it any more. She was much too tired. She'd just snooze by the fire for a little while, and then go up to bed. She hadn't the energy to tackle the stairs just yet.

*

Alice had no idea where she was when she woke. There was a bright pool of light by her right elbow, and she turned her head in that direction. Her cup and saucer were there, on the little table, lit by the gleam of the small lamp. Relieved, she sat up and looked around her. The familiar pieces of furniture in the sitting room arranged themselves in the shadows while she waited for her eyes to focus more clearly. She must have fallen asleep downstairs, then. Was it daytime, or night-time? The fire was out, and the room had grown chilly.

She glanced at her watch. Four o'clock. Cautiously, she took the rug off her knees and folded it over the back of the chair. Picking her way carefully across to the window, she pulled the velvet curtain open, just a chink. Darkness. It was still night, then. That fitted. Then she remembered: she had sat down after Gemma left, promising to go to bed straight away. Never mind, no harm done. She obviously hadn't gone wandering, and she was still in one piece. There were no gaps, either – she'd been simply asleep, so all her time was accounted for. It was like having an unruly child in the house again: it was exhausting, keeping track of what her mind might make her do at any moment, when she wasn't looking. She'd take a hot-water bottle up to bed with her now; her hands and feet felt completely numb.

While she stood in the kitchen, waiting for the kettle

to boil, she noticed that the tradescantia on the far window-sill was looking droopy: when had it been watered last? Immediately, she pulled the little yellow block of paper towards her and wrote, with difficulty, her fingers still stiff: *Water plants.* This she stuck beside the other messages on the tiles. She walked to the far end of the kitchen and took the plant pot off the ledge. She noticed how light it felt: it was obviously suffering badly from drought.

She couldn't work out what happened next. She'd her route all mapped out: back over to the sink, put plant on draining board, fill jug with water, water plant. She had begun that journey, she knew she had, but suddenly the world stood still. She watched, in slow motion, as the planter slipped from her fingers and came crashing down on to the hard surface of the red, glazed kitchen tiles. It seemed that the sound took a great deal of time to travel to her ears. When it did, she jumped, startled, as though she had made no connection between the shattered bits of plant pot and the explosion of sound all around her.

She looked at the floor helplessly. Dried soil had scattered everywhere, dangerous splinters of ceramic lurked in the grouting between the tiles. What if she forgot, and walked here in her bare feet? She reached in under the sink for the dustpan and brush. Within minutes, perspiration was beading across her forehead, and anger at her own helplessness was making her weep with frustration. No matter what she did, her two hands would not work together. The dustpan kept facing the wrong direction, the brush pushed the soil to the left, or to the right – wherever the dustpan was not. It was as though these two inanimate objects had acquired a mischievous mind of their own, and had decided to tease without mercy the old woman trying to clean up her kitchen at four o'clock in the morning.

She sat down, breathless, the job only half-done. Maybe Gemma would call again in the afternoon. If so, she'd get her to finish it. She was much too downhearted to continue. Alice reflected that her old age was now an inescapable process of becoming more and more aware of her own body. Even five years ago, she'd never have needed to think about it: her physical self had operated independently of her will. A few aches and pains here and there, sure, but she'd been lucky. Now her stroke had plunged her into a new knowledge of things that didn't function as they should. This was no longer dying in small steps. This was a huge leap into the darkness.

She filled her hot-water bottle very carefully, suddenly terrified of the kettle full of potential danger. She made her way slowly up the stairs. She'd love a bath, but even that simple pleasure was forbidden unless there were someone else in the house. She'd ask Gemma to stay a bit later, tomorrow. A shower wasn't the same thing, at all; she wanted to lie down and be soothed by lots of hot water.

Shivering, she climbed into bed. She must remember not to fall asleep downstairs, in future. She'd grown far too cold. She might even have to give in, at this rate, and put James's electric blanket on the bed. That is, if he'd let her. Everything seemed to be fraught with so much peril these days.

*

'Alice? Where are you?'

James made his way rapidly down the hallway to the kitchen. He opened the door and the clouds of smoke burned his lungs, made his eyes water.

'Jesus Christ!' he cried, frightened now. 'Alice? Alice?'

She was not in the kitchen. He opened the back door, and the smoke was sucked out into the stormy morning. A large saucepan had burned completely dry on the cooker. He fumbled at the switch underneath, turning off the heat. Then he grasped the handle of the pot in a bunched-up tea-towel and fired the whole lot out into the back garden. He looked around him, quickly. The floor was unusually dirty, bits of soil everywhere, but everything seemed to be safe. Now where was his mother? His heart pounding, dreading what he was going to find, he ran back to the sitting room and wrenched the door open.

A cup and saucer sat innocently on the table beside her armchair, her rug was folded carefully, and draped over the back. Gemma had given her tea just before she left, and her medication, so what had she done then, where had she gone next?

He took the stairs two at a time and paused for a moment outside her bedroom. He didn't want to frighten her. He knocked on the door, smartly.

'Alice? Are you in there?'

There was no reply. He pushed the door open and stepped inside. The bed had been slept in, thank God – for a moment, he felt a great wave of relief. He'd been terrified she'd gone wandering, out on the streets all night long. He felt the sheets – still warm. She couldn't be far, then, but why wasn't she answering the mobile? If everything was all right, why wouldn't she answer the phone?

He knocked on the bathroom door, and opened it almost at once. There was no sense of her being in the house – some instinct told him she was already gone, roaming around God only knew where. He was just about to leave when something caught his eye. Curiously, he bent down. What on earth was the mobile doing in the *bath*? He picked it up and put it into his jacket pocket. This was not looking good – the burnt saucepan on the stove, the mobile left behind, no sign of Alice anywhere. He'd try Mrs McGrath first, and then he was going to the police. He hoped he wasn't already too late.

*

Alice pulled her coat more tightly around her. It had gone very cold, and she didn't like the feel of the strong wind through her nightdress. She'd remembered to put her boots on, though, so at least her feet were warm. She hoped that Brutus and Rusty wouldn't get too restless waiting for her to come home. It was too bad that they'd run out of dog food: she wouldn't be a bit surprised if Peggy had done it deliberately, just to annoy her.

There were an awful lot of cars on the road this morning. There must be something going on in the village, but surely Mam would have told her? At least she wouldn't have to cross the road. She was only allowed to go as far as Mr Courtney's because it was on the same side as *Abbotsford*, and she didn't have to leave the footpath, not even once. But it seemed a much longer walk than usual, today.

Alice felt in her pockets for her mitts. They weren't there, she must have left them on the table in the hall. Instead, her fingers closed around a key that she had never seen before. What was it doing in her pocket? She buttoned her coat up to the neck, and stuck her cold hands into the sleeves. When she looked down, she saw that the ends of her dress were getting wet. She was puzzled: this wasn't a dress that she recognized. Had she taken one of Peggy's, by mistake?

She walked close to the kerb, stepping over every second crack in the stone, the way she and Peggy always did. You won if you got to fifty, without lifting your eyes from the ground.

The blare of a horn startled Alice, and she stepped off the kerb in fright. A car swerved, missing her narrowly, splattering her from head to toe with dark, mucky stuff. Dismayed, she looked down at her coat. It was ruined. Mam would be cross now.

She tried to brush herself down, using her sleeves, but her left arm didn't seem to be working too well. Maybe she'd be able to clean herself off once the muck dried. She was here, at last, and Mr Courtney's shop was open.

She pushed hard at the glass door, wondering why the bell didn't sound. She looked around her, puzzled. Things didn't seem to be in their usual place. And Mr Courtney wasn't behind the counter, either. Instead, there were two girls Alice had never seen before, giggling and nudging while they placed cans and bottles on the shelves, nodding in her direction. Dismayed, she looked down at her coat again. She must look like a right sight.

*

'Yes, sir, can I help you?'

James stood at the counter, a young garda half his age getting up to speak to him.

'My mother is missing. She's not well, she had a stroke recently, and . . .'

'How long has she been missing, sir?'

'I don't really know. At least, she slept in her bed last night, so she probably went off early this morning . . .'

'Have you checked with the rest of the family, sir, and the neighbours?'

'Yes. Well, not all of them – she's not in the habit of spending time with her neighbours . . . Look, she had a stroke a couple of weeks ago, and I'm afraid she's off somewhere, not knowing where she is. She knows she's to have this mobile with her, but I found it in the bath.'

He was beginning to get impatient. Were they going to wait for something ridiculous like twenty-four hours before they even *started* to look for her?

'What's your mother's name?'

James cut across him, rudely.

'When are you going to start looking for her?'

The garda looked at him levelly.

'As soon as we have her details and a physical description, I'll radio the local squad car to keep a look out for her. I can't do that until you give me some information, sir.'

'I'm sorry – I'm sorry. I'm just terrified that something has happened her.'

The garda nodded. James took a deep breath: what might Alice look like now, if she'd left the house heedlessly, unaware of herself?

'Her name is Alice Keating, she lives at "Woodvale", 27 Avonmore Grove. She's seventy-six years of age, tall – five foot eight – white hair usually in a bun.'

'Have you any idea what she's wearing, sir?'

'No, I'm afraid I never even checked. She has a green raincoat, and a heavy tweed overcoat which she wears in the winter . . .'

He stopped. He was aware that he was babbling.

'I'll check to see which coat is missing. I'll phone you.'

'When did you last see her, sir?'

'Last night, about eight o' clock – my daughter saw her. She said she was fine. I rang the house phone this morning and then the mobile, when I got no answer. That was about ten o'clock.'

'And you went to the house?'

'Yes – and a saucepan had burned dry – the place was full of smoke. There was dirt all over the kitchen floor – it's not like her.'

'All right, sir. I'll put the word out. If you think of anything else that would help, let us know.'

'Should I make sure there's someone at her home, in case she comes back?'

It seemed such an obvious thing to do that James felt immediately foolish.

'Don't answer that,' he said, grinning in spite of himself.

The garda smiled back at him.

'Go back and phone everyone you can think of that she might have gone to see. Have the neighbours keep an eye out. And I suggest you check out the local shops. Don't worry – she won't have gone far.'

James hoped he was right. He remembered Alice telling him of a time when he had gone missing as a toddler, when the whole road had turned out in force to search for him. She had been distraught: she'd even sent someone to get his father from work when they'd been searching for over three hours without success. Eventually, they'd found him: asleep in a neighbour's garden shed, clutching a small fistful of dinkies, totally unaware that he'd strayed.

Now it was time to pray for the same again: only this time, their roles had been reversed.

*

Alice had forgotten whatever it was she was looking for. Perhaps if she walked up and down the aisles once more, it would come to her. She didn't think she'd run out of tea – she'd never run out of tea, not once in all her married life. Bread, perhaps, or milk? She continued her search, stopping now and then to peer at items on the well-stocked shelves.

Suddenly, someone caught hold of her elbow, but gently. She turned to face a blonde young woman with brown eyes.

'Mrs Keating?'

Alice thought for a moment. She was doubtful. She started to shiver, suddenly cold to her bones.

'Are you sure?' she asked the young woman. It wasn't a name that felt familiar to her, but then, nothing felt familiar right now. She noticed the way this young woman was dressed in a very sensible rain-jacket: big and bright yellow, one that no one could miss on the dark country roads.

'Your first name is Alice, isn't that right? I'm Ann. Why don't we get you home now and out of those wet clothes before you catch cold?'

Alice looked around her. There was no one she knew here. The shop was almost silent, the two young girls chewing gum, staring at her. She began to feel frightened. Alice was a nice name, and this Ann seemed kind.

'Yes, yes – that's a good idea. I need to go home – I'm in a hurry; my children will be waiting for me.'

'Let me give you a lift. My car is just outside. It's an awful day, isn't it? You must be absolutely soaked.'

Alice allowed herself to be steered out of the shop. There was no sign of Mr Courtney – neither he nor Mrs Courtney was anywhere to be seen – and she didn't like it here any more. The young woman opened the rear passenger door of a waiting car. There was a man standing beside it, taking a last pull on the cigarette cupped in his right hand. She had known someone else, once, who used to smoke like that. The half-memory disturbed her. But this man was clean, not covered in coal-dust, and his blue uniform reassured her. She looked again at the young woman who was holding her arm. She smiled at Alice, and Alice felt that she might know her, after all. That smile reminded her of someone, too, someone she had once been fond of.

'We're going to drive you home now, Mrs Keating. Your son is waiting for you.'

Alice frowned. She fingered the key in her coat pocket. She struggled to make the connection that was prodding at her, trying to break the surface, like a swimmer coming up for air. Suddenly, she got it.

'I live in a house with three others!' she said, triumphantly.

The woman called Ann turned and smiled at her.

'That's fine; we'll have you back there before you know it,' she promised.

Relieved now that she had said what was important, Alice put her head back and closed her eyes. So tired, so very tired.

*

James was standing at the front door, waiting. Thank God they'd found her so quickly. Wandering around the local Spar, of all places. It wasn't even the one she normally went to; there was another one much closer by. Luckily, the owner had spotted Alice, dressed in nightie and tweed coat, white hair flowing, and had had the sense to call the Gardai. James had wept with relief.

'She's not hurt, Mr Keating, just very confused. I don't think she knows who she is. She told us she lived in a house with three others.'

The young garda spoke kindly, in a low voice, before she opened the car door for Alice. James nodded, shocked into silent grief as a pinched face, framed with wild white hair, peered up at him from the back seat. For one insane moment, he thought of the witches from *Macbeth*. This was the wrong woman: this was some other poor mother who'd plodded off into the murky distance, looking for something to understand, something that finally made sense.

'Thank you, thank you both very much. I'll look after her now.'

'Do you need a lift to Beaumont Hospital, sir?'

The driver spoke courteously to James, his arms folded, leaning on the roof of the squad car.

'No, thanks, Guard – I'll get her cleaned up first. Our GP is meeting us there in an hour.'

'Goodbye, Mrs Keating.'

Ann had held out her hand to Alice. She shook it gravely.

'Goodbye,' she said.

She turned to James, smiling.

'What a nice young woman,' she said.

Then her face clouded over. She peered at him, tucking strands of hair behind her ears as the wind caught them. She was looking at him shyly, half-quizzically, her head a little to one side. For a moment, she resisted his hands on her arms.

'Do I know you?' she asked.

*

James brought her straight into the kitchen, where it was warmest. He had no idea how he was going to approach the idea of a bath, or a change of clothes: to her, he was a complete stranger.

'Would you like a cup of tea?' he asked politely, keeping his distance from her, terrified she would take fright, and bolt like some startled animal if she felt crowded.

'Yes, please,' she said, pulling her coat around her, folding her arms decisively.

Carefully, he took things out of the kitchen presses and off the dresser shelves that he knew would be familiar to her. One of her best china cups with its fluted saucer, the yellow teapot, the willow-patterned plate she always used for biscuits. He took the carton of milk out of the fridge and placed it on the table in front of her while he filled the kettle.

'Where's the jug? You know I hate cartons or bottles on the table!'

Her sudden tone was sharp, the way James remembered it from time to time when he was a child.

He wheeled around from the sink to face her.

'Alice?' he said, hardly daring to hope.

'James?' she asked, suddenly inhabiting her own face again.

He must take this carefully. He didn't want to alarm

or upset her. He knelt down beside her chair, taking both of her cold hands in his.

'Are you all right?' he asked her gently.

'I seem – have I had another turn?'

Her voice was full of dismay, like a child's.

He nodded.

'Just a little one. You went out . . . into the back garden with just a coat over your nightie. I'm afraid you've got a bit mucky.'

She looked down at her boots.

'Oh, dear,' she said. 'That's a bit of a mess.'

He smiled. He felt that her return was fragile, he didn't trust it.

'Not to worry. We can get you cleaned up after our cup of tea.'

'Yes. That would be nice.'

They sipped at their tea silently. James hoped she would remember something, that she would ask a question – anything, about anything at all – so that he could try and reassure her. He felt edgy, not at all certain that his mother was solidly planted in herself, sure of who she was again.

Finally, she put down her cup.

'James?'

At least she still knew him, still remembered his name.

'Yes?'

'It's getting very late. It's time for Elizabeth to come home for her tea now.'

She stood up very carefully, while he fought for control of his face, his words. He couldn't speak.

'I think I'll go and finish watering the garden,' she said.

She was standing at the kitchen window now, watching the rain pour down the glass in little zig-zagging rivulets. Before he could stop her, she had reached the back door. He moved towards her, but he could never have been quick enough. She crumpled from the knees up, it seemed, and her head was the last to hit the floor. She hit the tiles with such a sickening crack that James was rooted to where he stood, unable to move at first for the wave of terror that pinned his feet to the floor.

'Alice!' he cried, finally down on one knee beside her. He felt for her pulse. Still beating; she was still alive. Frantically, he pulled the mobile phone out of his pocket and dialled 999.

'Ambulance, please. It's an emergency.'

*

'James?'

He recognized Ellen Crowley's voice at once.

He sat up, lifting his face from his hands. He fumbled for his glasses in his top pocket.

'You look exhausted,' she said, kindly. 'You should go home and rest. There's nothing you can do here tonight.'

'Has the specialist seen her?'

She nodded.

'We won't have final results for twenty-four hours or so, but I think it's pretty conclusive. It looks like a massive stroke. She came round for a moment or so, and I got the impression she knew who I was. I spoke to her, and I told her that you and Beth were outside. I hope that's okay?'

He nodded.

'God, yes, more than okay. I'll call Beth as soon as I get home. I know she'll be over straight away. Will Alice sleep? I mean, is she likely to ask for us during the night?'

Ellen shook her head.

'I doubt it. They've sedated her, to help her cope with the shock. You'd be much better off at home for tonight. If there's a crisis, I'll make sure they know to call you.'

'Thanks. Can I see her before I go?'

'Of course. She's down here.'

*

It was ten o'clock when James finally left. Alice had been peaceful, warm and clean, almost childlike in her complete repose. Her hair had been braided neatly, and her face was her own again, despite the downward curve of her mouth. He felt an enormous pity as he looked down at her, shocked by her sudden, childlike vulnerability. He was glad to leave, to make his uneasy escape from the face with the wild white hair that had begun to haunt him.

Automatically, he made his way back to her house. It was the only place that now felt anything like home; besides, it would feel wrong to phone Beth from anywhere else. He felt guilty, too – he should have ignored Alice and let Beth know how things were, at least a couple of weeks ago. But Alice had always managed to get him to do exactly what she wanted, bending his will to fit smoothly into hers.

Twelve hours. He couldn't believe that she had been reduced to almost a shell in such a short space of time. She'd looked so old suddenly, so fragile. The heavy crack of her head against the tiles wouldn't leave him, made him feel nauseous, over and over again. He couldn't stop replaying the moment, his eyes and ears full of her. He knew it was a sound he would never forget.

He sat down again at the kitchen table, cups and saucers, biscuits, milk carton still where he had left them. And he hadn't even had time to fill the jug for her.

He waited until he was in control again. Then he pulled the phone towards him and began to dial. It was answered at once.

'Beth? It's James. I'm afraid I have some bad news for you.'

*

'What is it, Mum?'

Beth hadn't moved since the phone call. Everything around her was spinning gently, distorting what had once been familiar surroundings. Every feeling she had ever had now seemed to be concentrated in the pit of her stomach.

'Mum?' said Laura again. This time, Beth saw her daughter's pale, delicate face, heard the fear in her tone.

'It's Gran, love. She's had a stroke.'

'What's that, exactly? Is it like a heart attack?'

Her eyes were wide, frightened. Beth tried to remember James's explanation on the phone. But his words were still floating around the room somewhere. She hadn't quite got hold of them, yet. She had to make an effort – Laura was waiting to understand.

'It's more like a brain attack, a sort of seizure, I suppose. Sometimes, people become paralysed on one side, or lose the power of speech.'

Beth's mind was racing. She had to go home, of course. As soon as possible. She must ring Tony, get him to look after Laura for as long as she was away. And how long might that be? She couldn't go before tomorrow, obviously, she'd have to organize the office – and, Jesus, she'd a VAT inspection on Wednesday. Thursday, she'd go Thursday.

And what if her mother died in the meantime? Well, she'd have fucked up once again, wouldn't she? Beth dragged her hair back from her forehead, her head already beginning to ache.

'Mum? Are you all right?'

'I'm fine, love – just a bit shocked, that's all.'

'Is Gran going to be okay?'

'I don't know – from what James said, I think it might be serious.'

'When are you going over?'

'I'm trying to work that out, right now. It looks as though Thursday might be the earliest.'

Laura's eyes widened.

'Mum – you have to go *now*.'

'I can't go now – I have too many things to sort out, first.'

'Are you going to ring Dad?'

Beth looked at her watch.

'Yes – but not now. I'll ring him first thing in the morning.'

'It's not even half eleven, Mum – he'll still be up. You should go *now*.'

Beth shook her head.

'I'd rather wait.'

'Can I go over with you?' Laura asked, suddenly.

'I don't think so, love – I could be gone for some time. We'll have to play this one by ear. I'll talk to James again tomorrow and see what the story is.'

It would probably be better to wait for the test results, anyway. As long as her mother was unconscious, there wasn't really a whole lot she could do. And besides, she should have a clearer picture of everything by the middle of the week.

'Would you like a cup of tea?'

Laura was standing by her mother's chair, her small face filled with anxiety. Beth hugged her.

'Thanks, love, but I'm going to pour myself something a lot stronger. I can't think straight at the moment.'

Her brain felt waterlogged. All the ifs and buts and maybes were swimming around the inside of her head, panic-stricken. She could make no sense out of anything James had just told her. Her mother was only seventy-six: that was still young, these days. She couldn't be snuffed out, just like that. They had too many things unfinished between them.

'Why don't you go on up to bed – there's nothing

we can do tonight, really. Don't you have to be up early for band practice?'

Laura nodded.

'Yeah, but I don't want to leave you on your own.'

'I'll be fine – in fact, I think I need to be on my own right now.'

Beth wanted her daughter gone: she wanted to sit in silence and loosen the grip of anxiety that was coiling around her insides. She needed a drink.

Laura bent and kissed her.

'Sure you're okay?'

'Sure. We won't know all the test results for twenty-four hours, anyway, so I have some breathing space.'

She could see by the look on Laura's face that that was not the point. God, she was so like her father. And she didn't push it, either.

''Night, then.'

''Night, love – sleep tight.'

Beth waited until she heard her daughter's bedroom door close. Then she bent down to the drinks cabinet. Nothing but whiskey. It would have to do. There was nothing she could do to help, really. James had said their mother was more or less unconscious; the hospital had even sent him home. She'd make her way through this, a day at a time. Let's see what tomorrow would bring.

*

Finally, on Thursday evening, she rang Tony. He came over immediately.

'I'm sorry, Beth,' he said, his hand carefully on her

shoulder. 'Your mother's a great lady. I really hope she pulls through.'

'Thanks,' she said automatically, not able to shake the feeling that they were talking about someone else, someone who had been her mother only briefly, occasionally.

'When's your flight?'

She had her back to him, spooning coffee into the cafetière.

'I haven't booked yet. I want to talk to James again, first.'

She poured the boiling water carefully.

'What on earth are you waiting for?'

His tone was astonished, verging on angry. She was taken by surprise. She'd always been the one with the short fuse. When Beth didn't answer, Tony spoke again, this time more quietly.

'How long have you known?'

'Just since Monday night. I've had a whole lot of stuff to sort out – I can't up and go, just like that, you know.'

'Why not? That's wasting three whole days for heaven's sake! You've an office full of people to do your bidding! Use your mobile tomorrow if you must keep in touch – you're only going to Dublin, not outer Mongolia.'

She became angry, then. He was backing her into a corner, leaving her no option but to face what she desperately didn't want to see.

'I'll drive you to the airport, right now. I've brought my stuff – I think it's better if I stay here, with Laura –

less of an upset for her. You don't need to wait any longer. Are you packed?'

'No,' she said, furiously.

'Come on, Beth,' he said, his tone more gentle now. 'You're suffering from shock. That's why you're not thinking straight. Throw a few things into a case, and I'll get you a flight. You can ring James on the way. Go on.'

She walked stiffly into her bedroom, and closed the door. She still felt as though she were moving through quicksand. The last three days had crawled past, in a mist of unreality, punctuated only by phone calls to and from James. He had been very good about keeping in touch with her, calling twice a day, telling her the same things over and over. He hadn't hurried her, hadn't bullied her. What gave Tony the right? Had Laura said something to him, something she shouldn't have? But even her anger wasn't real; it trickled away as, mechanically, she folded clothes and filled her suitcase. She could keep James company, she supposed. At least that would be a useful thing to do.

Tony was waiting, Laura beside him in the hall.

'Can I come with you to the airport, Mum?'

'Of course,' said Beth.

But she'd been put out, just for a moment, when she'd seen the two of them standing so close together. There was the whiff of conspiracy in the air.

'Have you done all your homework?' she asked.

Laura nodded, looking surprised. It was years since her mother had asked her that.

'Okay, then, let's go,' Tony said, picking up the suitcase.

Beth shrugged on her winter coat.

'I'm ready,' she said.

*

Alice was moving in and out of the darkness. Sometimes, she felt that she could break through to the brighter light which was just out of her reach, just on the other side of the surface. But the effort was too much. She felt awake from time to time, conscious inside her head, alert behind her heavily closed eyelids. Those were the times when she knew that James was beside her. His voice was soothing, he always took her hand.

Once, to make sure he was really there, she pressed his hand with hers. She was aware of his closeness then, as never before. She made a huge effort and willed her eyes to open. He was looking at her, his face poised just above hers.

'James,' she said softly.

She wanted to raise her hand, to stroke his face, but her hand was too heavy to lift. Her eyes closed again almost immediately, and she allowed herself to drift away again on the stream of bright water. Floating like this was so much easier than wrestling with the weight which so often pressed against her.

Occasionally, she was aware of being turned, of feeling warm towels rubbed all over her skin. She was sure she heard voices then, indistinct, bubbling, as though trapped under water.

Why didn't Elizabeth come?

Once, her eyes opened fully, without her willing it. She had got a strong sense of being in a different place, that things had shifted. All around her was familiar: this was a place she knew. Instantly, James was at her side.

'Welcome home, Alice,' he said, and stroked her hair back from her forehead.

She wanted to say 'Thanks'. Her sense of relief was enormous, filling the whole room. Home. She wanted to say it out loud, but her mouth kept sloping away from her, refusing to form the word. She felt that she had patted his hand, instead. She hoped so.

*

Now she could feel the struggle to the surface begin all over again. She had felt a different touch, a lighter one. This was what she had been waiting for, saving her energy for. She turned her head to where the light appeared to be strongest. Suddenly, everything seemed to come into focus.

'It's all right, Mam, I'm here.'

She felt her eyes flicker open, and there she was. There was Elizabeth. Alice felt the silence all around her fill up with joy. She made a tremendous effort and pressed her daughter's hand as hard as she could. She had something to tell her, something that couldn't wait. She felt her fingers merely flutter.

'Letter,' she whispered urgently, making her mouth do as she willed it.

Elizabeth was smiling down at her.

'Of course I will. Don't worry. I'm not going anywhere.'

Alice felt trapped inside a body that would not behave as her own. She hadn't made Elizabeth understand her. She began to grow angry.

'*Letter*,' she whispered again, with a fleeting return of her old energy. For a moment, she could feel her face move, could see by Elizabeth's eyes that she had finally made contact.

'Don't worry. I will. It's all under control, I promise you.'

She heard her daughter's words, felt her hold her hand close. Exhausted, she gave herself up to the river again, and floated.

*

Jack was busy planting.

'*Clematis jackmanii* – this one's after me!'

Alice heard the deep, black crunch of spade against soil as Jack dug a trench against the garden wall.

'This one grows like wildfire. It'll cover the wall in no time.'

'What colour are the flowers?' she asked, raising her face to the warm sunshine of an Indian summer. She had plenty to do inside, but she liked being out here with him, chatting as he pottered his way around the huge garden. She loved the way he really connected with the soil, the way he delighted in getting his hands in deep under the plants, settling them, covering them, being protective. He took the watering can from her and drenched the area he had just planted.

'Purple-blue,' he said, 'and they'll bloom from July to September.'

'I'm beginning to feel left out,' she teased him. 'Elizabeth has the rhododendron, James has the water-lily, and now you've got the clematis named after you – what about me?'

He grabbed her by the waist and kissed her suddenly, theatrically, on the mouth.

'This one's for you – don't go spoiling the surprise.'

'You found one called Alice – really?'

She was delighted. It had become a game between them. He'd promised to find her the one that suited her best. He pointed to his wheelbarrow.

'Better again. See this?'

He lifted out a bushy plant, prettily-shaped.

She nodded. In those days, she could never bring herself to tell him that, to her, every young plant looked the same as the next one. He was the only one with the green fingers then, the one who coaxed each small beginning into its full glory.

'This is called *hebe speciosa*. Know why I chose it?'

She shook her head, waiting.

'Its English name is Midsummer Beauty. Just like you.'

He smiled at her in the same way as the night he'd arrived at *Abbotsford*, her engagement ring hidden nervously in his jacket pocket. She fell in love with him all over again now, in their own garden.

There was the faint trace of a childish voice that Alice couldn't quite make out, coming from the west-facing wall of the garden. She tried hard to focus, but her attention was distracted by a strange feeling in her hands. A soothing feeling. At the same time, a little voice was telling her of a teddy bear, one with a glorious red ribbon around his neck. Alice sighed. She could feel her eyelids flicker, and she tried once more to move her head towards the light.

Suddenly, Jack was gone and she was standing alone by the garden shed, the patch of wildflowers before her swirling into a delicate maze of shape and colour. She heard his voice tell her all over again how wildflowers thrived in poor soil; you could kill them with kindness, he said. The less pampering they got, the more vigorous they became. A bit like us. And she could hear the smile in his voice, see the bright gleam of mischief in his blue eyes. The day had gone silent again; a bright sun filled the huge sky.

Jack's garden seat was empty. She was surprised. She was sure he had come there to wait for her. She needed to sit down. Gratefully, she turned her face to the light, and closed her eyes.

She sighed deeply, and rested.

SEVEN

Holding on

'GOODBYE, MRS MCGRATH, thank you for coming.'

They saw the last of the neighbours out, and closed the front door gratefully. There had been a constant stream of people all day: Beth had been amazed at the extent of her mother's small world. She and James, Keith and Gemma, and, from time to time, Olive, had spent the past fourteen hours boiling kettles, making sandwiches, pouring drinks. There had been no end to the kindness of people, who arrived with covered plates and dishes, a steady army of tin-foil offerings, like some ancient tribal tribute.

Starting with the priest, Ellen Crowley and a tearful Peggy at ten o'clock that morning, and ending with the last of the neighbours after the removal to the church, they had fed, watered and comforted well over a hundred people. Beth had been very moved by the appearance of men and women she hadn't seen in over twenty years; but of course, James had. She was finding it difficult to remember that she was the outsider here: she kept forgetting, kept thinking of it as her home.

She hated the thought of this house being locked up, stripped bare, waiting to be sold to strangers. She had grown to love it again, as she remembered doing when she was a small child. And this time, coming home, she had, finally, felt truly welcome. She looked around the warm, slightly shabby kitchen. Someone would come in here and rip it all out; its guts would be spilled into a waiting skip. They'd probably turn it into something white and minimalist and painfully trendy, all glass and brushed stainless steel. She shivered. She wished she could keep it just as it was, for her and Laura to come back to. Alice would like the thought of them visiting more frequently, keeping in touch.

Old Mrs Collins from the house at the corner had come into the kitchen while Beth was busy making tea and raging silently against the ghosts of potential house buyers. The stooped old lady was leaning heavily on her walking-stick.

'Elizabeth?'

Beth had turned around, startled at the unfamiliar voice.

'I just wanted to say that you're the image of your mother. She was very proud of you, you know.'

She'd nodded at Beth, several times. Then, without saying anything else, she'd turned around slowly and made her way back out into the hall.

'Thank you,' was all Beth had managed to call after her. She didn't even know if the old woman had heard her.

'Drink?' asked James.

'Make it a double.'

He handed Beth her glass and then threw more turf briquettes on the fire. The gesture reminded her of the night she'd arrived. Only five days ago, and now it was all over. The funeral tomorrow was the last marker, the final acknowledgement of this rite of passage from daughter to orphan, from child to grown-up.

'I can't believe she's gone. I can still feel her everywhere.'

Beth sipped at her drink. She was comforted by the thought of the photographs at the top of the wardrobe, the letters which could be read and reread. They weren't finished with each other, yet. She didn't need to let Alice go, not for another while. They were still keeping in touch.

James sat in the armchair across from hers.

'Jesus, I'm absolutely knackered.'

He took off his glasses and rubbed his eyes. It was only then that she remembered how much more he was dealing with. The last couple of days had been so frantic that she'd forgotten all about him and Olive. Now that she and the kids had gone back home, Beth felt it was time to ask. No more beating around the bush, either – Alice's death had taught her that. Time was no longer an unlimited luxury.

'What about you and Olive? Have you had a chance to talk?'

He shook his head.

'No, not really, not yet. I'm going to go over for a few hours tomorrow evening.'

He finished his drink in one gulp. He gestured towards her glass.

'Another?'

'Why not?'

She was beginning to wind down, to feel almost normal again. She liked the feeling in the room. It was comfortable sitting there, just herself and James, surrounded by the bright shadows of Alice.

'I don't know whether you have given this any thought, but I'd rather we didn't sell the house.'

She felt a little shiver of delight. Had he read her mind? She let him continue: he didn't look as though he would welcome being interrupted.

'I've spent a lot of time recently thinking about the rest of my life. Alice's death has brought everything into focus for me: including the things I've been leaving on the back burner. I'm not prepared to live like that any longer.'

His tone was quiet, but Beth could see the depths of his determination. She was glad for him, glad that he was finally learning to put himself first. It was time for him to shape his will around himself, and not be always moulded by others.

'I don't know about me and Olive – I don't know what's going to happen with us in the long run. In the short term, I don't want to go back there to live. I've moved out, and I want to stay moved out. I'll meet her and talk to her often, of course, and I want to stay close to my kids. But I'm not going back until I get my life sorted out. At least – ' and he stopped, looking at Beth, 'that's what I'd like to do, but a lot of it depends on you.'

She wanted him to ask, wanted to be able to say 'yes'.

'How?'

'I'd love to live here and do this old place up, bit by bit. I could make it very comfortable.'

'Would there be room for me and Laura?' she teased.

He smiled at her.

'There's room for anyone you want. It'll always be half yours. Think it over.'

She shook her head.

'I have thought it over. I've thought about nothing else all day. I hate the thought of strangers moving in here, particularly as I've only just begun to feel that it *is* my home. I don't want to let it go.'

She was still curious. She wanted to ask him something, wasn't sure how appropriate it was. She decided to ask it anyway, seeing more and more of her mother's blunt tongue in herself.

'Does this have anything to do with Alice's letters? – don't answer that if you don't want to: I'm just wondering how astute she was.'

He grinned.

'She was no fool. But no, it's not directly because of anything she said. Just the realization that I have choices – and she did remind me of that. You don't have to spend your life trying to be something that you're not. I think the whole awful experience of her death has given me back a part of myself.'

'Me, too,' Beth said softly. 'And I'm really glad that no strangers will get the chance to start ripping the heart out of this lovely old house. We're the third generation to live here – I'd love to think of it going on for ever.'

He raised his glass.

'Here's to the fourth and fifth generations, then.'

She smiled over at him.

'Let them wait their turn. Here's to the third.'

*

Beth was looking out her bedroom window anxiously. Laura was late. She had insisted to her mother that she'd take a taxi from the airport, and now Beth was worried. She shouldn't have listened to her; she should have gone and collected her. She glanced at her watch. Nine twenty. The funeral Mass was in forty minutes.

She and James had stayed up most of the night, only snatching sleep between six and eight. They had shared memories of bikes and swings, of ice cream and glasses of fizzy lemonade. They remembered their jobs of shelling peas and collecting summer loganberries in the welcoming shade of the walled garden. They'd shared some of the different Alices they had each known, too: the all-efficient housewife, sharp-eyed on the lookout for unfinished chores: sharper-tongued when she found them. The working mother, rushing from one job to the next, but still insisting on checking all homework, all the time. The proud parent: nothing was more important than doing well at school. And then the adoring grandmother, completely oblivious to the faults of her grandchildren. One generation had seemed to be enough for Alice to soften her expectations, to gentle the edges of her words. They had laughed a lot, too, which surprised Beth. She'd never thought of funeral days as a time for laughter. It had buoyed them both up, made them ready to face the last bit, which Beth was now dreading. She needed Laura beside her during the Mass; she wanted all of her family around her, even Olive. Today was not a day for divisions.

It was raining, naturally. The mourning car was due in fifteen minutes. Where *was* Laura? Beth was about to ring the airport when a taxi swung through the gates and came to a noisy stop on the gravel. At last.

She ran to the front door, ready to welcome her daughter. She was surprised to see the outline of two figures on the porch step. She opened the door, curious, not knowing what to think.

Laura stood there, in floods of tears as soon as she saw her mother. And there, with one arm protectively around his daughter's shoulders, was Tony.

'I hope I didn't need to be invited?' he said.

*

Beth closed her bedroom door behind her. She looked out into the gleaming street below, beyond the low walls of the front garden. The rain had been relentless, all day. Somehow, she had preferred that; there would have been something very insensitive about sunshine on the day of Alice's funeral. She closed the curtains, shutting out the glow of the streetlight that had comforted so many of the long winter nights of her childhood.

There was a strong feeling of Alice, all around her. Beth did not believe in ghosts; what she felt in this room now was not some eerie restlessness of the spirit, but rather the warm glow of reassurance and acceptance. This was where her mother had written her letters, after all, where she had groped towards something beyond the years of bitterness and mistrust. Beth sat at the same little desk now, wanting to finish the conversation that her mother's letters had started. She remembered as a child, throwing pebbles into the pond in the back garden, watching the way the ripples had widened, growing larger and larger as they reached the edges of the little pool. She had always liked to see the process in reverse: she imagined the ripples reproducing themselves in smaller and smaller circles until they reached the stillness at the centre of the storm. She felt now that she and Alice had just negotiated the outer circles successfully. Now she wanted to come close to the centre, to complete the something which still pulled at her, nagging for her attention. She'd be leaving soon, too soon, and there were some things that just couldn't wait. And she wanted to be on her own to attend to them.

She had sent Laura off with Gemma, relieved that the two girls' white, pinched faces had recovered as soon as the funeral formalities were over. Both of them had begun giggling at nothing, each of them goading the other on to helpless laughter, reacting in their own way to the stress of the awful last few days. James and Tony had caught Beth's mood quickly, and gone off together for a pint somewhere, leaving her to herself.

She got up from the desk and pulled open the wardrobe doors, taking time to look at everything the way Alice must have seen it. It was as though a sudden shift in her perception had taken place, as though she were looking out through borrowed eyes. On the top right-hand shelf, there were half a dozen photograph albums, the old-fashioned type. Beth took down one of them and glanced through it quickly. Faces, names, places that meant nothing to her, until she suddenly caught sight of a young woman that could only have been Alice. She looked at the photograph more closely. A group of young women, all neatly gloved and hatted, smiled out at her from 1945. She'd take these albums back with her if James didn't mind. She was curious to track down Arthur Boyd, and she had a strong feeling that this was where she would find him. And she wanted to take her time doing it.

There was the famous sewing basket, on its own on the bottom shelf. Beth knelt down and opened it, the varnished cane lid creaking in the way it had always done. Neatly arrayed in all the little compartments were shirt buttons, fasteners, old-fashioned hooks and eyes, safety pins. Beth smiled to herself; Alice had always been a hoarder, not even throwing away the small safety pins that came attached to dry-cleaning labels. Underneath the first hinged tray lay bits of petersham, tailor's chalk, a measuring tape. She would take these back with her, too. She'd never be any good with her needle, not like Alice had been, but she liked the sense of connection she got when she handled these strangely intimate bits and pieces. She put the sewing to one side. She'd pack it with her last-minute stuff in the morning.

Reaching up to the top shelf, she found the two bundles of photographs which Alice had mentioned in her letter. And there, right where she'd said it would be, was the photo of the four of them, taken by a passer-by in the Phoenix Park on that magical day in May 1957. Little girl with eyes creased against the sunshine, smiling into the camera. Holding one of her hands was the eight-year-old James. The two of them were standing between Alice and Jack, who looked oddly formal in good clothes. Jack was wearing a shirt and tie under his new jumper, and Alice had on a dress and jacket – hardly picnic wear. Beth was almost sure she remembered the dress her mother was wearing: it looked strangely familiar. Then she got it. She did remember it: it had been cut down and made into a winter coat for Beth the year she'd started primary school. Beth felt the photograph as something of a reproach. How had everyone learned, in the space of one generation, to be so utterly wasteful? She smiled in spite of herself. She was even beginning to think like Alice. She put her bundle of photographs into the sewing basket. She would look at these back home, in her own time. There was no longer any rush.

She made one last sweep of the top shelf and her hand caught at something on the final arc of its search, something pushed almost to the back, right at the wall. Alice must have stood on a chair to do this. Beth stood on tiptoe and finally managed to get her fingers around the soft corner of a cardboard box. She pulled, and the box slid willingly to the outer edge of the shelf.

It was big, and quite heavy. She toppled it into her arms and carried it over to her waiting desk. She had begun to feel acutely nervous: what other surprises might Alice have in store for her? How much self-knowledge was one wilful daughter supposed to acquire in just one week? Cautiously, she lifted the lid of the box. There, wrapped in tissue-paper as Alice had promised, was Dolph. She laughed out loud in relief, pulling back the layers of thin paper, which were marked with some strange black lines. She looked more closely: Alice had used old dress-patterns as Dolph's blanket. Beth could hear the words clearly, in capital letters, as Alice would have spoken them. WASTE NOT, WANT NOT. But they had wasted, hadn't they? At least thirteen years, which were only now beginning to be recovered.

There were three little jewellery boxes here too. Beth opened the midnight-blue one, first. Sellotaped to the lid was the word 'Gemma', and a highly polished gold locket and chain rested on the velvet covering. She put it to one side. The next box was wine-coloured, the lid not quite held in place by the unsteady hinge. Inside was a tiny solitaire, with 'Laura' printed in wavering capitals on a piece of card bent to fit the lid. Beth recognized it as having belonged to Margaret. It was the perfect choice for Laura, whose hands must be every bit as delicate as her great-grandmother's. The final box was bigger and flatter than the others. It contained a wide gold bangle, with delicate engraving. There was a folded envelope too, with 'James' written in large letters across it. Nothing for Olive; Beth wasn't surprised. She didn't need to read the contents of the envelope to know that Alice had left that decision up to James. Quite an astute old cookie, her mother. It comforted Beth to know that however devastating her final illness had been, she had held on to all the sharpness of her judgement right up until the last minute. That was something to be grateful for. Such a complete drawing together of loose ends was just what she would have wanted for herself.

The final package was wrapped in brown paper. She

opened it carefully, full of curiosity. Inside were three well-worn books. A Biggles compendium belonging to James – she'd have to tease him tomorrow about his politically incorrect reading matter; *The Turf-Cutter's Donkey* by Patricia Lynch, which she had read and reread as a child until she knew it practically by heart, and a very old, well-worn copy of *The Ugly Duckling*. Where on earth had Alice found that?

Her eyes began to fill as she leafed through the familiar pages. The binding was falling apart, and something slid on to the desk's surface as she turned the book's final pages. Another envelope, her name written in spidery strokes across the front. Her heart began to thump painfully now. She put the book on her bed and ripped open the envelope's flap. Why was it here? Why not with the other letters? For a moment, Beth had a painful sense of foreboding: what if this was just gibberish? What if Alice had written this when she was no longer herself? She held her breath as she unfolded the pages carefully, and was flooded with relief to see her mother's careful, distinct handwriting. She began to breathe again: this was the real thing. She was shocked when she saw the date: just one day before the first stroke, the beginning of the end that had taken everything that mattered away from her.

'Woodvale'
6th September 1999

My Dearest Elizabeth,
I've just come home from Sunday dinner with James and Olive. It was a lovely day – Eoin and Shea were

home from New York with their girlfriends, and they're all heading off to the West of Ireland tomorrow morning. I have to say, I was quite amazed by them. Shea has an American accent, quite a strong one, too – after only a year? Is it just me, or is that a load of old nonsense? He's so like his mother. Anyway, they both seem to be doing very well for themselves, earning 'a pile', as Shea put it. Eoin is the quieter one, getting more like James every day. He said to me afterwards: 'The Stock Exchange is a real young man's game, Gran – the pressure's too much. I'll be out of it in five years' time, at the latest.' Their girlfriends were friendly enough, but without a great deal to say for themselves. They were all long blonde hair and painted nails. And they never stopped smoking! I thought the Americans were too health-conscious to smoke? They ate hardly anything, either, and Olive had gone to a lot of trouble. Maybe they were a bit overwhelmed, we were all there – Keith, too, who's got the place he wanted at university, and Gemma, just back ten days ago from a summer job in London.

Sitting there, with all of them, I was struck so forcibly by how much times have changed. Of course, I knew that before today, but somehow the meal this afternoon might have been taking place in another time, another place. I felt very disconnected from everybody – as though there was no place for me in my own life any more. Olive and James seem to be able to let their children come and go so much more easily than I ever could – is it because there was always the two of them, or because they are better parents than I could ever be? I can't understand how I could have got it so wrong. I keep remembering you and James as toddlers, small children – anything up to the age of twelve. After that, it's like there's a great big gap.

I rushed up here to your room as soon as James drove me home, because I wanted to search for photographs, certificates, letters – anything from the time that you, particularly, were older. I have nothing. And yet I know that you did well at school, you were always a good student. You got a good Inter Cert, and an even better Leaving – and yet there are no signs of all those achievements. Do you have them?

Watching Gemma today was a too painful reminder of your own summer, the one when you'd just finished school. You were determined to go away, to spread your wings in London. I saw it as something very different. I was hurt that you wanted to get away from me and, to be truthful, I was afraid of being left on my own. James was twenty-three by that stage, just about to start his PhD, and I was so proud of him. He'd already met Olive, and I could tell it was serious. When you finished your exams, I was so pleased – I wanted the same for you as I'd wanted for James. My daughter – a university woman, maybe even a doctor or a lawyer. I'd learned how important it was for everyone, men and women, to be able to earn their own living.

Instead, to my horror, I saw you disappearing off to a big city with a boy you hardly knew. It had never even occurred to me that he was part of any picture, any plan of yours. In my imagination, I saw happening to you what had happened to so many before you – you'd get pregnant and that would be the end of any ambitions you might have. I didn't want that for you – I wanted you to have a better life, one with more ease and comfort than the life of an unmarried mother.

Why couldn't I tell you that? Had we really not been speaking for so long that it was impossible to say anything that the other would listen to? I regret that, Elizabeth. I regret it more than I can tell you. You were the young person, I was the adult, and I had a responsibility to behave better. If I had, we'd probably not have lost almost thirteen years. Thirteen years! It seems incredible that we punished each other for that length of time. I know you came back from time to time, and we had a tacit agreement not to mention the unmentionable. Those visits were hard for both of us, weren't they? But we kind of settled into the routine of them. I'll always be grateful to James for being the one to keep up real contact with you – and I've told him so, in my letters. He made sure you were back for each of the Christenings, in '76, '80, and '82, and I know he and Olive have lots of photographs of their babies and the doting aunt. I asked him for them today, and he promised to drop them by at the weekend. I'm looking forward to seeing them, and to filling in some of those gaps for myself. I feel saddened by the waste of it all, and I've nobody to blame but myself.

The real ray of sunshine came in '85, when you married Tony and had Laura later the same year. I really liked Tony, I thought he was good for you. I still do. And your wedding was lovely, so intimate with just the ten of us. Do you remember phoning me to tell me you were pregnant? I was overjoyed –

and I really began to feel that we still had time, that your baby would pull us back together again. And she did, really, didn't she? I used to look forward to your visits so much! Laura was such a lovely little girl, she reminded me so much of you. I felt we had a real connection at last, and I wanted to be very careful of it, to make sure I never did anything to weaken it. Christmas and summer became something to look forward to, and I felt I could show you through Laura just how much I'd always loved you. Over the years, it seemed to me that we no longer needed to talk about what had driven us apart. It's only now, when I feel I may never see you again, that I must acknowledge how wrong I was.

I know that when you read these letters, it is highly unlikely that I will be able to speak to you; perhaps I won't even recognize you. But that doesn't matter so much now, because I can feel you are listening to me; I feel that you will forgive me.

Your loving mother,
Alice.

Beth folded the pages and replaced them in the envelope. She tucked the letter into the back pages of *The Ugly Duckling*, and placed the book under her pillow. She gathered the jewellery boxes and James's book and took them downstairs to the sitting room, leaving them on the shelf beside the fireplace, where he was sure to find them. She'd talk to him in the morning.

Right now, she felt as though she were swimming in slow motion, making difficult progress through heavily moving water. Alice's final letter had left her too calm, almost without emotion. She knew that all the outer ripples of their stormy relationship had opened up and closed again, that she and Alice were now at the centre of things, just like the pebble at the centre of the pond in her father's walled garden. She would be back inside her other life soon, would find the time to be quiet and still: time in which she would look for, and discover, the daughter and mother she was now in the process of becoming.

*

'Are you ready, Laura?'

'Coming!'

She and Gemma appeared from the kitchen, eyes bright, faces flushed with laughter.

Beth couldn't help smiling at both of them.

'Do you think you can save some of that hilarity for our next visit? We might need it.'

'Are we coming back for Christmas?' Laura's voice was high, excited.

Beth hesitated. She was conscious of Tony standing in the hall behind her. He had been quiet and unobtrusive for the last three days: she had noticed on more than one occasion his discreet helpfulness, his kindness to elderly neighbours and his sharp-eyed concern for herself and Laura. She was glad he'd come; she suddenly didn't want to make any plans for the future.

'I'm sure we'll meet up sometime over the holiday – Gemma might even want a few days on her own in London sometime soon?'

The two girls shrieked and hugged each other.

'Come on, you two,' grumbled James. 'You're in my way.'

He was carrying Beth's suitcase down from her room, and the two girls were jumping about by the bottom step.

'I'll take that, James.'

Tony stepped forward and took the suitcase from him. He turned to Laura.

'Have you got all your stuff down to the car yet?'

She nodded.

'Yeah. I put it in the boot *ages* ago.'

'Come on – let's check that we haven't forgotten anything.'

Laura threw her eyes up to Heaven and Gemma giggled again. Beth looked at him gratefully.

'Go on, Laura,' she said. 'I'll be out in a minute.'

She and James were left on their own in the hallway. He held out his arms to her.

'Come here to me, Sis.'

He hugged her tight.

'You know that man still loves you, don't you,' he whispered into her ear, not letting her go. It was not a question. 'Hold on to him this time: do you hear me? Don't fuck it up. This is your second chance.'

Don't give yourself something to regret when you're eighty.

She shook her head, her eyes fixed on the bit of wall above his shoulder.

'I dunno, James. There's a lot of water under that particular bridge.'

'Not as much as you think,' he said quietly, kissing her cheek. 'Take my advice and start swimming.'

She drew back and looked at him, doing her best to smile.

'Will you be okay?'

He nodded.

'Yes, I will. I'm going to do nothing between now and Christmas: just use the time and space for myself. And by the way, send Laura over anytime you want to, on her own. It'll be good for her.'

'I'll do that. I'll be back soon, James – don't do any clearing out without me.'

He shook his head.

'I won't. I intend to leave everything exactly as it is until you come back. I'll be doing nothing that I don't have to.'

She could feel tears threaten.

'Thanks for everything, James.'

'Thanks to *you*. I don't know what I'd have done without you.'

She could see that he meant it, too.

'Ready, Mum?'

'Coming now, Laura.'

'Bye, Uncle James. See you at Christmas.'

'Or sooner. Look after your mum, won't you?'

He bear-hugged her and she smiled up at him, suddenly Alice's smile.

'I will.'

Tony was waiting, standing by the hire car, which looked ridiculously small beside his large frame. He came over at once, and shook hands warmly with James.

''Bye, James. Thanks for your hospitality. Take it easy, won't you?'

'See you soon, Tony.'

Beth looked at her brother. His eyes were full of mischief.

'Have a safe journey,' he said.

'Do you want to drive, Beth?'

Tony was holding the keys towards her. She had a brief, unpleasant memory from hundreds of years ago of a man with dirty fingernails and a cement lorry. The rain was running down the cracks and lines of his face; he smelt nauseatingly of diesel.

'No, thanks,' she said, 'I think I'll sit this one out.'

She blew James a kiss. He smiled, bent down and waved to Laura and watched as the car pulled away slowly towards the gates.

Beth looked behind her, waving until they reached the road. Watery October sunlight burnished the rioting leaves of the Virginia creeper. Her last glimpse was of the prolific ivy and woody-stemmed clematis all along the smooth capping-stones of her parents' walled garden.